'Tell me, are you married or promised to any man?'

Such impudence took Judith's breath away. And while she was struggling to form a reply he coolly stretched across the table and lifted up her left hand.

'Ah, you have no rings. That's good,' he said, scrutinising her fingers.

She snatched her hand back as though his touch had burnt her. ''Tis outside of enough, sir!' she protested, outraged by his manner as much as by his impudent words. 'I don't know how people conduct themselves in Holland, but your manners are far too saucy for this part of the world.'

'Why? You think that I'm too blunt, perhaps? But if you had been wed or betrothed it would be most improper for me to try to know you better. Why aren't you betrothed yet? You are not, are you? or you would have said so by now. Is there some good reason? You are old enough. Seventeen, perhaps? Eighteen? And you do not look sickly.'

'You go too far, Master van de . . .'

'van de Scheldt. You'll soon get used to it.'

'No, I will not, sir, because I've no intention of ever uttering it—or ever trying to utter it—again!'

DAY OF RECKONING

Elizabeth Lowther

MILLS & BOON LIMITED
ETON HOUSE   18-24 PARADISE ROAD
RICHMOND   SURREY   TW9 1SR

First published in Great Britain 1989
by Mills & Boon Limited

© Elizabeth Lowther 1989

Australian copyright 1989
Philippine copyright 1989
This edition 1989

ISBN 0 263 76486 9

Set in Times Roman 10 on 10¼ pt.
04-8907-86674 C

Made and printed in Great Britain

CHAPTER ONE

1642

IT WAS no easy task edging the flat-bottomed boat through the shallow water. An icy February wind blew straight across the Fens from the German Sea, making Judith thankful that she was wearing a thick cloak and her grandmother's quilted petticoat. Even though she was so heavily shrouded against the cold there was no disguising the slender litheness of her figure, as with deft, sure strokes she propelled the little craft through the current. Gradually her exertions made her blood flow again, bringing warmth to her limbs and a glow to her cheeks. Her activities had also caused soft tendrils of dark hair to escape from beneath her cap, forcing her to stop briefly while she tucked them back in place. Her task completed, she prepared to continue, but then the beauty of the fen overwhelmed her and, with the boat-pole still grasped in mittened hands, she paused to look about her.

The people of Sedgewick St Peter called this region the Summer Grounds, because in the summer months the land was firm and dry, giving fine pasture for the cattle and sheep. Now in winter, though, all the land was drowned by heavy rains and the overspill from sluggish rivers. It was this annual flooding that gave richness to the summer pastures, so the villagers patiently suffered the waters that surrounded them each year, taking to their boats as the best means of transport.

For those who knew it, however, there was a path, a difficult, treacherous track that wound its way along a scant strip of firm ground. A horseman now plodded along this narrow route, weariness in every line of him. Judith took one look at the powerful figure in the well-worn leather coat, and at the fox-red hair glowing in the wintry sunshine, and her heart leapt with happy recognition.

'Adam!' she called, steering the boat in his direction. 'Adam!'

At the sight of her the horseman straightened in the saddle and urged his tired beast to a trot; when he was level with her he hastily dismounted. Leaning forward, he flung his arms about her slight waist and clasped her to him, a dangerous manoeuvre that made the boat rock perilously.

'You'll have me in the water, you fool!' laughed Judith.

'Not I.' He tightened his hold on her. 'I've got you clasped here, next to my heart. I'll never let you go, so how can you fall into the water?'

He bent and kissed her with lips that were cold and tasted of the fen winds, but there was no coldness in the ardour of his embrace, nor in that of Judith's response to him. Hungry mouth met hungry mouth, until breathlessness drove them apart.

In spite of what he had said, Adam did release Judith, steadying her until she had regained her balance, but he did not loose his hold completely.

From her position in the boat Judith looked with love at Adam Digby and thought for the hundredth time how handsome he was. Even though mud-spattered and pale with fatigue, there was no man his equal in Sedgewick, nor for miles around. Although of little more than medium height, his rich russet hair marked him out in any crowd, that and his eyes of a blue so intense they were almost piercing. Everything about him suggested latent strength and power, from the hawk-like curve of his nose to the muscular set of his shoulders beneath his coat. Fire and energy and passion, that was Adam Digby!

'You were not expected until tomorrow,' said Judith, her hazel eyes bright with happiness at this unlooked-for encounter.

'Ely's no place to be at this time of year, not when you've got a decent fireside of your own and a beautiful sweetheart waiting for you.'

Adam changed his hold on her, grasping her wrists possessively with strong, work-roughened hands. Ardour made his grip painful, but not for the world would Judith have protested or pulled away. Instead she asked, 'And what news is there from Ely?'

'Naught but rumour upon rumour of the King's quarrel with Parliament.'

'So, your business done, you left this morning?' Judith prompted.

'Aye, and a long, hard ride we've had of it, eh, lad?' He addressed his horse which, too weary to wander off, stood beside him, its head drooping. 'But what of you? What brings you this way today?'

'I'm looking for Ruby. Why she should break out of her warm byre and come exploring among the sedge-banks, I'll never know.'

'No doubt she has a lover. Some fine young bull, with whom she is keeping a tryst at this very moment. Leave her to it and go home!'

'What, and face Aunt Ketty without her?' laughed Judith. 'You know that of all our cattle Ruby is her pet and her darling. I would just be sent out again to fetch her. Besides, I doubt if there are any fine young bulls out here now, not in this cold weather.'

'Ah, love's its own furnace!' Again Adam pulled her to him. 'You'll find that out soon enough when we're wed. We'll have no need of flame or fire, not with our love to warm us.'

As if to prove the truth of his words his mouth covered hers, so demanding and urgent with desire that her head reeled.

'That day cannot come too soon for me,' she whispered at last.

'Oh, when will your aunt give her permission? Why is she being so tardy? You are old enough! We've been of a mind to wed these two years or more! There's a fine home waiting for you at Old Place. You'll never want, yet still she waits!' Adam's tone was anguished.

Judith wished with all her heart that she could give him a sound reason, but, in truth, she found her aunt's reluctance as inexplicable as he. Her dear Aunt Ketty, who had loved and cherished her since she was a small child, and given her everything else she could have wished for, was strangely unwilling to give her consent for Judith to marry Adam.

'I'm all she has,' said Judith. 'I think she's loath to lose me.'

'You're scarce going any distance! We're neighbours.'

'Aye, but it wouldn't be the same, would it?'

'No it wouldn't be the same!' Adam's eyes sparkled wickedly. 'Which is why I want you as my wife and not just my neighbour. Still, if we must wait then I suppose there's no help for it ... And now, what about Ruby? Shall I help you look for her?'

'No, thank you. I can manage well enough alone. Get you home, you and your horse, to some warmth and rest. You both need it by the looks of you.'

'I confess there's not a bone in my body without an ache,' admitted Adam. 'And doubtless old Jupiter here feels the same. Very well, off you go and find your cow. But take care not to stay out too long. You're too precious to be wandering the fen in the dark.'

Judith watched him go, leading his tired horse now, for he was close to home. As his beloved figure receded she felt such happiness knowing that Adam Digby had chosen her as his future wife. Since her earliest years she had idolised him. There were some who called him arrogant and proud, but she could never see it. In her eyes Adam was perfect. He stood head and shoulders above any other man in the village, in character if not in stature. He had been educated at a proper school in Ely, for one thing, and not scrambled into some hasty learning in the church chancel when the curate had a mind, like the other youngsters. His farm, bordering the cottage where she lived with her Aunt Ketty, was acknowledged to be the best in the district, though, to be honest, much of the credit for that lay with Marjorie, his elder sister. There was not a girl for miles around who had not cast flirtatious glances in his direction, yet Judith was the one he had chosen.

She returned to the search, standing in the stern of the craft, feeling her way through the channels that had to be relearned each year.

Once she was in the broader waters of the river, where she did not have to pay such close attention to her navigation, she allowed her senses to wander. The colour and beauty made her catch her breath more sharply than the east wind had done. She could never understand why some folks thought of the Fens as dull and drab; to her they were a mass of colour, particularly in winter. This afternoon the sun glowed a dull, fiery red, touching the fronds of sedge with a fine ruddy glow, and casting great splashes of fire across the water that stretched as far as the eye could see. On the clumps of reeds the hard frost still clung in crusts of white lace. Above all this was the endless sky, shaded now from blood-red to a blue as pale and chilling as the centre of a lump of ice.

Something in her always responded to such colours; it was like a deep hunger that made her long to preserve them in some way, to keep them by her always; but she had no means of doing so except with her needle.

The meandering course of the river was easy to follow, edged as it was with sentinel willows trunk-deep in the floods. As she negotiated a wide bend, Judith dragged her senses from the beauty around her and concentrated on the search for the cow. Ahead of her was an island raised enough above the waters to allow sedge, willow, and rough grazing to flourish. It was here she hoped to find Ruby.

Movements among the scrub raised those hopes, but when she pulled closer she was surprised to see a group of men standing on the spongy bank. Alongside, a boat was moored, and in it two boatmen waited patiently.

'Mercy on us! What have we here?' demanded one man when he caught sight of her. He was an elderly gentleman, with a fine cloak lined with miniver pulled tightly about him. His cheeks were mottled with the cold, despite his rich garments and many scarves. At the sight of Judith, anxiety was added to the cold and misery already etched on his face. 'Whoever are you, child? And what are you doing in that boat alone? I'm sure it can't be safe. Come, come, what's your name?'

'Judith Pentelow, sir,' Judith replied reluctantly. She was not sure of these men so unexpectedly met with on the fen.

'Judith Pentelow, eh? Well, well, well!' The old gentleman did not seem any easier in his mind. 'I'm surprised at your family letting you do anything so dangerous. Why are you out here in this desolate wilderness?'

'I'm looking for our cow, sir. She's wandered away. But you needn't worry, I've been handling boats since I can remember.'

'Is that so? I have heard that you fen folk are more at home on water than on land. Just the same, I am sure that it isn't safe for you to be alone. Have you come far?'

'From Sedgewick St Peter, sir.' She was curious about the presence of these men, for they carried no guns or nets, and had no dogs with them. What purpose could they possibly have out on Hanser Fen in winter other than hunting or wildfowling?

'Sedgewick St Peter, eh?' The old gentleman was persistent. 'Do you hear that, Sir Walter? The maid is one of your people.'

Judith started at the name, then looked with curiosity at the sour-countenanced man who stood close by. So this was Sir Walter Massingham, squire and richest landowner in these parts! He was just as much a stranger to her as the others, for Sir Walter found the fens too dull for his tastes, and preferred to spend his time at Court. It was said that he was very close to King Charles himself, and to the French-born Queen, Henrietta-Maria. His presence on Hanser Fen was all the more baffling.

Sir Walter scowled at Judith. 'Can't be expected to recognise any of 'em,' he snapped.

'Well, damme! If it isn't the prettiest thing to see! The maid handles the boat as neatly as you please!' The third man in the group spoke up. He was as jovial as Sir Walter was sour, and just as richly dressed. Stout and merry, he had a purple flush about his cheeks that spoke of too much good living. He went on, 'You've come to the right place, my dear. There is a cow about somewhere.'

'There is, certainly.' The elderly gentleman nodded in agreement. 'I was quite anxious lest it proved a savage beast and attacked us all.'

Judith had to smile at this. 'You had nothing to fear, sir. She is very gentle.'

'I am relieved to hear it,' said the old gentleman. 'Boatman, up you go and see if you can catch the beast. And you, fellow, take a tight hold of the maid's boat. I am so afeared she'll drift away. Oh, dear! This is such a risky business!'

'I have her secure, master.' The second boatman stretched over and took a firm hold on the gunwale, treating Judith to a bold leer as he did so.

'I can get the cow easily enough, sir, if your boatman will only get out of the way,' called Judith.

But the old gentleman was too intent upon watching Ruby to hear her.

As Judith had feared, the other fellow was making a very poor show of catching the cow. He was rushing about, with much shouting and flapping of arms, and Ruby, who soon recognised an inexperienced adversary, was leading him a merry dance. Encouraged by whoops and halloos from the stout gentleman, she tossed up her heels and galloped about, splashing over the soft ground.

'Stand still! Stand still, I say! That's the only way to catch her!' Judith called to Ruby's pursuer. But her advice fell on deaf ears. She watched with impatience. Given the chance she could have captured the truant cow within minutes, but the leering boatman still barred her way.

'Make room, if you please,' she requested. 'Take your boat a way off so that I can land, else we'll be here all day!'

But the boatman persisted. 'Didn't you hear the gentleman? I've to take hold of your boat, lest you drift away. Them's my orders, so I must obey. Mind you, I'd sooner take hold of you. You'd make a pretty little handful for any man by the looks of you.'

'Oh, yes?' said Judith scornfully, all too well aware that his lustful eyes had taken in every curve of her body. 'Well, I fear I'd be too much of a handful for the likes of you. Unhand my boat when I say so!'

The man made no move, so Judith raised her foot and stamped hard on the back of his hand. The man gave a yelp of pain and let go, nursing bruised fingers. Quickly she pushed the other craft away, and brought her boat alongside the only suitable landing-place on the firm ground. As she was tying the mooring rope the fourth man in the party made a move.

Until then she had taken little notice of him, for he stood apart from the others. He was more soberly dressed than his fellows, yet there was not the air of a servant about him. Whatever his situation, he obviously deemed himself not above catching cattle; in a few strides of his long legs he had reached Ruby, who was thoroughly enjoying herself by now. She tossed her head evasively, but he was too quick for her; he dodged and caught her by the horns. She gave a few sharp shakes, trying to free herself, then, finding it was useless, she submitted peacefully enough and trotted calmly along at his side.

'Thank you, sir.' Judith was relieved to have the matter settled so swiftly. 'If you hold her there I'll bring the boat alongside and take her on board.'

The man nodded and led Ruby closer to the water's edge. He was certainly not the one for unnecessary conversation. Judith glanced at him curiously. He was an unusual-looking man, striking rather than handsome, with thick corn-coloured hair. His high-cheekboned face was clean-shaven, and he stared back at her with hooded green eyes that were bold yet held none of the lecherous familiarity of the boatman. Something in that stare caused an uneasiness to stir within Judith. She looked away abruptly.

'I'm sure it's much too dangerous,' protested the old gentleman. 'Surely there must be some other way?'

But his stout companion was delighted at the prospect. 'A cow in a boat! I don't believe it!' he cried.

'She's quite used to travelling so,' Judith insisted.

As if to prove her right Ruby, encouraged by a slap on the flank from the tall man, stepped daintily in beside her. Other cattle often had to be swum from one pasture to another, but Ruby, pampered creature that she was, preferred to travel in a boat if she could.

'I don't believe it!' repeated the stout gentleman, shaking with merriment. 'It's like What's-her-name and the bull that came out of the sea in the story. I'll dine out on this tale for many a night when I get back to London, that I promise you.'

'Oh, it's not a bull, is it? I thought the maid said it was a cow!' The old gentleman went into fresh pangs of anxiety.

'Perhaps I should go with her, just to see she gets home safely, eh master?' suggested the over-familiar boatman, who was still favouring his bruised hand.

Judith felt her heart sink. She did not like the look in his eye—there was vindictiveness there and a lot else besides. The boat and the cow she could handle with ease—a lustful companion was a different matter. It was a fair way back to the village, and lonely too. The kindly old gentleman, though, was very much in favour of the idea.

'Yes, that is a splendid notion,' he said.

'Please, there is no need,' stated Judith firmly.

But the boatman was already moving towards her.

Determined not to have him aboard, she grasped the boat-pole purposefully, ready to fend him off. Fortunately she had no need for such measures, for the tall man intervened.

'The boat is too small. Get back on your own craft, fellow.'

It was the first time he had spoken, and she should have felt grateful—he had saved her from a nasty situation—but instead she was suddenly wary. His voice was pleasant enough, deep with a melodious ring to it, but his words were clipped and spoken with a foreign accent. He was a Dutchman, no doubt about it. And a Dutchman out on the fens meant only two things— drainage, and trouble.

Judith glared at him across the body of the cow. Back came a clear, unwinking stare. He must have seen the sudden hostility in her expression, yet his gaze did not waver. He studied her frankly, assessing her from the top of her dark curls down to her stout country boots. His expression betrayed quite clearly that he liked what he saw.

'I'd best go,' said Judith, irritated by such attention.

'Aye, it grows dark, and you have some way to go, I think.' He leaned forward and pushed the boat away from the bank.

As she eased her craft back into the sluggish current, Judith's thoughts were too much disturbed for her to speak again. Before she rounded the bend she could not resist one last look back. Three men were looking in her direction—the old gentleman anxiously, Sir Walter sourly, and the stout gentleman jovially. Only the Dutchman had turned away, and he was nonchalantly examining the fen mud that covered his boots.

Judith's backward glance cost her dear, for in that moment she dug the boatpole too deeply in the muddy riverbottom. Before she recovered, it had stuck fast and the momentum of the boat had snatched it from her fingers. It was a stupid error, a novice's mistake, and Judith, who was proud of her boatmanship, was furious with herself. There was more at stake than bruised pride, though, for the current tugged at the boat, pulling it beyond the reach of the pole. She did not relish the prospect of drifting helplessly with the stream or trying to control the craft by paddling it with her bare hands in the icy water. There was no need for her to suffer either, however, for the Dutchman must have been paying her more attention than had seemed apparent. He waded in, shin-deep, and retrieved the pole, then ran through the shallows in pursuit of Judith.

'I fancy you will need this, mistress,' he called, holding out the pole to her. 'Without it you could find your journey home a mite difficult.'

Judith managed to grasp it, wet and slippery though it was.

'Thank you, sir,' she said. She expected him to let go of the other end, but he did not. Beneath her the boat swung round in the current, and she realised that he was drawing her in towards the bank.

'Have a care what you are doing, sir,' she protested. 'Else we'll have Ruby escaping again!' Then, because she felt she had been ungracious, she said, 'I am much obliged to you, sir. You've saved me from a difficult situation, but I assure you I'm all right now. I can continue perfectly well on my own.'

'You are sure? You would not like me to call one of the boatmen to assist you?' Still he did not loose his grip, but continued to regard her with steady green eyes.

'You know I would not, sir. And you choose a curious place to jest, standing there up to your knees in water.'

'Oh, so I do!' He looked down at the fen water swirling round his long legs as though noticing it for the first time.

'Then I pray you, let the pole go so that I can reach home and you get to a place of warmth and comfort before you get chilled to death.'

'I pay little heed to the cold, particularly when I'm conversing with a pretty maid.' His gaze, more assessing than ever, rested on Judith's dark curls which, now that she had lost her cap through her exertions, tumbled in profusion across her shoulders. 'A lovely maid in disarray,' he went on. 'Can there be a more pleasing sight to any man?'

'You are impertinent, sir,' she snapped. 'I am beholden to you, but that does not give you the right to be saucy.'

'Saucy? Impertinent? What words are these when all I speak is the truth?' He sounded aggrieved.

Judith was beginning to feel angry, and a little uneasy. She did not know how to cope with this huge man, whose face was so impassive yet who said such outrageous things to her. She looked about for someone to intervene on her behalf, but the three gentlemen had wandered away out of sight. Irritably she tugged sharply at the pole, hoping to take him by surprise, but he continued to hold it tightly.

'Is the grazing here good for your cows?' he suddenly asked in a conversational tone.

Surprised by the abrupt change of subject Judith replied, 'Not now, but in the——' She stopped sharply before reaching the vital word 'summer'. What was she thinking of, giving such information to a Dutchman? 'It's good enough,' she said tersely.

'I thought it must be,' he nodded. 'I've heard these fens of yours are famed for their butter and cheese.'

'And what is that to you, sir?' she demanded. 'Why are you so interested?'

'Why?' The green eyes widened in innocence. 'Because I've no wish to eat dry bread, of course. What is a crust without butter and cheese to make it more palatable?'

Judith began to suspect that this man was either mad, or had a very strange sense of humour. Either way, she had no wish to stand there in the cold wind talking to him.

'Sir,' she said in her sternest tone, 'I have been from home long enough. Let me have the pole, if you please.'

She gave another tug, but still he would not let go. At that her patience snapped. 'Oh, stop your foolish pranks!' she cried. 'I refuse to be dangled on the end of a pole like a . . . a hooked pike!'

'You are too pretty to be a pike,' protested the Dutchman. Then, for the first time, he smiled. It was a surprisingly attractive smile; it lit his face and made his eyes seem to spark green fire. 'Though I suspect that you may have sharp teeth,' he grinned.

'You must be sadly lacking in amusement to have to stand here in the cold playing silly games and keeping me from a warm hearth!' she exclaimed.

'But who is keeping you, mistress?' he protested, holding both hands in the air to show that he had released her.

'And in good time, too!' she declared, pushing the boat back towards the mainstream and making sure her fingers gripped the pole tightly.

The Dutchman splashed his way towards the meagre high ground, and stood there balanced precariously on two tussocks of grass, like a colossus in black broadcloth.

'Who would have thought to see roses in February,' he said.

'Where?' asked Judith, looking about her.

'Why, in your cheeks, mistress. Where else?' He took off his hat and swept her a bow so low that she could not tell whether he was grinning or not.

With an angry snort Judith set the boat towards home.

'The man's wits are gone,' she muttered to herself.

'Farewell, mistress. I am glad to have made your acquaintance,' she heard him call. But this time she took good care not to turn round.

She was desperate to get home, to spread the news of the Dutchman's presence. She could see the low mound of the village of Sedgewick ahead, rising out of the surrounding water, but it seemed a long time drawing closer. She could not bear to think of the fenland way of life, with all its freedom and independence, being destroyed. There had always been men who sought to gain land and gold by draining the marshes, but so far the fens had defeated them. In recent years a new breed of speculator had emerged who employed skilled Dutch engineers to plan their work. Already there had been dreadful tales of starvation from up Axholme way, where men had found their marshes drained, their rights gone, and the new land seized by the Crown. Now, with the unexpected presence of the Dutchman and his richly dressed companions, it seemed the people of Sedgewick must be on their guard.

Judith's arms ached with poling the boat through the flood water, but she did not slacken the pace. She had to get to Adam to tell him what she had seen, then they could decide what to do. At last she reached her home, and moored the boat at the little landing-stage below the garden hedge. Judith and her Aunt Ketty owned the two cottages nearest to the Summer Grounds. They lived happily in one, and the other, which had been left to Judith by her grandmother, they let to the village shoemaker at a modest rent, along with its land and grazing rights on the fen. Beyond, sheltering among a clump of trees, was Adam's farm, Old Place, and further still lay the village, with the outline of St Peter's Church sticking up, a lonely sentinel in the sky.

Ruby tripped ashore unbidden and Judith followed her, hurrying up the path to the cottage. Already her aunt was looking out for her.

'There you are, my lamb! I've been that worried about you. No sooner had you gone than I'd a dreadful feeling that something was wrong. I've been in torment ever since. In fact, I'd half a mind to come looking for you.'

She hugged the girl to her round plump bosom, and pulled her indoors beside the glowing peat fire. She was not really Judith's aunt, nor even any relation, but she had brought her up from the time she was in leading-strings, with such love and kindness that the girl had never really felt the loss of a mother she could not remember.

'Come you by the fire, child,' Aunt Ketty insisted. 'See, I've baked you a nice apple. It's standing in the hearth.'

Despite her tiredness and anxiety, Judith had to smile as she saw the apple in its earthenware dish. Aunt Ketty was a great believer in food as a source of comfort. The fact that she had specially cooked one of their precious store of apples for her showed how worried she had been. Judith marvelled, too, that once again her aunt had known something was wrong.

It was Aunt Ketty's curse that she had the ability to see events before they happened. It was a talent which distressed her greatly, and one that she would have gladly been without. It was too much like witchcraft, and had not the Church spoken out strongly against such unnatural practices? Poor Aunt Ketty, she could not help but practice her art, for it came unbidden. Of course, she had told no one other than Judith of her unlooked-for gift—only a fool would have broadcast any hint of possessing supernatural powers.

Now she looked at Judith apprehensively and said, 'Tell me what happened out on the fen. It's no use trying to hide it from me. I know full well that there was trouble.'

'No trouble yet, though I feel there will be,' said Judith. 'I met a Dutchman on the fen. He was with some finely dressed London gentlemen. One was Sir Walter Massingham.'

There was a moment's silence as Aunt Ketty took in the full implications.

'They were wildfowling?' she suggested, but there was no hope in her voice.

'With no nets or guns?' Judith shook her head.

'Can you be sure he was Dutch? Perhaps he was from some other land.'

Again Judith shook her head. 'He was Dutch. I heard the accent often enough when we stayed with your sister.'

They had once visited Aunt Ketty's sister who kept a small eating-house in Lynn. At the time many of the customers had been Dutchmen, but they had been welcome visitors, seamen and merchants, sheltering in the port because of prolonged gales.

'Surely no one can be planning to drain Hanser Fen, not after all these years? That would be trouble indeed.' Aunt Ketty's face wrinkled with concern. 'What was he like, this Dutchman? What age? Was he well-favoured?'

Judith thought back. 'I don't know—I mean, he was such a strange-looking fellow that there was no saying whether he was comely or no. As for his age, he could have been anything. He was big in stature and flaxen-haired, and he had a bold look to him, too, the saucy fellow.' The memory of those assessing green eyes roused Judith's anger once more.

'He can't be the one, then...'

'He can't be which one?'

'The Dutchman who came before. You won't remember, you were but a child at the time, but some ten years ago there was a serious scheme to drain Hanser. A rich merchant from London was to undertake the affair, and he brought over a Dutch engineer.'

'What happened?'

'Thankfully it all came to naught. The merchant took sick and died; there was some squabble over who would inherit. Anyway, the money dried up and the Dutchman went off elsewhere without a spade being stuck into the ground.'

'And you think it is the same Dutchman?'

'From what you say, it can't be. That fellow was well on in years even then, and very red in the face... Oh, dear, I do hope it's not the start of another such wrangle!'

'We must stop them if it is. We can't let anyone drain our fen. I think I should go and tell Adam at once.'

'But he's been gone to Ely these three days.'

'No, he's back. I saw him as I set out after Ruby.'

'In that case his feet will bring him here soon enough, if I'm any judge. Bide there, love, finish your apple and get warm. There's no point in fighting the fen drainers if you get a chill while you're about it. You'll have chance enough to talk to Adam soon.'

She was right. Judith barely had time to empty her bowl and tidy herself before there was a knock at the door. She flew to open it knowing that Adam would be there, he came most nights to see her after his work was done. It was gratifying to know that even the after-effects of his long ride from Ely had not kept him away.

'Adam, how I need to see you! Come you in!' she cried.

'Now, that's a warming welcome for a man,' he grinned.

Stooping, he kissed her full on the mouth. The temptation to return his kiss in equal measure was overpowering, but Aunt Ketty was standing by watchfully. Reluctantly Judith had to restrict herself to a response that was both seemly and chaste.

'Did you ever doubt your welcome?' she asked, when Adam released her.

'I hope no other man is more welcome here, but who is to know how many suitors come knocking at your door when my sister finds business for me in Ely?'

Adam always teased Judith about her supposed sweethearts, though he knew full well she never had eyes for any other man. Content at his confidence in her, Judith smiled back.

'Judith met one who was certainly far from welcome,' said Aunt Ketty.

'You did? How so?' Adam made himself comfortable on the long bench by the fire, then drew Judith down beside him, his arm firmly about her waist.

'While I was out on Hanser Fen I met a Dutchman,' she told him, and went on to relate her encounter. She did not tell him all that had happened; she thought it best not to mention the Dutchman's strange flirtatious behaviour.

'His being here could mean drainage, couldn't it?' she concluded.

Adam struck his knee with his free hand. 'Undoubtedly! Why else would he be out there at this time of year? Someone plans to drain the fen, and to the devil with the poor souls who must live off it! Well, they'll find they've bitten off more than they can chew this time, these fancy London gentlemen with money to throw into our marshes.'

'One was Sir Walter Massingham,' Judith said.

'Massingham? Our beloved squire? That makes it doubly certain!'

'Why? What difference does he make?'

'Our dear Sir Walter is a toad-eater of the Papist lover, Charles, that's why. 'Tis a well-known fact that the King has long had his eye on our fens. He's always in dire straits for money to squander on trumpery pleasures. Draining the marshes will gain him gold.'

'The fens are ours, held in common right,' Judith protested.

'Try telling that to King Charles. It's my belief that Sir Walter is acting as his agent, and those prettily dressed London gentlemen are the ones to venture the money. They'll make handsome profits, the King will get his share of the land, and we'll be cheated out of our birthright.'

'Then we'll stop them!' cried Judith.

'Aye, we will.' Adam sprang to his feet and began pacing the tiny cottage, scattering the floor rushes with his boots. 'We must call all the Fen Commoners together and fight. It's a pity 'tis so late now, else I would have my men out rallying them all. Tomorrow must suffice, yes, early tomorrow.' He was thinking aloud now, oblivious of Aunt Ketty and Judith. 'We'll have a meeting by the church wall, and organise ourselves. We must have vigilant patrols, then we'll know what's happening—and arms, we'll need plenty of arms and ammunition. Best see what each man can provide. Some form of signal must be decided upon, too, to rally everyone to the fray——'

'Arms? Ammunition? Surely it won't come to that?' Aunt Ketty protested.

'How else can it be? I'll get matters in hand at first light tomorrow,' stated Adam.

'Let's not be hasty,' cautioned Aunt Ketty. 'In truth, we've got very little to go on. We can hardly call the countryside to arms just because Judith met a Dutchman on Hanser Fen!'

'What do you suggest we do? Wait until they've dug their ditches under our very noses before we act?'

'Nay, nay. I agree we must do something,' said Aunt Ketty. 'But let's find out more details before we cry murder!'

Her words struck a calming note in Judith's senses. One Dutchman and a few London gentlemen on Hanser Fen were hardly cause to start a revolt. Reluctantly her glowing image of Adam as a hero and leader of men faded as she had to acknowledge her aunt spoke wisely.

'A few days' delay can make little difference, can it?' she said. 'After all, the drainers, if such they be, can do nothing until the waters go down.'

Aunt Ketty looked at her approvingly. 'That's right, my lamb. Where can we find out the truth, though?'

'The Fen Office at Ely would surely know,' Judith said.

"And you think that they'll tell us the details just for the asking?' Adam's voice was scornful.

'Of course not! We don't need to go to their door cap in hand. There must be rumours flying around. Something as important as the draining of Hanser can't be proposed without there being talk,' replied Judith.

Their cautious arguments were beginning to have effect, and Adam stopped his restless pacing.

'I've only just come back from Ely,' he said. 'To be away from the farm again so soon...I'm not sure I can manage it.'

It had not occurred to Judith that Adam would be the one to go. She had missed him sorely these last three days, and the thought of being parted from him again so soon was unbearable.

'Who else is there who could go?' she asked hastily. 'Someone trustworthy, of course... Toby, perhaps?'

'No one better,' replied Aunt Ketty with such alacrity that Judith suspected she had had him in mind all along.

Toby Brazier was a wildfowler, a fenman born, and as cunning as a bagful of foxes. If anyone could get at the truth, he could.

'Mm...Old Toby's reliable enough,' Adam considered carefully. 'As fly as they come. Perhaps we should see if he's agreeable.'

'I'll go and ask him in the morning,' said Judith. 'I'm sure he'll go, it's a scheme that will appeal to him. One thing more—we don't want to worrit folks unnecessarily, do we? So perhaps we should keep this matter to ourselves until we're sure. I don't count Marjorie, though,' she added, catching Adam's eye. She knew that he kept no secrets from his sister.

'Another wise notion!' Aunt Ketty gave her a hug. 'You're getting a good head on your shoulders, my pet.'

She began damping down the fire for the night. This was her sign that she thought it time for Adam to go.

Taking the hint, he rose. 'Will you walk as far as the gate with me?' he asked Judith.

This was a nightly ritual also, but the girl still waited for her aunt's nod of approval before she ran for her cloak.

The winter sun had all but set as they walked along the rough path towards the gate which divided Adam's property from Aunt Ketty's. It was no more than a field's width away, so the young lovers walked slowly, their arms entwined about each other. Everything was so peaceful, with just the soughing of the wind in the reeds, and the brief call of a solitary wild goose out on the flooded fen to break the silence. It was hard to believe that this quiet way of life could be threatened. As she thought of what drainage would mean to everyone in the village, Judith felt the secure future that made up her dreams for the past few years begin to waver.

'Do you think we'll have to fight?' she asked.

'I do indeed. Every man will have to play his part.'

'Just every man? Why not women, too? After all, it touches us just as deeply. We'll all fight together!'

Adam turned his head. 'No, love, there'll be no fighting for you, not while I'm here to protect you,' he said firmly. 'A fine sort of fellow I'd appear if some hurt befell you! No, I'll do all the fighting for the pair of us.' He turned and pulled her tightly to him, and his lips began to trace the outline of her cheek. 'I only wish I had the right to protect you as my wife—— Oh, Judith! We should have been married long since. I have been very patient. When will your aunt agree? At least, would she not consent to our betrothal?'

Judith could not reply immediately, for his kisses got in the way, driving all thought of mere words from her mind. When at last she freed her mouth she caressed his chestnut-bright hair and whispered breathlessly, 'You know I am as eager to wed as you are. To be your wife, to work with you by day and lie in your arms at night, that would be the most perfect life I could wish for. It's agony to part like this each evening, but I beg you, be patient a little longer——'

'Haven't I been patient long enough? I tell you, Judith, I can't stand it much longer. I've bided my time this age, waiting upon the whims of your aunt. But I am a mortal man, with needs and longings. If you won't speak to your aunt again then I must.'

'Oh, no, I pray you, don't,' begged Judith. 'You know that when you did so in the past it led to harsh words——'

'Only because your aunt is stubborn.'

'Adam, Aunt Ketty has given me so much over the years, in love as well as material things, yet she's never before asked for anything in return. Even the rent that Peter Renshaw pays for my grandmother's cottage has been carefully saved for me; Aunt Ketty hasn't touched a farthing in all this time. Now, if she wishes to keep me by her a little longer then I won't defy her, nor will I cause her pain.'

'You don't mind how much suffering you cause me, do you?'

'Oh, Adam, that's not so, and you know it!'

'All I know is that you won't wed me.'

'Not until my aunt gives her consent. She'll not keep us long, I'm sure.'

'I wish I was of the same mind. I fear she'll keep you tied to her apron strings until you're an old maid!'

'So you don't think I am worth the wait?'

'That depends for how long! I confess I grow impatient, and I tell you if you won't have me there are plenty of girls who will.'

'You mean Susan Osborne, I suppose?' retorted Judith. 'With her big blue eyes and her boasts that her father is the richest man in Sedgewick!'

'Aye, Susan, for one. If I asked her to be my wife she'd not keep me waiting an eternity.'

'That she wouldn't! Her mother would be so fearful
lest you escape she'd have you down the aisle so fast
your shoes would scorch!'

They faced each other, their bodies tense as they
hovered on the edge of a quarrel. Then suddenly Adam
chuckled.

'Aye, Mistress Osborne would do that right enough;
but it might be worth it. Hal Osborne keeps a good drop
of ale at the Lamb, and as his son-in-law I'd be able to
sup my fill.'

'Not if Mistress Osborne caught you drinking the
profits. No, you'd best forget Susan and stay with the
sweetheart you know.'

'Perhaps I should.' Adam suddenly enfolded her in
his arms. His body was warm and urgent against hers,
sending the blood coursing through her veins. 'Please
ask your aunt again,' he whispered desperately. 'You've
no notion of how much I want you and have need of
you. Ask her soon!'

'I will, I will,' promised Judith, her voice husky with
her own longing.

The last trace of colour ebbed from the sky, the signal
that they must part. One hard, desperate kiss, then Adam
strode towards Old Place, while Judith returned to the
cottage. A tiny spark of candlelight guided her back
safely, but as she picked her way across the field she was
uneasy. She and Adam had come close to quarrelling.
They had done so before often enough and made it up
with tears and kisses. But this time it had been different;
for the first time Adam had hinted that he would not
wait forever for her. He was not a patient man, she had
long known it, and now it seemed his scant patience was
wearing thin. It had always been a secret fear of hers
that one day he would forsake her for some other maid,
and she dreaded to think that her fear might come true.
She decided to tackle Aunt Ketty again as soon as possible, for she was certain of one thing—to her, all other
troubles, even the drainers on Hanser Fen or the King's
quarrel with Parliament, faded into insignificance beside
the threat of losing Adam's love.

CHAPTER TWO

NEXT morning Judith awoke full of resolve, ready to ask Aunt Ketty for permission to marry Adam. There was no point in broaching the matter before noon, however. What with tending to her own chores and seeing that all was well with their neighbour, Loveday Renshaw, who was soon to give birth to her eighth child, Aunt Ketty would not be still for two minutes together. There was no help for it, she would have to bide her time.

The day had dawned dank and chill, with a light mist curling wraith-like from the drowned land. Even so, as she looked over the watery surface Judith found a pale, shimmering beauty, and she thought how hateful it would be to lose it all. Not that she had much time to muse, though, for she had to do the morning milking, and feed the fowls and the animals. Her hands were red and smarting with the cold long before she had finished because she had mislaid her mittens. In the end she had to make do with wrapping her poor fingers in the folds of her cloak whenever she could.

'When will you go to see Toby?' asked Aunt Ketty. 'If he's to go to Ely it must be soon.'

'I'll go now. I've just finished collecting the eggs.'

'Be sure to put the matter to him carefully. I'm convinced he'll find out how things lie better than anyone. But you know what he's like—he needs a bit of coaxing, he's that obstinate.'

'I understand. I'll use great tact,' Judith promised with a grin.

Her path lay along a causeway that in summer was raised well above the surrounding land, but today it was almost overlapped by flood-water. Judith took no notice of how slippery it was underfoot, she was used to such conditions and had walked that way a thousand times.

As she went she watched out for Adam, hoping against hope for a glimpse of him. The memory of those angry words they had exchanged the previous evening was still with her, making her vaguely uneasy. She would feel more content if she could see Adam for a moment, just to assure herself that all was really well.

She was out of luck, there was no sign of him. The figure she noted in the distance was far less welcome—she could not mistake that height or those heavy shoulders clad in black broadcloth. The Dutchman was out on the fen.

There was no chance of an actual encounter, for a wide expanse of marsh and deep water separated them, to Judith's great relief. She had no wish to cope with his nonsense again. In fact, she hoped that he had not seen her, for he was walking slowly, his attention focused on the spongy ground beneath his feet. He might simply have been taking care where he trod, but Judith stopped in the shelter of a clump of alders to observe him in case he was measuring, taking notes, or doing anything else that might indicate possible drainage. He did none of these things, though.

She knew at once when he spotted her, because he straightened up and advanced towards her until he was on the very verge of the boggy fen. He took off his hat and waved it to attract her attention, calling as he did so words that were whipped away by the wind.

Judith felt embarrassed to have been caught watching him. She turned and began to stride along the path, her head in the air.

To her annoyance he kept pace with her, checking his long stride to keep level with her. When she hurried he hurried, when she slowed he slowed. She did not welcome his presence, even when distanced by a sizeable stretch of marsh. In desperation she stopped completely, as though the strap on one of the pattens that raised her feet out of the mud needed tightening. It did no good; he stopped too.

'Oh, go away!' she eventually yelled in protest.

At this the Dutchman cupped his hand behind his ear, pretending that he could not hear, though Judith was convinced that the wind was carrying her words towards him.

'Very well, Master Dutchman, if all you want is a fruitless tramp across the fens then who am I to stop you?' she said under her breath. And she began to walk briskly in the direction of Toby's cottage.

As she expected, the Dutchman again took a parallel path, but she was at great pains to ignore him—at least, she tried, but she could not help watching his progress out of the corner of her eye. She was very familiar with this stretch of fen and she knew that the going on his side of the watery mud would soon get very rough. She was right. She walked easily along the path, muddy and crumbling though it often was, but he soon found himself having to avoid pools, and leap from one clump of turf to another to keep up with her.

At last she heard a splash, and turned to see what had happened. The Dutchman was standing on a small hillock wringing water from the skirts of his coat. Judith wished she had had the satisfaction of seeing him slip, but she contented herself with giving him a mocking wave before hurrying off towards Toby's house, leaving him to watch her go, his face as enigmatic as ever.

What his purpose had been in following her in such a fashion she could not imagine, unless it was part of the curious lunacy which seemed to afflict him. She had no intention of letting the Dutchman's minor eccentricities bother her, though. It was his purpose in coming to the Fens that concerned her, for she feared he was up to no good.

Toby's tiny cottage lay outside the village, perched as close to the fens as it could possibly get, for it was here that Toby won his living by catching all manner of game and wildfowl.

The door opened before Judith had a chance to knock, and Toby greeted her warmly. 'I saw you coming, mawther. You're a sight for sore eyes on such a bleak morning. Come you in by the fire.'

She followed him into the single room which served him as parlour, bedchamber, and kitchen. It was obvious, even in the dim light cast by the small horn window, that there was no woman to care for the place. Scattered about were nets, traps, and baskets of every description, the tools of Toby's trade.

With a sweep of his arm Toby cleared a space among the clutter on the table and set out two tankards. 'Will you take a drop of something...? No? Then do you mind if I take one myself, just to drive away the rheumatics? You darned brute! I'll have your hide, that I will!' Toby's genial tone changed swiftly to one of blazing anger as he stumbled over the dog which clung close to his heels. 'I'd put a shot through its miserable brain only it would be a waste of good lead!'

The old dog listened to these bloodthirsty threats, and continued to look up at its master with adoration shining from its one good eye. There was a strong resemblance between master and dog. Neither of them was young, and whatever looks they had possessed in their youth had long since been obliterated by the numerous fights that were lamentably the chief delight of both fenmen and their dogs. But the scarred and grizzled exteriors hid much true loyalty and warm-heartedness.

Judith sat down opposite Toby. She longed to blurt out the true reason for her visit, but she knew that she had to bide her time. Toby could be cantankerous if he had a mind. Patiently she answered as he asked after Aunt Ketty and talked over the gossip from the village, until she began to despair of ever bringing the conversation round.

Eventually Toby wiped his mouth with his hand and said, 'Right, now you can tell me what's burning the tip of your tongue.'

Taken by surprise, Judith stammered, 'W-what do you mean?'

Toby's eyes twinkled. 'Come, my mawther, you can't fool me. You've been dying to speak your piece ever since you got here. What is it that's agitating you so?'

She had to chuckle. 'So much for my guile and cunning. Very well, I'll tell you. We need your help and advice. You see, yesterday, when I was out on Hanser Fen, I met a Dutchman...'

Toby listened in silence until she had finished, then he said quietly, 'That's quite a mess of fishes!'

'Do you think it means draining?'

'Maybe...maybe not...'

'We thought—Aunt Ketty and I—that someone should go to Ely and find out for sure. There's bound to be gossip flying around...' This was the part where she had to be particularly crafty. 'We thought that maybe Adam should go.'

'No, young Adam isn't the one to send. I'll go myself. That's what you've been angling after, isn't it? You and Ketty had it all worked out.'

'Well——'

'Of course you did, you saucy jade! Don't think I was fooled for one minute.'

'I confess you're right,' admitted Judith. 'Do you think there's need to be concerned?'

'Who's to tell? It seems a crazy time to start such a scheme, the country being in such a turmoil with King and Parliament at loggerheads. But stranger things have happened. I'll know better when I've had a few hours in Ely.'

'How will you set about it?'

'Mercy on us, was there ever such a wench for asking questions! The Fen Commissioners have servants, and those servants have eyes and ears. I'll just find the ones with the longest tongues—doubtless they'll have thirsts to match.'

'You make it sound so easy.'

'Don't fret you now, there's no call to get anxious before we're certain.'

'In that case I'll wish you Godspeed and a safe journey.'

'I don't know when you can look to see me again. It'll depend on what I can ferret out...and how good the ale is. I'll come back with the truth of the matter, never fear.'

Judith left Toby's cottage feeling happier. As he had pointed out, it was useless to worry too soon. Besides, whatever the future held, life still had to go on, so instead of going straight home she made a detour to one of the fields that she and Aunt Ketty cultivated each year. Digging at it with the heel of her boot, she decided that perhaps they would be lucky and be able to start ploughing early.

Much as Judith and her aunt revelled in their self-sufficiency, the early ploughing was one task where they needed help. They hired a day labourer. Usually it was Humphrey Chester, a somewhat unpleasant character, whose nickname of Dewdrop owed much to the rheumy state of his nose and nothing at all to poetic origins. He was more or less honest, if they kept an eye on him, and he gave a good day's work for a good day's pay, which was why they employed him. Adam would have gladly undertaken the ploughing for them, had not Aunt Ketty's sense of propriety forbidden it.

'It would not be seemly. He'd never accept payment. And for a man to give his labour is the same as giving a costly gift. We couldn't accept it, him not being a kinsman. No, far better we pay our own way while we can.'

Judith wished for the closest of all kinship with Adam, but that did not stop her agreeing wholeheartedly with her aunt's independence.

Aunt Ketty was churning butter when she arrived home.

'Toby'll go?' she asked, not ceasing her task.

'Yes, he's setting off immediately.'

'And what did he think of the matter?'

'That we should wait until we have just cause before we start worrying.'

'Very wise. I thought last night that young Adam was taking matters a bit far. He's all fire and fight, that lad!'

Judith chose to ignore this criticism of Adam. Instead she changed the subject.

'I had a look at the top field on my way back. It's fit for ploughing.'

'So soon? Now, that is good news. We must call on Dewdrop as soon as possible, before anyone else speaks for him.'

'I may as well go now, since I've my cloak on already.'

'Yes, you go at once, my love—but why aren't you wearing your mittens? Your hands look frozen.'

'I can't find them.'

'Can't find them? There's a nuisance! If they don't come to light soon I must start a new pair for you, else you'll be getting the chaps and chilblains. Here, take mine for the time being.'

'Thank you. I won't be long, though I might call at Old Place.'

'As you please, dear.' Aunt Ketty's tone was mild, but Judith knew that she was not fooled. She was well aware that her eagerness to run errands was just an excuse to see Adam.

As it happened Judith was disappointed on both counts. Dewdrop Chester was out, she had to leave word with his wife. Then, when she reached Old Place, Adam was not at home, either. She had to content herself with seeing Marjorie, his sister, who was in the wash-house supervising the laundry, her cool, unblinking eyes missing nothing.

If anything clouded Judith's hopes of happiness with Adam then it was the prospect of having Marjorie as a sister-in-law. She was ashamed of feeling so, and forced herself to look only upon the older woman's good qualities, trying hard to love her for her brother's sake— but with little success. Marjorie was a worthy woman. Few would have done what she did—given up all thoughts of marriage, in spite of being handsome and having a good dowry, to bring up her young brother. Marjorie and Adam were the extremes of a large family, the eldest and the youngest, with nigh on twenty years separating them. No other Digby child had survived, a comment on the harshness of life on the Fens. When poor Mistress Digby had passed away Marjorie had given

herself up to the care of her baby brother, then, some
years later when their father had died also it was Marjorie
who took up the reins of the farm with characteristic
efficiency. She was much respected for her skills at
husbandry, as well as for her virtue. Indeed, there were
some who claimed she was the 'strongest man in
Sedgewick'. But she lacked all the softer, more gentle
qualities. Her love for Adam was the only sign of
womanly tenderness in her, and for that alone Judith
could forgive her much.

Many women, especially those as dignified as Mistress
Digby, might have felt awkward at greeting a visitor in
the wash-house, but not Marjorie. She nodded to Judith
without once taking her eyes off the perspiring maid who
was scrubbing sheets in a welter of steam.

'I had hoped to see Adam,' said Judith, when she
made no move to speak.

'He's out. Is it important?'

'Yes. No doubt he told you of the business on Hanser
Fen?'

'He did indeed.'

'Well, Toby has agreed to go to Ely.'

'I wonder if Tobias Brazier is really the best person
to send on such an errand.' There was disapproval in
Marjorie's voice. 'Whom does he know? What contacts
will he have? None but boatmen and low creatures who
frequent the riverside taverns. You should have chosen
someone with more standing and influence. One with
education, with friends in high places where the truth
could really be learnt.'

She meant Adam, of course. As far as Marjorie was
concerned the Digbys were one of the foremost families
in the country. They had indeed been a noble family
years since, but no one remembered their past glories
now, save Marjorie. She still spoke as though they were
among the mighty of the land instead of being yeoman
farmers.

'I'm sure Toby will do the job well. He knows a great
many people.' Judith sprang to the old man's defence.

'Perhaps—perhaps...' Marjorie began taking off the coarse apron that covered a spotless linen one. 'I am glad you came today, though. I have something to show you. Come you into the house.'

Mystified, Judith followed her. As its name suggested, Old Place was very ancient, and even though the existing dwelling was no more than one wing of the original structure it still gave an impression of how grand it must have been. Under Marjorie's stern control it was beautifully kept, washed, waxed and polished by harassed maids, but to Judith it always felt cold. There was a starkness and lack of colour about the house that she found depressing.

Judith imagined how Old Place would look under *her* tending. How she would transform it with colourful hangings against the dark panelling, posies of bright flowers to bring colour to gloomy corners, bowls of fragrant herbs to drive away the ancient mustiness. She would bring out the family silver, too, the remnants of the Digbys' great wealth, that lay wrapped in flannel in the huge court cupboard, and have it polished and shining so that it reflected the light of the fire and the candles. For a moment she was enchanted by her vision of the future, until her eyes focused upon Marjorie's poker-straight back going before her, and the dream faded abruptly.

She knew that Marjorie longed for Adam to marry and have sons. Judith knew just as well that she would not easily relinquish the reins of the household to anyone else. In her imagination she could hear Adam's sister querying every innovation in that crisp voice of hers, 'It does well enough, but of what use is it?' Then Judith realised that she was being critical again. Concentrate on her good qualities, she rebuked herself; learn to love her for Adam's sake if not her own.... It was a heavy task.

Marjorie stopped so sharply that Judith almost cannoned into her.

'This is what I want to show you,' she said, and led the way into one of the upper rooms.

The wood panelling showed tantalising traces of colour here and there, long since faded, but they proved that Old Place had been bright and colourful. Apart from that there seemed to be nothing out of the ordinary.

'There it is!' cried Marjorie triumphantly pointing to a carved inscription on one of the panels. 'It has been hidden for goodness knows how long, and only came to light when we moved the great bed. Read what it says!'

Judith had a fair knowledge of reading—Aunt Ketty had insisted on her learning so that she could at least make out the Commandments that were written up in church—but these letters were so old and ornate that she could scarcely decipher them.

Marjorie's impatience overcame her. 'It says "Judith de Gibié" and the date—1492.'

Judith did not see the significance, other than it being her Christian name, and Marjorie became even more impatient at such stupidity.

'Don't you see? De Gibié is the old form of our name; that is how it was in the good old days when we had our rightful position in the land. I thought that you would like to see that we had a Judith in the family then. A long way back, it is true; she would have been in the times of Henry VII, grandfather to the great Queen. Perhaps discovering it now is a sign that it is time for another Judith to join us.' She smiled her wintry smile.

Judith was delighted at the discovery, and traced the letters with her fingers. She was equally delighted to find how much Marjorie favoured her as a wife for Adam— until that moment she had had her doubts.

'It's time Adam was wed.' Marjorie seemed to have read her thoughts. 'He has set his fancy on you, and I've no objections. You are from good Fenland stock. I do not think you are indifferent to him, so why don't you become betrothed? Adam is a fine catch for any wench.'

'I know, and I am indeed far from being indifferent...'

'Jane Kettering is the stumbling block. Don't try to deny it! I know. Why won't she give her consent?'

'She was childless for so long, and I know she felt it sorely, then I came to her...' Judith gave the only reason she could think of.

'So, she's loath to let you go. Understandable, I suppose, but it's high time Adam was wed. So often men who delay marriage end up by getting themselves entangled with someone entirely unsuitable—that is my fear!'

It was Judith's fear too, and she felt a frisson of unease at hearing her own misgivings so expressed.

'She is no kin to you, is she?' demanded Marjorie suddenly.

'Aunt Ketty? You know she's not!' Judith looked at her in surprise. 'She took me in after my grandmother died, when I was but two years old.'

'Have you no folk of your own living?'

'Not that I know of... It was the plague that orphaned me as a babe; only my grandmother and myself were spared. Two years later she was taken too. There were some cousins up Grantham way, I believe, who were elderly and had no wish to take on a little child. They were more than happy to let Aunt Ketty have me. Without her I'd have fared very badly.'

'But you were not left penniless?'

'No, the cottage where Peter Renshaw lives is mine, and all its land.' Judith was puzzled. Marjorie had known her all her life and was as familiar with her history as she was herself—so why was she asking such questions?

'Have you any legal papers making Jane Kettering your guardian?'

'Naught was done with lawyers that I ever heard of,' Judith replied, still mystified.

'That solves it, then!' Marjorie was triumphant. 'You can be married as soon as you wish. Jane Kettering has no right to stop you, she is nothing to you!'

'Nothing to me!' cried Judith aghast. 'She is but the woman who has brought me up for the last sixteen years! My natural mother couldn't have given me more affection and kindness! Maybe Aunt Ketty has no papers with a lawyer's signature on them, she has no need of them. I owe her more in love and gratitude than a thousand lawyers' letters would grant. I love Adam too, aye, and wish to marry him more than I have words to tell, but to do so without my aunt's approval would cause me nothing but unhappiness. I am prepared to wait until she sees fit to give her consent. If Adam truly loves me in return he'll wait too!'

'You've too free a tongue for a maid of your years,' Marjorie snapped, then she added, 'You're loyal, I'll give you that! I suggest, though, that you set about persuading Jane Kettering to give you her blessing before Adam becomes too impatient.'

Judith left Old Place in a state of disquiet.

Aunt Ketty saw that there was something amiss the moment she stepped over the threshold. 'Why, what has vexed you, my lamb?' she asked.

Judith felt that she could not tell her the full truth so she said, 'I didn't see eye to eye with Marjorie.'

'There are few who do, I fear, love. But never mind, forget her for now. It's such a raw day we'll bank up the fire and spend some time warming our toes after dinner, shall we? And maybe we could roast some chestnuts on the shovel into the bargain.'

Aunt Ketty's faith in food as a solace yet again— Judith found it a cheerful prospect after her wearing morning. It had the added advantage of presenting an excellent opportunity for her to broach the subject of her marriage to Adam.

They were very snug that afternoon. The dank mist swirled outside, pressing against the windows, making the cottage seem even more warm and comfortable than usual. Their meal over, they settled down beside the glowing turves of peat. Aunt Ketty began to make replacements for Judith's mittens, which still could not be found, while the girl took out some sewing.

One advantage of a long spinsterhood, thought Judith wryly, was that her dower line would be something out of the ordinary. She already had sheets and coverlets in plenty, stored in the big cedarwood chest, and now she was working on an embroidered hanging. The doors at

Old Place were stout and strong; they were also twisted with age and let in the biting Fen winds most cruelly, and a hanging would be both practical and good to the eye. The fabric was of a heavy cream linen, and on it she had sewn as many flowers as she knew—roses, blue-bells, daffodils, gillyflowers, and many more—a veri-table garden of stitchery. In her mind's eye she could see it completed and hanging against the age-darkened panelling of Old Place, the pale linen lightening the gloomy background, the multicoloured flowers bringing warmth and brilliance to a sombre room.

But, she reflected, if I don't get Aunt Ketty's per-mission to wed soon, all this work will be for naught.

She threaded her needle to start on a clump of violets.

'Marjorie has found the strangest thing at Old Place,' she began. 'It was an inscription that no one knew was there, carved into a panel. It said ''Judith Digby'' and it was dated years and years back in olden times, only it was not writ ''Digby'' in those days but ''de Some-thing-or-another''. The ''Judith'' was the same, though.'

There, she had played her opening gambit. With luck she could soon move the conversation round to the subject of marriage.

Aunt Ketty, however, had other ideas. 'A fine old name is Judith. A Bible name, one to live up to.'

'Aye, but don't you think it was curious——?' She got no further, for she was interrupted by a knock at the door.

'Answer it, my love,' said Aunt Ketty. ''Tis not a day for anyone to be kept standing outside.'

'It'll be Adam, as like as not,' said Judith, hurrying to do as she was bid. 'Though I'd have thought he'd be too busy to call...'

Her voice faded away as she opened the door, for it was not Adam standing there. It was the Dutchman.

'Good day, Mistress Pentelow,' he greeted her in his clipped accent.

Judith was too astounded by his presence to do more than gape like an idiot.

'Good day, mistress,' he repeated. 'You didn't expect to see me, I think.'

Judith swallowed hard, but still the words would not come. She just stared back at him, at his huge sombrely clad figure, which filled the doorway in a way that was almost sinister.

'Judith, my love, bid whoever is there to come in,' instructed Aunt Ketty. 'There's a draught whipping through here keen enough to cut bread.'

The Dutchman needed no second invitation. Without hesitation he stepped in, removing his steeple hat as he did so, but even then he was so tall he had to duck to avoid the beams. His hunched posture did at least make him look less threatening.

Seeing a stranger, Aunt Ketty rose and gave a neat curtsey.

'Good day, sir...' she began, then it dawned on her just who was standing before her. 'Judith, is this...this...?'

'Aye, this is the gentleman I met on Hanser Fen, or one of them, at least. I fear I cannot formally present him to you, for we weren't introduced.' Judith had recovered her composure with a vengeance, and was angry with herself for having been taken aback.

'Indeed we were not, to my regret,' said the Dutchman. 'Your servant, mistress. I am Maarten van de Scheldt, of Amsterdam.' He bowed to Aunt Ketty in a gesture which threatened half the furniture in the small room. Then he waited calmly for the introductions to be completed.

Stung by his impudence, Judith replied in an icy voice, 'May I present my guardian, sir, Mistress Kettering?'

Again the Dutchman bowed low as he kissed her hand, and again the furniture rocked perilously.

'You will sit down and take some wine with us, sir?' asked Aunt Ketty, her innate sense of hospitality superseding her astonishment and suspicion.

'That would be most welcome, I thank you.' The Dutchman settled himself down in a chair and stretched his long legs out towards the fire. Then he looked at Judith.

'I am glad you reached home safely,' he said. 'I hope your cow behaved herself.'

'She behaves well enough when properly handled,' replied Judith, her tone still unwelcoming. 'I hope you didn't come far out of your way to visit us?'

'I didn't come out of my way at all. I came to your house on purpose.'

'Am I permitted to know why?'

'Of course. I came to return these.' From his pocket he drew her missing mittens.

'How kind of you. I have been looking everywhere for them. Where did you find them?'

'In your boat. I took them.'

'You did what?' Judith's icy politeness deserted her.

'I took them. While you were tending your cow.' He spoke in a matter-of-fact manner, as though he had done nothing out of the ordinary.

'I don't understand this!' cried Judith angrily. 'You steal my mittens! You know where I live! You know my name! What mischief is this?'

'No mischief. You told us your name yesterday, when we met.'

'I did not—' Judith began to protest, then remembered that she had indeed told her name to the anxious old gentleman.

'And I didn't steal your mittens,' said the Dutchman, taking an appreciative sip of the wine Aunt Ketty had set before him. 'I merely took them.'

'If there is a difference it escapes me.'

'It's quite simple. I didn't mean to keep them. Why would I want to keep your mittens? They are far too small for me. Look!' He spread a large strong hand over the mittens covering them completely.

'Having established that you didn't steal my mittens but simply took them, would it be asking too much for you to tell me why?' asked Judith, controlling her voice with an effort. She strongly suspected that this man was mocking her even though not one muscle of his face betrayed laughter.

'That I can explain. I wanted an excuse to call on you. I'm not well accustomed to the ways in this part of the country. I feared it would not be proper to knock on your door without good reason.'

'You wanted a reason to call?'

'I did. I like pretty women and I think you are very pretty. Your spirit I like too. I think to myself I would like to know Mistress Judith Pentelow more—no—to know her better,' he corrected himself. 'Tell me, are you married or promised to any man?'

Such impudence took Judith's breath away. And while she was struggling to form a reply he coolly stretched across the table and lifted up her left hand.

'Ah, you have no rings. That's good,' he said, scrutinising her fingers.

She snatched her hand back as though his touch had burnt her. ''Tis outside of enough, sir!' she protested, outraged by his manner as much as by his impudent words. 'I don't know how people conduct themselves in Holland, but your manners are far too saucy for this part of the world.'

'Why? You think that I'm too blunt, perhaps? But if you had been wed or betrothed it would be most improper for me to try to know you better. That's why I engineered an excuse to come to call. Mistress Kettering is here to guard your good name, so everything is as it should be.... Why aren't you betrothed yet? You are not, are you? or you would have said so by now. Is there some good reason? You are old enough. Seventeen, perhaps? Eighteen? And you do not look sickly.'

'You go too far, Master van de...'

'van de Scheldt. You'll soon get used to it.'

'No, I will not, sir, because I've no intention of ever uttering it—or even trying to utter it—again. I have had enough of your nonsense! I ask you to finish your wine and go. But for my aunt's hospitality, I would never have let you over the threshold!'

'Why? You don't know me, you cannot dislike me yet?'

'I have no wish to know you!'

'After we have met more often, then you will be able to decide properly.'

There seemed to be no getting through to the man. Nothing she said to him registered.

'I *have* decided!' she cried in exasperation. 'I want you to go away now, this minute!'

'But I haven't finished my wine yet, and it would be most impolite to leave it. I have nearly done.'

The Dutchman took a leisurely sip of wine. He seemed so completely at his ease that Judith had difficulty in curbing her annoyance. Her censorious eyes took in the quality of his clothes. No country tailor had cut the fine broadcloth coat that covered his well-muscled back. His linen, too, was immaculate, and the buckles on his shoes were of silver and highly polished.

So, you're vain, thought Judith contemptuously. You want me to note that you've got good shoulders beneath your coat and that your legs are well-shaped. I fear you've knocked on the wrong door this time. I've better things to do than ogle some Dutch popinjay.

At that moment she felt the Dutchman's eyes upon her. He was not in the least disconcerted to be caught staring. On the contrary, he continued to regard her steadily, his eyes lingering approvingly over every line and curve of her body.

'Sir!' Judith began to protest at this bold scrutiny, but then the Dutchman's gaze settled on the tendrils of her hair which, as usual, had escaped from her cap. His expression made her feel suddenly embarrassed. She was not used to being subjected to such patently masculine admiration. Her hands flew up to tuck away the offending curls—then she stopped, furious with herself for being so discomfited.

'I don't know how you found our house in the first place,' she snapped.

'I found it very easily. I just asked a man "Where is the house of Mistress Judith Pentelow?" and the man said "There, across that field".'

'The man? What man?' asked Judith suspiciously.

'There was a man on the path by the water, a shabby man, with perhaps a cold in the head. Oh, and he had a message for you. I was to tell you he can come on Friday if no one is took. I do not understand it, but I am sure that is what he said.'

Dear heaven, thought Judith, he has asked the way of Dewdrop Chester, of all people. The biggest gossip in the parish! It will be all over Sedgewick that we have entertained a Dutchman.

Aunt Ketty, who had been stunned into silence by their strange guest, spoke at last.

'The man is our day labourer,' she explained. 'He is also the village gravedigger, so he can only come to us if no one is to be buried.'

The Dutchman turned again to Judith.

'This is your land? You own these fields, yet no man has spoken for you?' He shook his head in surprise. 'Is it that you have no wish to be wed? Or maybe no man has asked for you? Though I think your land would be attraction enough to many.'

'Out!' exploded Judith, picking up his hat and handing it to him as she made to open the door. 'Go, and pray you—I beg you—do not come back!'

'I've finished my wine now, it was very good. I thank you.' He rose, once more seeming to fill the small room with his presence, and bowed to Aunt Ketty. Then he noticed Judith's embroidery lying on a stool. He looked at it critically. 'You did this, Mistress Pentelow? It's a good design, very good. Your flowers, they seem to grow, and the colours are pleasing. It's a garden you are sewing, but why are there no tulips? All gardens, even embroidered ones, should have tulips.'

'I had no idea you were such a judge of stitchery, else modesty would have made me hide my work from you,' Judith said sarcastically. 'As for including tulips among my flowers, that would prove difficult, for I don't know what they look like.'

'I think you joke with me. I'm a poor judge of embroidery, though sometimes I make patterns for my mother and sisters to sew. I am sorry you've never seen a tulip, for it is a flower with a pleasing symmetry. The colours, too, are fine and varied. I will bring you one.' He turned to Aunt Ketty. 'I bid you farewell, Mistress Kettering. My thanks for your wine and the comfort of your hearth.'

'It was my pleasure, sir. You—you must feel a long way from your home at times.'

'I do, Mistress Kettering. All my family are in Amsterdam, and I miss them sorely.'

His hand was on the latch. He was going at last. Then Judith realised what an opportunity she had missed. The Dutchman had been sitting by their fireside for half an hour and never once had she questioned him to find out what he was doing in the district, or whether he knew aught of plans to drain the fen. But it was still not too late.

'You seem to spend much time on our marshes,' she said. 'To what purpose?'

'To what purpose, mistress? Why, to take the air.'

'Is that what you were doing this morning, when you pursued me?'

'How could I pursue you when there was water between us? I fear that is but one of your fancies, Mistress Pentelow.'

His eyes glinted with mischief and she knew that he was baiting her. Well, it was a game that two could play.

'I'm so glad it was the imaginings of my foolish brain,' she said sweetly. 'I declare that the splash when you fell in was most lifelike. I could have sworn I saw water dripping from your coat. How fortunate you suffered no inconvenience.'

'Some imaginings are clearly much stronger than others. I'll admit that a small mishap did befall me. I lost my footing, nothing serious.' The spark of mischief burned brighter now, and with it Judith detected a look of frank admiration as he continued, 'But I would gladly have endured greater hardship for the pleasure of looking at Mistress Pentelow, even from afar.'

This was not the conversation she had hoped for; they were moving yet again from the important issue she wished to pursue. It looked as though she would lose her chance, for his hand was once more on the latch.

'Wait! I would speak with you,' she exclaimed.

'There, I was convinced you would grow to enjoy my company eventually,' he said.

'You are the most provoking man I have ever met!' exclaimed Judith. 'I gain no pleasure from your presence, nor ever will do. What I want is to ask you a question.'

'Ask what you please.'

'What brings you from Holland?'

'Business, mistress. A need to earn my living.'

For the first time she sensed evasiveness in him. Very well, she thought, I'll provoke the truth from you.

'And isn't Holland where all the villainous drainers come from?'

'Holland is where all the *best* drainers come from,' he said with quiet emphasis. Then with a courteous nod he left the cottage.

His answer had not satisfied her. 'So——' she protested. Then, when he did not hear her, 'Master van— Master van——' She could not remember his confounded name! And, anyway, hadn't she said she would never again utter it? She was suddenly glad the wind had whipped her words away. She did not want him to think that she was summoning him back to the cottage—above all she did not want him to think that!

'Well,' declared Aunt Ketty, after Judith had closed the door. 'Well, if the world isn't full of surprises. Fancy, the Dutchman coming here in such a fashion!'

'If he had come in any fashion he would have been just as unwelcome. Did you ever meet such a rude, saucy fellow?'

'He was certainly forthright, though I don't think he meant aught uncivil by it; it was just his manner.'

'Aunt Ketty, if the devil himself walked in here you would try to find something charitable to say about him.'

'Well, I've heard it said that all drainers are in league with the Devil,' chuckled Aunt Ketty.

'Then I'm sorry for the Prince of Darkness, having to put up with that one!'

'Come, child, where is your Christian kindness?' reproved Aunt Ketty gently. 'The fellow can't help being a Dutchman. He is somewhat blunt in his manner, it's true, but I found him comely enough. There's no denying he's a fine set-up lad. He certainly speaks our language well enough; if it wasn't for his bit of an accent, I'd have taken him for English born and bred. He seems to have taken a proper fancy to you, my love.'

'I'll not thank him for that!'

'So you made clear.' Aunt Ketty chuckled again. ''Twas an entertainment to hear the pair of you tossing words back and forth; far better than the mummers.'

'I'm glad you were amused! You don't think he was serious about bringing us a tulip, do you?'

'He was bringing *you* a tulip, as I recall. From what I gather of that young man, I don't think we have seen the last of him.'

'That's what I fear, but at least we might get another chance to tackle him about his business out on the fen. Oh, just think, Aunt! We had him here, under this very roof, and we never said a thing about Hanser Fen or those London gentlemen, or anything of importance. We could have found out so much!'

'In truth, my love, he did take the wind out of our sails, didn't he? What with him coming so unexpectedly and all. Besides, I doubt if we'd have learned much. He seemed to be one who keeps his own counsel. Did you notice that when you mentioned drainers he seemed to close up?'

'Perhaps you're right. But I still think I should have tried.'

Judith picked up her embroidery again. But as she stitched at the clump of violets she found it hard to concentrate, her mind was too full of lost opportunities and, to her consternation, tulips.

Only when her head touched the pillow that night did she remember one more opportunity she had let slip by— she still had not asked Aunt Ketty for permission to marry Adam.

CHAPTER THREE

DAWN had barely broken when there was a loud hammering on the cottage door.

'Mercy! Who can that be?' wondered Judith, pausing in her task of lighting the fire.

'My guess is that it'll be Peter Renshaw, come to fetch me to Loveday's lying-in,' said Aunt Ketty. She was right. When she opened the door there was the tall, angular figure of Peter. 'No need to say why you've come, lad. Hold a minute while I get my cloak, and I'll be with you.'

'And send your little ones here to be out of the way. I'll care for them,' called Judith.

'Thank you—oh, thank you both!' Peter sounded harassed.

In no time the cottage was filled with a host of little Renshaws waiting to be fed, not giving Judith a minute to call her own.

It was way past noon when a weary Aunt Ketty returned home, a satisfied smile on her face.

'A little boy,' she said, kicking off her shoes with a sigh of relief. 'As strong and as lusty as anyone could wish for, and bawling fit to deafen the parish when I left. Loveday's in fine fettle, too, the Lord be praised! Your father says you can go home now,' she told the children. 'But go you quietly, mind, in case your new brother has ceased his noise and fallen asleep.'

She could have saved her breath. They dived out of the door like savages in their excitement to see the new member of the family.

Aunt Ketty shook her head and smiled. 'You'd think the novelty would have worn off by now, there being so many of them, yet they're all as merry as crickets. To see Peter you'd think he'd just become a father for the first time, he's that delighted.'

'I don't know how they cope,' said Judith. 'I'm worn to the bone after just one day.'

'There will be no dancing a jig for me, either, that I promise you. My poor feet, I fear they'll fall off!'

'Here, put them up on a stool while I get you something to eat. I have saved you some mutton stew, but it was a close run thing. I've never seen food disappear so quickly as it does with those children around the table.'

'Ah, there's a good creature you are, and such a blessing to me.' Aunt Ketty beamed at her fondly as she took the steaming bowl.

Judith felt a stab of sadness when she saw that loving smile. Her aunt would miss her sorely when she married. They had dealt so well together, the pair of them, with scarce a cross word, so how would Aunt Ketty fare when she was on her own? Judith pondered the problem. Perhaps she could come to live at Old Place, it was big enough... No, she discarded the idea almost as soon as it was formed. There was no imagining Aunt Ketty and Marjorie Digby under the same roof. Judith gave a sigh. Aunt Ketty's eyelids were drooping even as she ate her meat. There would be no discussion of marriage, or aught else, this day.

Aunt Ketty was still sleeping by the fire when Adam came to call. With one glance in the direction of the old lady he pulled Judith into his arms. His embrace was so charged with passion that Judith could not help but respond. Her body cried out for him with such a sudden animal urgency that for a while all else was obliterated... Then a sudden snore from Aunt Ketty reminded her that they were not alone. Reluctantly they loosed their hold on one another, until their ardour had lessened and they had grown calmer.

'Do you deny that it's time we were wed?' whispered Adam, his lips tantalisingly close to hers.

Judith shook her head. 'When did I ever deny it?' she whispered back.

'What has your aunt to say on the subject?'

'I haven't spoken to her yet.'

'Not spoken!' Adam's exclamation made Aunt Ketty stir and murmur in her sleep. 'Why not?' he went on, lowering his voice. 'You said you would!'

'I know, and I fully intended to, but so much has happened of late. Today it was the Renshaws' new baby and yesterday it was the Dutchman calling——'

'Dutchman! What Dutchman? Surely not the fellow you saw on Hanser Fen?'

'The same.'

'What did he want? He didn't trouble you in any way, did he?'

'No, of course not!'

'You are sure? The nerve of the man! I'll break his head for his impudence!'

'There's no need for that. He only came to return my mittens that he'd found. He was quite civil. Ask Aunt Ketty.'

Judith felt that this was not a truly accurate description of the Dutchman's behaviour, but she was reluctant to dwell too much on the visit. Adam was such a fiery character there was no knowing what he would do if he got angry.

'Your Aunt Ketty was here?'

'All the time.'

Adam's annoyance faded a little. 'I don't like that fellow sniffing around here. Keep out of his way, my sweet, I beg you.'

'I've no wish to seek out his company, that's certain. I hope I never see him again.'

'Amen to that. But be on your guard. Satan can work in the most devious ways. This man—you saw no sign of the Devil about him, did you? You know that these Dutchmen have evil powers? It's how they can set about draining, and other black crafts.'

'There was no whiff of sulphur about him, I assure you. He seemed a normal enough man, not one to be feared for himself, though his part in any draining might be another matter.'

'I'll write you something from the Scriptures to keep about you, just the same. That'll ward off any evil... But what of the draining? Did you question him? Did he say aught?'

'In truth, I was so surprised by his presence that I didn't think to say anything until it was too late. I cursed myself afterwards.'

'You seem to have grown skilful at not asking vital questions.' Adam's tone turned sour. 'You neglected to ask your aunt about our marriage, too, as I recall.'

'I will ask her, I promise.'

'When?'

'Soon—tomorrow.'

'Aye, tomorrow, and no later! Do I have your word?'

'You do.'

'That's my lass,' said Adam, suddenly pulling her so close that the breath was crushed from her lungs. 'For that is what you are, you know. My lass, and mine alone. I'll kill any man who tries to take you from me.'

'As if anyone would dare,' Judith whispered, unable to remember a time before Adam, or imagine a future without him. 'Nor would I let them,' she added.

She slid her arms under his leather coat to encircle his chest, so that she could savour the warmth of his body. Adam's mouth was on hers at once, hot and demanding. At the same time his hands strayed down over her hips to caress her thighs. His exploring fingers dug painfully into her flesh, despite the thickness of her petticoats.

'Ouch!' She flinched, easing away from him. 'Take care, else I'll be black and blue!'

'So what harm's a bruise or two? Who's to see?' Adam's questing mouth settled on her throat, his hands still gripping her, pulling her harder against him.

'But you're hurting me!' Judith protested, pushing him away.

Adam slackened his hold, his eyes bright with desire.

'I know wenches who like a bit of rough and tumble,' he said.

'No doubt you do. But they must bruise less easily than I do.' Judith rubbed the painful skin, then she grinned. 'You great oaf,' she said fondly. 'You're supposed to be wooing me, not pinching lumps off me. I can scarce ask Aunt Ketty for liniment to ease my hurts, can I?'

'Very true. Your pardon. I forgot what I was doing for the minute.' Adam's face was all innocence. 'You see, that's how I'd choose a prime heifer, by taking a good handful of flesh——'

He got no further, for Judith began pummelling him with her fists, and their laughter awoke Aunt Ketty.

'Judith, is that you?' Aunt Ketty gave a yawn then looked about her. 'Why, I've almost sat the fire out. Adam, you are here?'

'I was just leaving, Mistress Kettering. I bid you good day.' Adam bent and kissed Judith. Before Aunt Ketty's gaze it had to be far more restrained than the embraces they had exchanged earlier.

'Until tomorrow then, sweetheart,' he said. 'Nay, don't come with me to the gate. The rain is falling in torrents. You stay here in the dry.'

Adam departed. No sooner had Judith closed the door behind him than he knocked to be let in again.

'Did you forget something?' she asked.

'Aye, one question. If you and the Dutchman didn't discuss draining the fen, what did you talk about?'

Judith thought quickly. It would not do to let Adam know how personal their conversation had been; that would only rouse him to anger again.

'Flowers,' she said at last.

'Flowers? Oh!' It was a subject in which Adam had no interest, so he went away without another word.

During most winters part of the Lynn road was impassable for weeks at a time. This year was different. This year it was unusually dry, so Judith revelled in the fact that she could deliver some of Aunt Ketty's herbal remedies on foot instead of having to go by boat. Her pleasure was soon dimmed when a horseman came into view. At first she did not recognise the Dutchman—for some reason she had never imagined him on horseback—but as the mounted figure drew closer there was no mistaking him. If she could, she would have avoided meeting him, but although the Lynn road was above water the surrounding land was not. She had no alternative; she had to continue.

'Mistress Pentelow! Now my day is complete!' The Dutchman reined in his horse and looked down at her.

'Pray don't start all your silliness again,' begged Judith.

'If it is silliness to admire you then there is little I can do in the matter. I fear I must remain a fool, and be happy to do so.'

Judith looked at him sharply. She was never quite sure if he was teasing her or not. Attack seemed the best way to quell her doubts.

'Is there no getting a sensible conversation out of you?' she demanded.

'*You* may have any sort of conversation from me that you please,' he said.

Judith groaned in exasperation. 'That is exactly what I mean,' she replied. 'Your foolish compliments... Oh, never mind. Let me pass!'

'Won't you keep me company for just a moment? You aren't afraid of me, are you?' he asked.

'Certainly not!' retorted Judith. She was surprised to find that it was true. There was power in this man, his large frame obviously possessed great strength, yet somehow she could not picture him as being violent. Any unease she had ever experienced in his company had now dissipated, although he still irritated her beyond endurance.

'Good, because I mean you no harm. Tell me, then, why are you so wary of me?'

'Because you are a Dutchman.' The response was out before she could stop it.

A brief smile flickered across his face.

'Is that your only reason?' he said. 'I assure you that we are much as other men, more clever and more handsome perhaps, but we are certainly no more wicked or depraved.'

'I find that hard to believe!'

'Oh, why is that? Just because a man comes from another land doesn't mean he differs much from men hereabouts.'

'If he were a Turk or came from Araby I would believe you—but Dutchmen are different.'

'In what way?'

'Because they always mean trouble.'

'Oh, come! Have I ever been a trouble to you?'

'Yes, you've been a constant nuisance to me since the day we met. But I'm talking about graver matters than ruffled nerves—draining the fens, for example.'

'But these fens are not drained. In fact, they look decidedly watery to me.'

'Don't make a jest of it. Can you deny that is why you are here? To drain Hanser Fen?'

Judith stepped back a little, the better to scrutinise his face for some sign of guilt, or perhaps a fleeting expression of unease.

The Dutchman's imperturbable calm did not falter.

'Why should you assume such a thing?' he asked. 'Do you think that we Dutchmen can do only one thing, dig ditches in the mud? We are a capable race, you know, able to turn our hands to many different skills.'

He was playing with her, she knew, but whether that was to cover the fact that her accusation was correct, or not, she could not tell for certain. It might have been just his normal perversity.

'And what is your skill, that you must practise it here on Hanser?' she demanded.

'My talent is the ability to seek out the prettiest maid in all the Fens, which by some strange chance I find I can only do in the vicinity of Sedgewick St Peter.'

'Don't try such flummery on me, it won't work!' cried Judith angrily. 'I tell you this—if you're planning to drain Hanser you'd best think again.'

If the Dutchman was alarmed by her warning he did not show it. Instead he leaned across his saddle and gazed down intently at her face.

'Your eyes are beautiful,' he said.

'My eyes have nothing to do with the matter. We were discussing Hanser. And I swear to you that you will never drain the fen!'

'In that case, since it will never happen, the draining of Hanser Fen is an unworthy subject of conversation. Your eyes, now, they are a very different matter. I have never seen their like before. How would you describe them? Light brown touched with green—and so large and clear, like beryl. There is an English word for such eyes but I can't think of it. See what a turmoil you have me in? I pride myself on my command of your language—you have noticed, haven't you, how well I speak it?—yet here I am, unable to utter the most important word of all, the one that would describe your eyes.'

'Sir!' exclaimed Judith. 'I do not wish you to say such things! There are more important matters we must speak of——'

'More important than your eyes? Never! Ach, I have it—the word I couldn't remember. Hazel, of course.... Oh, but how unworthy, how inadequate! I must seek another. Just as I must find other words for your complexion—silken, the petals of a rose—they're all too ordinary. Tell me, how do you keep it so in the harsh fen wind? Do the supernatural powers tell you their secrets?'

'No!' snapped Judith. 'But my patience needs supernatural powers to deal with you!'

The Dutchman gave a sudden snort of laughter.

'Bravo, mistress!' he cried. 'Not only beautiful but spirited. A fine combination.'

This was the first break in his imperturbability, and also it was the first time that there had been any sincerity in his words.

'I see what you are about,' said Judith evenly. 'You would make me agitated and angry just for sport. Well, sir, you must find your sport elsewhere. But I beg you, in all seriousness, to take heed of my words. Have nothing to do with the draining of Hanser. You are the most tedious man I've ever met, but you are a stranger in this land, so I give you warning as a Christian—take heed for yourself. Put your spurs to your nag and ride as far away from here as you can, before you bring misery and disaster to everyone with your draining.'

The smile vanished from his face.

'You still insist I am here to dig ditches, yet a moment ago you said the draining of your fen was impossible. I confess that I am confused. Or is it that you have such faith in my talents that you think me capable of doing the impossible?'

'I refuse to let you annoy me,' said Judith. 'But I speak as much for your benefit as for ours—do not think that you'll manage to destroy Hanser Fen unscathed.'

'Your concern for me touches me deeply, and I thank you for your warning, though against what I'm not sure.'

There was a stillness about the Dutchman that made Judith suspect that perhaps she had touched near the truth after all.

Then he said, 'I must protest at having to depart on horseback, however. It's a mode of transport I'd sooner avoid if possible. The horse, though doubtless a noble animal, isn't built for comfort. Besides, it always seems to me to present hazards in every direction. Now a nice boat——'

'I care not what mode of transport you use, just so long as you go!' interrupted Judith, maintaining her calm with increasing difficulty.

'But think—if I go we would never meet again like this. Then who would tell you of the beauty of your eyes? Or how enchanting your chin is when you tilt it up in that determined way?'

Judith realised then that she would get no closer to the truth with him. Despite his flippant speeches he was a master of evasion.

'Oh, a fig for you and your horse!' she exclaimed, forgetting her resolution to remain calm. She gave the horse a hard slap, sending it, and its rider, along the road at great speed.

To her disappointment the Dutchman proved to be a better horseman than he had intimated. He did not fall off.

Later that day, Toby, with his dog beside him, returned from Ely. Judith saw him poling his boat towards their hythes, so she ran to meet him.

'Well?' she demanded, as he made his way over the rickety staging to the path.

'Well? What sort of a greeting is that? Let me get my puff...'

'I'm sorry. I didn't mean to be rude, but we've been so concerned. I'm glad to see you back safely, and so soon. Come you into the house and get warm.'

They had scarcely reached the cottage door when Adam arrived too, hot and breathless.

'I...I saw you coming,' he panted. 'I...I ran all the way from Far Meadow. What news?'

'Not good, I fear. Not good at all.' Toby's leathery face was set in deep lines. 'There are plans to drain, right enough, with our own Lord of the Manor, Sir Walter Massingham, at the centre of things. You hit the nail on the head, Adam boy, when you guessed he'd be involved.'

'Oh, no! I was dreading this! That wretched Dutchman was so devious when I spoke to him!'

'The Dutchman? When did you see him?' demanded Adam.

'I met him by chance on the Lynn road earlier today. This time I did as you said and tried to get the truth from him, but it was no good. He's not a man to give a straight answer, and I fear that one who is so evasive must have something to hide. Now Toby tells us it is so. The drainers are coming.'

'Then we must act to stop them right away.' Adam made to leave, but Judith pulled him gently down on to the bench beside her.

'Hear it all,' she insisted. She turned to Toby. 'Have we no rights in law?'

'In law, aye, but the rich and powerful are ever a law unto themselves,' said Toby.

'At least it will take time. That should give us breathing space,' Judith pointed out.

'Time to build up arms and men,' said Adam firmly. 'We'll need every minute.'

'Like you, I hope we get a spell,' said Toby. 'Though I fear that trouble will come quickly.'

'How so?' asked Adam.

'Sir Walter has already formed his company—the Royal Hanser Company! That shows the sort of birds he's flying with! I hear they've bought up all the rights from the last attempt to drain Hanser Fen. And now they're claiming that, since Parliament gave approval then, it still stands, for they intend to use the old plans.'

'Can this be true?' Adam demanded. 'Is such gossip to be relied upon?'

'It's no tavern gossip, and my teller has no cause to lie. I got it from my niece's husband, who's body-servant to one of the Fen Commissioners.' Toby sounded irritated that his information should be questioned.

'They intend to use the old plans, you say?' said Judith. 'That means they'll be ready to start draining as soon as the flood-waters fall. They'll have no reason to wait longer.'

'You're right, mawther.' Toby nodded in agreement. 'They'll be on us soon enough. But for you seeing the Dutchman on the fen, we'd have had no warning at all.'

'I wonder at them going ahead with the scheme now,' Judith said, 'when the whole country is on the brink of strife, with the King and Parliament at each other's throats.'

'It shows that the King is confident who will be the top dog,' said Toby.

'It's wrong he'll find himself on that score once the snarling stops and the fighting begins,' put in Adam. 'What news is there of that matter, Toby?'

'Rumours aplenty in that quarter. It's said that the Queen has gone to Holland to try to raise an army there.

Aye, and that her Frenchie kinfolk have men amassed on the coast ready to cross the Channel for her benefit.'

'And is Parliament doing naught?' asked Judith.

'They've taken charge of the Army, so 'tis said.'

'That'll give the Papist lovers something to think about!' Adam was jubilant. 'We have right on our side and the Army behind us. How can we fail—at least, where Parliament against the King is concerned? Let us hope that strife does break out through the country. With Parliament holding the upper hand we stand a better chance of keeping our fens.'

'Shame on you!' cried Aunt Ketty. 'You'd wish the land torn by civil war? What sort of a solution is that? If such fighting broke out men would be killed here as well as anywhere else, you know. Aye, and doubtless women and babes too. War respects no one. Civil strife or the fen drainers—that's a pretty poor alternative, in my view!'

Secretly Judith thought that Aunt Ketty was right, but her loving heart would not let her side against Adam. She said, 'And what of the drainers? We've still them to contend with, and hastily.'

'The whole village must be told. We'll set the church bells ringing, that'll call them all in.' Eager for action, Adam jumped to his feet.

'But won't it be too late now for the folk to get here from Outer Fen?' Judith pointed out. 'The sun's already going down. Can't we call a meeting for tomorrow noon?'

'That's more time wasted,' objected Adam. 'Goodness knows, we have little enough of it!'

'I don't suggest that we waste time,' said Judith. 'But surely it would be better to have some firm plans drawn up to put before the people when they get here? Else you know how it will be, tongues wagging and folk arguing all day, and naught decided. If we have some schemes to put before them, for them to say aye or nay to, I'm convinced that we would save many precious hours.'

Toby nodded approvingly. 'There's much we can do today; telling folk of the meeting, for one thing——'

'And shouldn't we look out any maps or charts of Hanser Fen,' Judith interrupted. 'I'm sure I saw one once when I was little, and it might be of value to us.'

'I can see we'll have to watch out, else you'll be making all our decisions for us and be properly ruling the roost,' grinned Toby, while Aunt Ketty looked on with quiet pride.

Adam grinned too, and slid his arm around her waist.

'We'll have petticoat government this once, shall we? What time do you suggest for the meeting, Mistress General? Noon at the church wall? I'll send round the parish to let folks know, and I'll seek out the map. It was in the church last time I heard of it. Let's hope it hasn't been eaten by mice!'

'I'll do my share of passing the word at the Lamb, anon,' said Toby.

'Maybe, but only after you've had something to eat,' said Aunt Ketty sternly. 'To have had a long journey then go drinking Hal Osborne's ale on an empty stomach—I know what the consequences would be then!'

Toby gave a resigned shrug. ''Tis as you say, boy—petticoat government! That's what we're ruled by. Get you gone, and I'll be along to aid you as soon as my jailer here gives me leave.'

Adam left the cottage and Judith walked with him to the gate.

'Toby's really worried,' said Judith. 'Did you notice, he never once cursed his dog? That's a sure sign all is not well.'

'Who's to blame him for being anxious? These are worrying times for the whole land—and for us most of all.... I fear I'll not be able to call on you this evening, my sweet, not with so much to be done.'

'And can't I do something too? Must I sit modestly with my embroidery and my spinning, while you men do everything? This is a woman's fight too, you know.'

She saw the objections begin to form on his lips. Then his face relaxed and he smiled at her. Sliding his hands beneath her cloak, the better to caress her slim body, he said, 'Aye, love, you shall do your share. Go to the East Fen and rouse the people there. And, if we don't meet again today, I'll see you at the meeting tomorrow, perhaps?'

'Definitely!' she corrected him. 'Nothing will keep me away!'

Suddenly she clung to him, with as much apprehension as longing. Reality was intruding too painfully into her dreams of the future, and she did not like the prospect.

Adam's thoughts must have been running along similar lines, for his arms tightened about her. He whispered, 'Don't worry, my love, we'll win through.'

'I'm not worried,' replied Judith untruthfully.

'Good, because nothing is going to be allowed to spoil our happiness together, not if a horde of Dutchmen arrives to drain our fens. We'll fight 'em off, you and I together!'

He bent to her, and they kissed, a long lingering kiss made more urgent by their misgivings. When at last he released her, Judith found that her eyes had misted.

'One more task for you to do,' said Adam, wiping away the single teardrop that moistened her cheek. 'The most important task of all. Have you forgot? Today is the day you are to ask your aunt if we may wed. I had your word on it.'

'You did indeed! And when did I ever break my promise to you?'

'Never, which is why I long for more promises from you—to love, honour, and obey...' He gave a sigh. 'I wish we could stay for ever thus, but I must go.' He kissed her once more, then with a deliberate gesture held her at arm's length before he released her. 'Take care, my dear one,' he said. With a final wave he strode off towards Old Place.

Judith returned indoors with the taste of Adam's kisses still on her lips. She found Toby taking his ease by the fire, while Aunt Ketty filled his ale mug.

'What's this I hear about you having a new suitor?' he asked, his eyes twinkling.

'Which suitor is this? I have so many, he must have slipped my notice.'

'Not this one. Not a Dutchman ten feet high. Imagine the nerve of the fellow to call in such a way. Thank goodness young Adam wasn't about, else there'd have been fisticuffs for sure!'

'There would have been no need. I've no intention of encouraging Dutch suitors—and by the by, this one was not quite the Goliath you make him.'

'Goliath or not, he seems not to need much encouragement!' Toby chuckled. 'Mind you, he had a point.'

'What do you mean?' asked Aunt Ketty.

'Well, why isn't this lass wed yet, or betrothed at the very least? She and Adam have been willing a good two years to my knowledge. They've had time to be properly betrothed, wed and fill the cradle, yet she still has no ring on her finger. How so?'

Judith drew in her breath sharply. This was not at all the approach to the matter she had planned, but it was none the less acceptable. Eagerly she waited for the reply.

Aunt Ketty did not answer immediately, but turned away, pretending to be busy with the fire.

'I must indeed appear to be a selfish, unreasonable old woman,' she said at last in a trembling voice.

'No!' cried Judith. 'Never that! But you know how much I love Adam, and I can't think what you have against our marriage.'

Again Aunt Ketty took her time before she spoke, as if considering her words carefully.

'There's much to be taken into account before you go to Old Place as a bride. I'd like to see you of age, and mistress of your own affairs by then. Goodness knows, you've got a good head on your shoulders now. But I'd see you old enough, and with more knowledge of the world, so that you would not be downtrodden.'

'Downtrodden! Surely you can never think that Adam would treat me so?'

'Not Adam—his sister.'

'Marjorie?'

All at once the words came tumbling out as Aunt Ketty expressed the worries that she had been holding to herself.

'She's such a strong-minded woman, that Marjorie Digby, for all her genteel ways. She's eager enough for Adam to wed, but that's only because she wants him to have sons to inherit Old Place—you know what a maggot she has about their family—and I fear it is a maggot that will control her, you, aye, and your babes. You'd be less than nothing in the house where you should be mistress, Judith love, and you're not used to that. We've led a simple life together, you and I, but we've led it *together*, share and share about. It's not in your nature to be dominated, which would certainly be the case, and would lead to trouble, and I fancy Adam would always take his sister's part. It's what he's done all his life. And then where would you be with no one to speak up for you, you having no family?'

Judith was shaken by the intensity of her words.

'But I have a family!' she protested. 'I have you!'

Aunt Ketty shook her head. 'I am nothing to you in law. Just because I have thought of you as my child for all these years it doesn't make it so.'

'But Judith's grandam asked you to care for the child on her deathbed, we all know that! Surely that's binding enough?' declared Toby.

'You only know what I have told you,' Aunt Ketty contradicted him. 'Only the good Lord and I really know what that poor woman said to me as she lay dying, and that would never hold in any court of law. I did try to get things done legal-like once, Judith, my lamb, but those kinsfolk of yours had moved away, no one knew where. Then time went on, and we were so happy there seemed no need. I regret it now, though, for if you are to share a house with Marjorie Digby the time will surely come when you'll need someone to stand aback of you, someone with the right to take your part. A foolish old woman who has always loved you like her own flesh and blood won't do.'

Aunt Ketty's words were too close to Marjorie's for comfort. Judith did not know how to reply. She was glad when Toby spoke up again.

'I see what troubles you. I confess I hadn't thought of that before. I'd take anything you say as gospel, Ketty, but the law might think otherwise. Is it too late to make the lass your child legally? Even if you can't find these kinsfolk, surely sixteen years of looking after the wench must count for something? Why don't you speak to a lawyer?'

'That's a good idea . . . if Judith wishes it.'

'Of course I wish it. Though for my part I couldn't feel more your child than I do now. I am that, whether the lawyers say so or no. However, I confess that I, too, have my misgivings about living in the same house as Marjorie.'

'But not enough to give up thoughts of wedding Adam, eh?' grinned Toby. 'Well, then, if all else fails, a good marriage settlement, properly worked out so that Marjorie doesn't get more than her fair share of the hearth should do the trick. Besides, the lass is no milksop. I can't see her being downtrodden for long.'

'Oh, you've made me feel so much easier.' Aunt Ketty did truly look as though a load had been lifted from her shoulders. 'I should have spoken out long since, instead of keeping it churning inside of me. It has troubled me, holding back my blessing when I knew that Judith was pining to be wed. You're right, Toby. I'll go to a lawyer and see what he advises. Once that is settled, Judith, my love, you and Adam can set your wedding day.'

'Oh, thank you! Thank you!' Judith flung her arms around her aunt. 'May I tell Adam so?'

'Aye, though how you'll do that and leave out mention of Marjorie beats me,' chuckled Aunt Ketty.

'You could say that Ketty wants to go to law to make sure you inherit this cottage and her land all proper like,' suggested Toby. 'After all, 'tis no more than the truth.'

'Toby, that's a cunning mind you've got there, but a clever one!' observed Aunt Ketty with satisfaction.

Judith was so delighted she longed to tell Adam the wonderful news immediately, but there was no means of knowing where he would be by now. She would just have to curb her impatience until the morrow. She looked up to thank her aunt once more, and was disturbed to see a troubled expression on her face. It was only fleeting, and disappeared when Ketty saw her looking in her direction. But it was enough to make Judith's heart sink a little. Surely her aunt did not still have misgivings about her marriage? And if so, what could they be? Then Aunt Ketty smiled, and began setting a place at the table for her so calmly that Judith felt sure that she had been imagining things.

They were a very light-hearted trio as they dined on meat pudding and supped home-brewed ale. Then afterwards, Judith and Toby left the cottage together.

'Now then, mawther,' said Toby as they untied their respective boats at the hythes, 'who else has pointed out to you that you and Ketty have no legal ties?'

'What do you know of it?' gasped Judith.

'Only what your face showed. Don't worry, I'm sure Ketty didn't notice. Who was it?'

'It was Marjorie.' Judith told him of her conversation with Adam's sister, glad to be able to unburden herself, too.

'That's just about Marjorie Digby's measure, that is!' he said when she had finished. 'You doubtless gave her the sharp edge of your tongue?'

'I did, certainly, yet for all that Marjorie still favours me as a wife for Adam, and that puzzles me. I'd have thought she would have gone for someone like Susan Osborne, who can boast one of the richest men in Sedgewick for her father.'

'Ah, but Susan only has gold for her dowry. You'll have something that Marjorie values far more.'

'Whatever's that?'

'Land, mawther, land! Just think. When you wed you'll be taking your own portion, where the Renshaws live, then in due time you'll have Ketty's too! And all their rights to the fens, if they haven't been drained!

Joined on to Digby land, that will bring their acres right down to the very edge of the Summer Grounds. A fine addition like that, in size and position, would appeal to Marjorie, eager as she is to see her family great again. There's few maids your equal in Sedgewick, Judith Pentelow, when it comes to dowries. If Adam ever jilts you there'll be plenty of other swains knocking at your door. In fact, I'd most like be one myself.'

'Then the others would stand no chance,' teased Judith. 'I don't know how Aunt Ketty has resisted you so long.'

'Nor do I. It's against nature!' Then Toby became serious. 'You know, I thought that it was Ketty's fear for your future which was the stumbling block, so I gave her my word that you would still inherit her land if she wed me—and that holds should this legal business come to naught—yet Ketty still hums and haws.'

Judith took his hand. 'You are our dearest and best friend, and I know that Aunt Ketty is very fond of you. Be patient, I beg you. My aunt doesn't always see things in the same way as other people. She'll have her reasons for keeping you waiting.'

'That Ketty! Sometimes I think she sees too much!'

Judith glanced up sharply at this remark. But Toby's expression was as unruffled as ever.

They parted, Toby and his dog towards the Lamb, and Judith to do her rounds of the East Fen.

As she poled her boat through the water her thoughts were a long way from the drainers and possible strife on the fens. All she could think of was that the day of her wedding was coming closer.

Winter visitors were rare in the isolated communities of the East Fen, so Judith was welcomed at every lonely cottage, even though no one relished the news she brought. By the time she had finished she was cold and tired, and the flickering lantern that Aunt Ketty had hung on the mooring post of the hythe was a very welcome sight.

'Well, that's the folks of East Fen warned of what's coming,' she said, pulling off her muddy footwear in the doorway. 'Everyone has promised...' Her voice died away suddenly, as her eyes took in the table. On the scrubbed surface stood a blue and white Delft pot, and growing in it was a flower. A cup-shaped flower with a straight fleshy stem and large, beautiful petals, that seemed to have been made of scarlet silk.

'What is that? And where did it come from?' she demanded, only to answer the question in the same breath. 'The Dutchman!'

Aunt Ketty nodded. 'He came soon after you'd gone. He waited a while then said he could tarry no longer. He seemed sorry to have missed you.'

'I'm afraid I cannot say the same of him,' retorted Judith. 'And this, I suppose, is a tulip.'

'It is. Did you ever see such a pretty trifle? It brightens the place up a treat!'

'He should never have brought it. Why didn't you insist that he take it away again?'

'I tried, my love, truly I did, but I fear he's the most obstinate man I have ever met. And cunning, too. He even beats Toby. When I said that you would never accept it and that it was not to be left here do you know what he said? He said, "That is a pity, Mistress Kettering, for I've no wish to take it home with me. I'll simply leave it outside your door. It won't trouble you for long, the cold wind will soon blow away the petals. It will be dead in no time." And that's exactly what he did! Left it on the path and went!'

'Then, how did it get back indoors again?'

Aunt Ketty looked shamefaced. 'It's such a bonny thing it seemed a shame for it to be wasted. I thought that, perhaps, we could return it to him properly in some way.'

'And no easy task that will prove!' snorted Judith.

But her eyes could not tear themselves away from the brilliance of the scarlet petals. Aunt Ketty was right, their bright colour seemed to light up the whole room.

'It certainly is beautiful,' she agreed at last.

'And valuable, which is another reason why it must be returned. I hear that Sir Walter Massingham has some that he paid two crowns apiece for.'

'For one flower?' Judith was astounded.

'That's what Ned Ingham told me a while back. And he should know, being head gardener at the Hall,' Aunt Ketty assured her.

'You don't think this is one of Sir Walter's, do you?'

'You think the Dutchman's been doing a bit of night gardening? I hope not, my love!' Aunt Ketty looked anxiously at the flower in its pot, then shook her head. 'Somehow I think not. I believe the Dutch set great store by them, so maybe he brought some with him. The pot's good Dutch Delft, at any rate.'

'Well, he's having it back right away, pot and all,' said Judith with determination. 'I'd not accept the cheapest fairing from that Dutchman, let alone anything of value.'

'Properly spoken, my dear. But do you know where he lodges? Is he at the Hall or does he have a place of his own?'

'Ah, now that is a problem! I can hardly walk up to Sir Walter with the tulip under my arm and ask the whereabouts of the Dutchman, can I?'

'A proper hornets' nest that would stir up,' chuckled Aunt Ketty. 'Perhaps we should throw it away after all.' But there was no conviction in her voice.

'That would do no good. He would simply come to the conclusion that I'd accepted his gift. No, it must go back.'

Judith looked at the flower, so vivid in its blue and white pot, and she was unable to quell the feeling of pleasure it gave her.

'Perhaps we should keep it indoors until we find out where he lives. It will only be a matter of days before someone sniffs him out.'

'That's by far the best plan,' said Aunt Ketty. 'Until then it had better stay on the table lest any harm should befall it.'

'Aye, it musn't be damaged while it's with us,' said Judith gravely. But by then Aunt Ketty was lovingly polishing the pot with a cloth.

Leaving her to her task, Judith went to change her stockings, which were soaking wet, telling Aunt Kelly all about her trip to the East Fen as she did so.

'...and they are all determined to come to the meeting, even Granny Burns, who claims she is turned ninety. She can't be so old, can she?'

Getting no answer, Judith looked up and saw that her aunt was standing still, her face chalk-white, gripping the table to keep herself upright.

'What's wrong?' cried Judith, rushing to her side. 'Are you ill? Here, sit down. Let me help you. Have you a pain?'

Seeming unable to speak, Aunt Ketty just shook her head.

'It was that wretched Dutchman! He has upset you! What did he say? If he was saucy to you I'll seek him out at first light and box his ears, I don't care how big he is!'

Again Aunt Ketty shook her head. 'It wasn't the Dutchman,' she whispered faintly.

Judith knew then that there could only be one other explanation. Sinking to the floor at her aunt's feet, she took one of Ketty's cold hands in her own.

'You've had one of your feelings.' It was a statement, not a question.

Aunt Ketty nodded. 'Why, oh why, should I be so cursed?' Her voice was barely audible. 'I saw such sorrow as you wouldn't believe, with father against son, brother against brother. Sorrow, and death, and misery!'

Judith was alarmed. Her gentle aunt's pronouncements had never been so dramatic.

'Then we're going to have to fight to keep our fens?' she said.

Aunt Ketty looked at her and for the first time her eyes seemed to focus on the girl.

'The sorrow I see is not just on the Fens...'

'Then where?'

Aunt Ketty gave a hopeless shrug.

'Everywhere,' she said simply.

CHAPTER FOUR

PEOPLE were gathering on the church green long before noon the next day, and the hum of anxious voices drowned the cooing of the pigeons that were already jostling for nest sites in the church tower above.

'I wish the meeting would start soon, this wind is bitter.' Judith stamped her chilled feet.

'Here, I'll stand behind the pair of you, so's you shall have the benefit of my cloak.' Peter Renshaw spread the folds of his ancient homespun garment about her and Aunt Ketty. There was no forwardness in the gesture, just an eagerness to give comfort to his neighbours.

When the tall, gangling shoemaker had first arrived in the village there had been those who had mocked him, seeing his kindness and concern as a weakness. Peter had won them over by sheer consistency of character. No one had ever heard him utter a harsh word or known him do a bad deed to anyone, man, woman or child.

From her snug position beneath Peter's protective arm Judith kept a sharp lookout for Adam. Soon she saw him approaching. It was more than the rich chestnut colour of his hair that drew her gaze to him, it was some invisible magnetic force that attracted her attention, so that she was the first to cry, 'Adam's coming! Now we can begin!'

Other eyes turned to greet him, and questions bombarded him from all sides until he raised his hand in cheery protest.

'Anon! Anon! We must wait till all are here. There's a whole boatload of folk from Outer Fen just arriving; they'll be here within the minute.'

He caught sight of Judith and his face lit up with pleasure as she ran forward to meet him.

'I might have known you'd be here in good time,' he smiled, 'if only to make me look a laggard.'

'I hurried for no other reason,' laughed Judith. 'Who are you looking for now?' she asked, as Adam's eyes searched the crowd.

'Toby. I can see no sign of him.'

'He'll be here. He doesn't move so fast these days— or is it that his dog doesn't move so fast?'

Adam gave an irritable frown. 'You'd think he could leave the brute behind for once, wouldn't you?' he said. Then his face relaxed into a grin. 'But perhaps the dog thinks otherwise. It's hard to tell who's the master of that household.'

'I'm glad we've got a minute, for I've got such news to tell you. Aunt Ketty says...' began Judith. But then there was a stirring in the crowd as a group of late-comers arrived. Among them was the squat figure of Toby.

'Wait for me afterwards. We can walk home together and you can tell me your news then,' Adam whispered. Then in a louder voice he called out, 'Come on, Toby, you snail. We're waiting for you like a tardy bride at a wedding.'

'Well, I'm here now, so you can stop worriting and get on with things.' Toby flatly refused to be rushed.

The spread of the green just outside the church gates had been the villagers' natural meeting place for generations. The ground sloped gently upwards towards the wall, forming a platform. Now Adam leapt up on to the wall to tower above the crowd.

As soon as he appeared there was a cheer, and he raised a hand in acknowledgement.

Adam began, 'By now I'm sure you all know of the plan to drain Hanser Fen. Before we decide what to do about it let's listen to Toby here, for he's the one who went to Ely to discover the truth of the matter. He can tell us all about it.'

Cries of 'Good old Toby' were hushed into silence as the old man climbed up beside Adam. Once he started to speak not a cough nor a shuffle came from the crowd.

Even when he had finished there was a full moment of silence as the villagers took in the ominous details.

'Mercy on us, we'll starve!' A voice broke the stillness. Then a great clamour erupted as a hundred others expressed their fears.

Adam held up his hand for silence, and at once the people quietened down. He looked stern and handsome, standing there, commanding the attention of the whole village. From her position in the body of the crowd Judith felt her heart leap with love and pride, so that she was sure everyone could hear its beating.

'Friends,' began Adam, 'if Hanser Fen is drained we all know the consequences. There's not a family in the village, or the surrounding countryside, that won't be the poorer for it. Aye, it's true that once the fen is dry and under the plough the reclaimed land will be fertile and profitable but for the men of the Royal Hanser Company, not for us! Maybe we'll be permitted to keep part of the land. A quarter is what I hear they've been left with in other parts—a quarter! That's not much among all of us! Or we may be offered money. The going rate seems to be between four shillings and six shillings an acre, to share among the commoners. But I say this— an acre of grazing is there for ever; money, once 'tis spent, is gone for good. Then how will we find food for our families?'

As Adam paused for breath a groan broke from the lips of the crowd, and cries of 'Shame!' When the outburst had subsided he spoke up again.

''Tis said that in a couple of years grain will be grown on Hanser, even wheat. Think of it! When now we have to go five miles to see a wheatfield! But I ask you, how many of us will be able to buy bread of any sort?'

Uproar broke out again, as concerned voices cried out in protest.

Judith watched and listened with fascination. This was her Adam, who had all of them hanging on his every word. Even she, who adored and idolised him, had never suspected he was such an orator. Toby had informed everyone of the threat that hung over them, but it was Adam who explained the implications, so that even the weakest wits in the crowd could understand.

Suddenly a voice called out, 'How can they do it? That's what I ask! How can they rid the fen of water for ever?'

'A good point,' replied Adam. 'We all know how much water there is on Hanser, don't we? Have we ever known Hanser to be dry all year? Have we stories from our forefathers telling of a Hanser under the plough and growing crops? Of course we haven't! Because it is the Lord's will that Hanser should be fenland. Those who would have it otherwise must be going against the wishes of the Lord God Himself, and so there is only one way they can accomplish their plans—by the black arts! By witchcraft!'

Judith felt a frisson of fear down her spine at the idea of such a thing. Surely the powers of darkness weren't threatening them all...? Suddenly the memory of the tall Dutchman came into her mind. He was infuriating and insulting, yet somehow she had difficulty in thinking of him as anything other than a man, and a lusty, tiresome man at that!

All about her voices were crying, 'No, that cannot be! We'll fight! Fight! Fight!'

'For pity's sake, isn't there enough strife in the land already?' muttered Peter Renshaw. But no one heard him except Judith and Aunty Ketty.

'Aye, we'll fight!' Adam's voice drowned all the others. 'And we must be well prepared!'

Adam was in his element, his face flushed and his eyes glowing at the prospect of the fight ahead. His enthusiasm stirred the crowd to even greater excitement, so that Judith, too, was carried along with the general frenzy. Then, just as it had been decided to have the swift tolling of the church bell to raise the alarm, a woman's voice cut clearly through the noise.

'Must we be like savages and fight at the first sign of trouble? Is there no other way? Can't we go to law?'

A surprised silence fell upon the crowd, as everyone looked towards the speaker. It proved to be Marjorie

Digby, who, as usual, stood a little apart from the press of people.

'What, are you faint-hearted, Marjorie?' came a derisive shout.

Adam looked astonished at his sister's interjection. Judith sensed that had it come from anyone else the idea would have been given short shrift. But he had been used to listening with respect to Marjorie all his life, and so he raised his hand.

'We'll hear her,' he declared curtly. 'We'll hear anyone who has an opinion to offer.'

All eyes turned towards Marjorie.

'I agree we must act,' she said in her calm, clear voice. 'and doubtless blows will be exchanged before this business is settled, but it is all very well for you men to think of nothing but fighting and bloodshed. We women do the weeping when it is done.'

At this she gained a sympathetic murmur from many women in the crowd. She continued, 'I say we should try other ways. We could raise a petition stating exactly what hardships drainage will cause, and every fenlander from hereabouts can put his or her name or mark to it. Next, we'd need a good lawyer to take it to the Law Courts, or to Parliament if need be.'

This new approach caused some confusion, for most people had thought only of a physical fight.

'I know the law!' The voice of old Granny Burns rang out like a cracked bell. 'They can't drain Hanser Fen without we say so, for 'tis common ground. 'Tis not allowed! Hasn't been since the days of Good Queen Bess! My father told me that! That's the law, that is!' she finished triumphantly.

'In that case we'll need an honest lawyer all the more, to ensure that the law is upheld,' said Marjorie. 'There are good lawyers in Ely, and I know those who would recommend one who is worthy.'

'Perhaps the Curate would write out our grievances,' suggested someone.

'Not him!' cackled Granny Burns. 'He be more afraid of the Vicar and Sir Walter than he be of the Almighty!'

When the laughter died down Marjorie spoke again.

'We need not trouble the Curate. My brother is well schooled, he can write down our grievances.'

'That's a pretty enough scheme, but where's the money to come from?' called someone. 'Lawyers are never cheap.'

'I say there's no call for lawyers and such at all,' cried Adam. 'We can drive the drainers away on our own.' He was clearly spoiling for a fight.

Judith had been listening carefully. Adam's rousing words had stirred her blood, convincing her that violence was the only way to repulse the drainers. Now, though, the first flush of fervour had cooled down, and Marjorie's idea calmed her even more. As she thought about it one point became increasingly evident. She hated going against Adam, but she knew that this was something too important to be left unsaid. At last she spoke up.

'Doubtless we can drive the drainers away for a month, or a year, by ourselves, but if we want to be rid of them for ever we'll have to have the law behind us!' As everyone turned to look at her she felt herself flush, but she had gone too far to turn back now. She continued, 'Aye, we must fight with everything to hand to keep Sir Walter and his friends from starting on our fen, but they are powerful men. They'll keep coming back. The only way to defeat them for good is with the might of the law, else we'll find ourselves in this same predicament time after time.'

To her gratification she saw heads begin to nod in agreement, particularly among the older villagers who remembered previous attempts to drain Hanser.

'Aye, it's best to get rid of them once and for all!' cried a voice.

'But who's to pay?' persisted another.

'Every commoner with grazing rights could give a groat,' she suggested. 'And all others contribute a penny, or whatever they can afford. Then, when we've found a lawyer and know better what is involved, we can collect more.'

'A groat? Do you think we commoners are made of money?' protested one man.

'How many groats do you think you'll have in your pocket once they drain Hanser?' That was Toby's voice. 'The lass is right, of course. She and Marjorie between them have put a pretty plan to us, and I can't think of a better one. Adam, boy, let's have a show of hands to see who's for going to law.'

From his position on the wall Adam looked annoyed that the initiative had been taken from him, but as a forest of hands showed their approval he gave in.

'Very well, let's get ourselves a lawyer,' he said, then a grin spread across his face. 'But I fancy I can promise broken heads and fisticuffs enough for all you fine lads who don't favour such milk and water measures, eh?'

His words were greeted with an enthusiastic cheer from the younger men in the crowd, who for a minute or two had feared they might be cheated out of a good fight.

It was a long meeting, and everyone was cold and tired by the end of it, but as folk made their various ways homewards the talk was excited and animated.

'I'll be glad to get home by the fire,' said Aunt Ketty. 'Come along, Judith, let's be brisk.'

'Do you mind if I come directly? I promised Adam I'd walk home with him.'

'What it is to be young and in love,' teased Peter. 'The winter winds hold no chill, eh? Never mind, Mistress Kettering, I'll keep you company along the way. Loveday will be wild to know what's been happening.'

'I'll be glad to have you walk with me, Peter, I thank you. Just the same, Judith, don't you go tarrying too long, do you hear? There are some heavy clouds about, and I wouldn't be surprised if we saw snow before this day is done.'

'Stop your fussing, Ketty,' said Toby. 'The wench'll take no harm, not with young Adam to keep her warm. You were young yourself once! Besides, you've got Peter and me as your gallants on the road home. What more do you want?'

'I suppose a body of my age couldn't ask for more!' Aunt Ketty relented with a smile. 'I'll see you anon then, Judith, and there'll be a nice bit of supper waiting for you.'

Judith watched the three of them head off towards home, then she looked around for Adam. He was still so pressed round by villagers eager to talk that all she could see of him was the top of his russet head, so she stepped into the shelter of the church porch to wait for him. As she huddled into her cloak, pulling it about her, a figure approached and she looked up to see Marjorie standing there.

'I'm glad to have a word with you, Judith,' she said. 'I want to thank you for your support today. You spoke up well.'

'It seemed an obvious solution, and sensible.'

'It was that, right enough, but getting the menfolk to agree was another matter. All they think of is fighting. It needed us women to see beyond. You spoke the truth when you said those fen drainers have power and riches. They mean to get their way, and I fear this sorry business will end with more than just broken heads. That's why I don't want Adam involved.'

'I don't see how he can help it,' Judith pointed out. 'The villagers have chosen him as our leader.'

'To go to Ely and talk of our grievances with lawyers, or to organise the collection! 'Tis only right and proper that he, as a Digby, should deal with such matters—but I don't want him involved in any fighting.'

'You'll have your work cut out to stop him.'

'I know. He has such courage and spirit, he will be in the forefront of any skirmish. There will be no hiding away at the back for him. Where there's most danger, that's where he will be, where he will stand the greatest risk of injury or even... I couldn't bear anything to happen to him...' Marjorie's voice faltered to a halt.

Judith was surprised at her distress. Marjorie was not a woman who gave way to her emotions readily, and to see her so upset was rare.

'Don't fret,' said Judith gently. 'It may not come to serious fighting; even if it does, I'm sure Adam will be more than a match for any drainer. I don't want him hurt, either, but I'm sure he has the ability to come through any sort of struggle victorious.'

The words seemed to reassure Marjorie, for she smiled her chilly smile and drew herself upright.

'Of course he has. Thank you for reminding me, Judith. Adam is a Digby, after all, and we've been warriors right back to Duke William's time. Such blood must run true, mustn't it? Forgive me for my foolishness, but Adam is all I have. I have been more mother than sister to him. He has always been everything to me, so much so that at times I give way to silly fancies. Of course, if he was to wed and have sons, then my mind would be easier, for there would be someone to inherit Old Place and carry on our ancient name.'

She favoured Judith with a stare so intense that for a moment the girl was tempted to tell her that her fears were at an end, that Aunt Ketty had said she and Adam might be betrothed. But she held her tongue. Adam must be the first to hear such wonderful tidings, and from her lips alone. To Marjorie she said, 'I'm sure we won't have to wait much longer until we're wed.'

Marjorie, however, was not satisfied. 'It's Jane Kettering dragging her heels, nothing else,' she said sharply. 'You'd best tell her that times are getting critical. If she does not give her approval soon she'll cause you to lose the best match that's ever likely to come your way! Good day.'

Her farewell was stiff and abrupt, in marked contrast to her earlier fears, but Judith was too accustomed to her ways to be upset. She guessed that Marjorie was ashamed of having shown such emotion, and chose to smother it under a cloak of coldness.

Marjorie had not been gone five minutes when, at last, Adam freed himself of his admiring crowd and came hurrying up. Judith ran towards him eager to tell him her news.

'I feared I'd never get away,' he panted. 'When some folk from this village get talking there's no stopping them. Well, how do you think the meeting went?'

'You know perfectly well that it went splendidly, a triumph for Adam Digby, so you don't need me to flatter your vanity,' she teased.

'Stony-hearted jade, you don't appreciate my admirable qualities.' Adam pretended to be cast down, but his mood of euphoria overcame his play-acting. 'Yes, it did go well, didn't it?' he said. 'The whole village is behind me in the fight, not one dissenting voice. Isn't it encouraging?'

'It is indeed,' said Judith. 'Adam, I have such news...'

But Adam's thoughts were still fixed on the events of the day. Taking her hand, almost absent-mindedly, he went on talking as they made for the lane home.

'...Of course, we still have much to do. Ammunition will be our greatest problem. Those who can afford it will amass shot, and such like, but we must also collect up spare metal to be made into shot. Thomas the blacksmith says we can use his forge——'

'Aye, but Adam——'

'And we need some sort of signal to direct our men to wherever the drainers are. What say you to flags flown from the church tower? Perhaps red for the West Fen and blue for the East?'

'An excellent scheme. Now, Adam, will you *please* listen to me?' Judith was growing exasperated in her failure to get his full attention.

'Listen to you? Of course I'll listen to you!' Adam looked at her in astonishment. 'You've not had another of your fanciful ideas?'

'Some folk, including your own sister, thought my ideas other than fanciful today,' she retorted, a little hurt by his mocking dismissal of her contribution to the meeting. 'But what I have to tell you has naught to do with drainers. I've been desperate to tell you—Aunt Ketty has given her approval at last——'

'You mean we can be wed?' Adam stopped in his tracks.

'Well, not just yet. We can be betrothed now and as soon as Aunt Ketty's spoken to the lawyers——'

'Not more lawyers! What's amiss with the times? A man can't breathe without consulting the law, it seems to me. This nonsense about seeking legal advice against the drainers, it's a waste of time. All we need to do is crack a few skulls and break a few bones every time they show their noses on our fen. They'll get discouraged long before we will. The lads in the village——'

'Don't you want to know why Aunt Ketty's going to the law?' demanded Judith, losing her patience.

'Aye. Tell me.'

'She wants to adopt me so that I'm her legal child, and when she's done that we can be married.'

'Why does she want to do that?' demanded Adam, perplexed.

'So that I am certain to inherit her cottage and land after her,' said Judith.

'Why wouldn't a simple will do?'

'That's the way Aunt Ketty wants it,' Judith said firmly.

'So there'll be more delays, eh? She truly is a difficult woman to fathom. I suppose this means you trailing off to Ely? Well, you and Marjorie managed to ensure another trp in that direction for me too, so we may as well all go together.'

'That would be splendid... But aren't you pleased that we can be betrothed?' Judith watched his face anxiously for some sign of joy.

'Of course I am, love!' Adam put his arm around her and hugged her, but it was almost a brotherly gesture. 'However, before betrothals, and gallivanting off to see lawyers, we must gather in some funds. It will have to be a Sunday, that's the only day the folk from the outlying fens are certain to come into the village. Perhaps collecting it on two Sundays would be best. I'll ask Hal Osborne if we can use the porch at the Lamb...'

For the rest of the walk home Adam's talk was all about fighting the drainers. He scarcely seemed to have understood Judith's tidings. Her spirits plummeted. With a sinking heart she realised that for the moment, at least, she would have to take second place in his affections. The fight against the drainers came first.

Aunt Ketty greeted the news that Adam would escort them to Ely with enthusiasm.

'I confess I was not happy about us going alone, times being what they are,' she admitted. 'There are all sorts of strange folk wandering about these days, it's scarce safe to wander far.'

'Do you include the Dutchman among those strange folk?' asked Judith.

'Well, 'tis true, you don't meet many like him,' Aunt Ketty chuckled, deliberately misunderstanding her. 'Though he didn't strike me as the sort to attack two defenceless women.'

'If he attempted such a thing on us he'd have a very nasty shock,' Judith declared.

'That he would.' Aunt Ketty chuckled again. 'Not that there seems to be much sign of him at the moment. I half expected him to come a-courting you again.'

'Heaven forbid! But you're right, there's been no sign of him for days.'

'I did hear that he's moving house; perhaps that has something to do with it. He was staying at the Hall, so 'twas said, but Peter reckons he's living in the old Fen Reeve's place.'

'Well, that's far enough out of our way, thank goodness!' Judith eyed the tulip, still blooming in its blue and white pot. 'I suppose I'll have to trail out there before long to return that flower.'

'I suppose you must, my pet.' Aunt Ketty gave a reluctant sigh. 'I must say, I'll miss it sorely when it's gone. It's a pretty thing.'

Aunt Ketty had no need to bewail the loss of the tulip, for it was destined to remain on the table for some time to come. It was not that Judith forgot it; she simply did not have the time to return it to the Dutchman. What with tending the animals, preparing for their journey to Ely, and helping Adam collect the money for the fight against the drainers, she had barely a spare minute.

They set out for Ely on a cold, dank morning. The threat of snow had come to nothing, the worst of the winter rains seemed over, and already the water-level on the flooded fens was dropping a little, so they dared not delay longer. In spite of the discomfort, Judith felt a thrill of excitement as their boat made its steady progress towards the city. She had seldom been away from Sedgewick St Peter, and the prospect of spending time among the bustle and activity of Ely appealed to her. Her companions did not share her pleasure. Aunt Ketty's mind was occupied with all the instructions she had failed to give Toby, who was seeing to their livestock. As for Adam, he did not bother to mask his reluctance for the journey.

'I only hope naught of importance occurs while I'm away,' he kept saying. 'I don't know what will happen if the drainers come, for with only Hal Osborne and Thomas the blacksmith in charge, our response is likely to be a shambles. I shouldn't have allowed myself to be persuaded into this errand. Someone else should have come.'

'And who else would you have chosen?' asked Judith. 'Perhaps you are able to name someone you'd trust, but I can't.'

She knew, though Aunt Ketty did not, that as well as the visit to the lawyers Adam had also been secretly entrusted to buy powder and shot for the village.

'I suppose you're right.' Adam eyed the brawny shoulders of his servants, brought along for protection as much as their strength in propelling the boat. 'All the same, I'll be thankful to get home safely again.'

'Amen to that,' agreed Aunt Ketty.

The bustle of activity at Ely struck Judith like a blow.

'So many people! And why do they rush so?' she demanded in bewilderment, as they stood on the quay.

'They're just going about their business,' Adam assured her, laughing. 'You'll soon get used to it.'

Judith was not convinced, and she was thankful for Adam's steadying arm as he guided them to their lodgings.

'Now, you're sure you'll be all right?' he asked, delivering them to the door. 'Wouldn't you prefer to lie at the White Hart, as I am doing?'

'We'll be fine here, I thank you,' Aunt Ketty assured him firmly before Judith could speak. 'These be kinfolk of Toby's, and he says we're sure of a welcome.'

She had been determined from the start that they would not lodge in the same place as Adam. 'It would not be seemly. Tongues would wag!' she'd stated. 'And, in addition, Adam's pockets are longer than ours, he can afford to lay out money for feather beds at grand inns.'

Adam knew her reasons well enough, and his expression as he bade them farewell expressed his certainty that this was one more of Aunt Ketty's strange ideas.

Toby had been right, his kinsfolk welcomed them most hospitably, expressing delight at the dressed ducks, the eggs, the cheese and the honey that their guests had brought as gifts.

Judith was so bone-tired she was certain she'd fall asleep immediately, but Aunt Ketty was snoring loudly long before her eyes felt like closing. Her head was too busy with events of the day and the prospect of the morrow, but, above all, one thought kept her awake—this trip to Ely meant that she was growing closer to marrying Adam. The exciting thought of that alone was enough to drive away sleep.

Next morning, one of Adam's menservants came to act as escort to Judith and Aunt Ketty.

'Isn't Master Digby coming himself?' asked Judith.

'He sends his regrets, mistress, but says he has certain important affairs he must attend to,' replied the man.

What affairs can be more important than me? thought Judith, then realised that she was being silly. Adam had appointments to keep with gunsmiths and the like, as well as conferring with lawyers. However, she could not help being a little disappointed, and she hoped that such transactions would not take up all his time while they were in Ely, she so longed to enjoy something of his company. But at least he had ensured that she and Aunt Ketty were not without a guide and protector.

'We want to go to Master Nichols, the lawyer, at the Sign of the Glove. Do you know it, John?'

'Aye, Mistress Kettering, it's not but a step from the cathedral,' replied the servant, as the three of them set off.

Judith's early confusion at the busy streets soon gave way to interest and curiosity, so that she was almost disappointed when they arrived at the narrow alley alongside the glovemaker's, and found a small sign proclaiming 'William Nichols, Notary and Attorney At Law' on a small inner door.

Their hosts, Toby's kinsfolk, had given them Master Nichol's name.

'He's an honest man,' they'd been assured. 'He won't charge you a shilling for sixpenn'orth o' work.'

Master Nichols proved to be a shabby, frail-looking man, a little above middle age, and he listened to their story attentively.

'You do realise that I can easily ensure Mistress Pentelow inherits your possessions simply by drawing up a will,' he pointed out. 'It would be cheaper, and far easier.'

'I'd be grateful if you'd do that for me; I'd like to have my will done,' replied Aunt Ketty. 'But I'd also like to make Judith my legal child.'

'After having reared her for sixteen years without hindrance?' Master Nichols' eyebrows rose, then he looked shrewdly at Aunt Ketty. 'Well, you strike me as a sensible woman, Mistress Kettering, and nobody's fool, so I presume you have good reason.'

'I have.' Aunt Ketty was definite.

'Very well. I'll put matters in hand at once, though I doubt if we'll make much progress until the better weather comes. Grantham, you say Mistress Pentelow's cousins used to live? That can be a fearful road when it's wet—and none too easy when dry... Now, let us commence with the will, shall we?'

The procedure was long drawn-out and, to Judith, tedious. Master Nichols punctiliously wrote down all that Aunt Ketty listed, his quill scratching on the paper, and the fire crackling in the grate, being the only sounds to break the stillness of the room. Judith's attention wandered to the shelf of books above his head. Their leather bindings were worn and well-thumbed with use, and she wondered what it would be like to have books of her own that she could take down and read at will. It seemed a pleasure far beyond her reach.

At last they were finished, and the manservant asked, 'Where would you go now, mistresses? To the White Hart? Master Digby expects you to eat with him.'

'I would that we could,' said Aunt Ketty, 'for I can't recall when I last felt so weary. Who'd have thought that just sitting talking to a lawyer could tire a body so? But we've purchases to make, things we can't get at home, and it would be a great pity to miss the chance now that we're in Ely.'

'It would indeed,' agreed Judith. 'But we don't both need to go, do we? You could go back to the inn with John while I get what we need.'

'Would you? You'd not be afeared in a great place like this?' asked Aunt Ketty hopefully.

'I'm not afeared,' grinned Judith. 'And if I get lost there is always the cathedral to set my sights by. Now, what do we need? Spices mainly, isn't it?'

'Aye, in particular cloves, we've not a one in the house. And nutmeg, and saffron, and pepper, of course. And don't forget sewing needles—get decent ones even if they cost a penny more. The one I'm using now is like sewing with a piece of briar.'

By the time Aunt Ketty had finished, the list was quite a formidable one, but Judith did not mind. To be truthful, she was quite looking forward to exploring the city on her own. The manservant directed her towards the most likely vendors, and she set off.

The sights of the city delighted her, particularly the people hurrying by. The grandness of their dress made her open her eyes wide with astonishment and wish that she had something a little better to wear than russet homespun. She was far from dowdy, though; the rich warm hue of her simple country gown suited her dark colouring, and the immaculate crispness of her white linen cap and wide collar, adorned as they were by the narrowest band of lace, complemented her glowing complexion. More than one city gentleman touched his hat hopefully to her, but Judith was too wise to be caught by such flattery, and went on her way.

After she had made her first few purchases Judith discovered something that the manservant had forgotten to mention—that there was a lively market in full swing. In her eager pursuit of more bargains, she hurried in the direction of the colourful stalls and the bustling crowd. She decided to take a short cut down an alley, but as she was heading towards the square where the market was being held her path was suddenly blocked by two men staggering out of a small tavern.

'Well, and who's this tripping along as trim as you please?' demanded the first fellow in slurred tones.

'I wager—I wager such a pretty wench has got a—a kiss for me an' for you—an' a kiss for the whole world!' declared his companion, who was decidedly the worse for drink and unsteady on his feet.

'Let me through, I pray you!' said Judith sharply.

'Not—not until you've given us both a kiss. We're not—we're not going anywhere until you've embraced us both!' said the unsteady one, advancing towards her.

'Aye, I fancy you're wench enough for both of us,' agreed the other.

He was less drunk than his companion, more menacing, and Judith did not like the look of him at all. She was determined not to show her unease, so she said, 'The only thing I'll give the pair of you is a kick hard enough to make your eyes water!'

'Oh! She's a lively one!' leered the first one. 'They're the sort I like, the ones who fight.'

Then suddenly, just as Judith was beginning to brace herself for the attack that was sure follow, the lustful grin left the man's face. He and his unsteady friend stared in alarm at a spot just above Judith's head.

'If it's a fight you want I suggest we make it even,' said a voice behind her.

Of all people, it was the Dutchman. Gently moving Judith to one side he headed towards the drunken men. But one look at his large figure bearing down on them was enough. They fled.

He turned and grinned at Judith.

'They should be grateful to me,' he said. 'They did not recognise the spirit of their adversary. If I hadn't come along there's no knowing what damage you might have done them.'

'I never expected to say this,' said Judith, 'but I am grateful to you also.'

'It was nothing,' the Dutchman said lightly. 'You were in no danger. From what I've seen of you, I'm convinced you could have defeated them both with one hand, while holding a nosegay of flowers in the other.'

'I don't share your confidence in me, so I would thank you for being present at such an opportune moment.' Judith was loath to admit even to herself that her legs were rather shaky.

The Dutchman regarded her with his usual steady stare.

'There's a small inn not far away—no, not this rat hole that spawned your would-be attackers—but a decent place. I suggest we go and try their excellent spiced wine.'

'I am grateful to you, sir, but not that grateful,' replied Judith.

'I am your gallant rescuer. You cannot deny my request,' was his response. 'Besides, I need fortifying, my nerves are shot to pieces!' he added unconvincingly.

'Oh, very well,' said Judith, then added, 'I thank you.'

'I suppose there's no hope of you taking my arm, just to support me in my feeble state?'

'None whatsoever!'

'I could but ask. Come, the inn is close by.'

He did not wait to hear any more arguments, so, half-bemused, Judith went with him, convinced that she must be mad. It was too late to back out, though, and she had to admit that she felt in need of the wine.

The Dutchman proved to be right, the inn was a decent enough place, but even so Judith had serious qualms about entering it.

'There's a pretty sort of garden at the back, can't we sit out there?' she asked.

'In this weather, with frost still hanging on the grass? You fenland folk are hardier than I thought. For my part I'd prefer to be beside a good fire. Come, what is your real objection?'

Judith paused. So far she had regarded the Dutchman merely as a provoking character. Now she had to admit he was clearly a virile man, one that many women would consider comely.

'I have more than one, but the chief is that my aunt would not approve of me entering the inn with a strange man,' she said.

'But you are not with a strange man, you are with me!'

'That is another of my objections.'

He grinned. 'I thought it might be so. All right, I promise you we will sit privately, and if you have any further misgivings I am sure we can prevail upon the landlord's wife, or one of the maids, to remain with us to observe the proprieties. Not only that, I feel you should sit a little and have refreshment for your health's sake. You have gone quite pale, and I would restore the roses I admire so much to your cheeks.'

'If you talk in such a manner I will not come!'

'Very well, I'll behave, but under protest.'

He was clearly no stranger to the inn, for he led her straight to a side room in which a fire burned brightly.

'There, is this not better than sitting chilled in the garden? We won't be disturbed here, and the wine will come directly.'

The Dutchman was completely at his ease, but Judith still felt uncomfortable.

A small, brisk woman brought their wine.

The Dutchman looked at Judith, his eyebrows raised. 'Would you have mine hostess stay with us?' he asked.

Suddenly Judith felt that her fears were nothing but foolishness. After all, what was the Dutchman to her?

'There will be no need, I thank you,' she said. 'I'll not tarry here long.'

'Then that will be all, thank you, mistress,' he said to the woman.

'Very well, sir. Just call if you require aught else.' The woman made for the door. 'There—I nearly forgot! Your letters are come, Master van de Scheldt. I've put them in your room,' she said as she departed.

Judith was aghast. 'You've brought me to your lodgings!'

'Of course. I didn't know anywhere more respectable.'

'I like not your notion of respectability! I am leaving!'

Judith rose to go, but the Dutchman caught her hand to detain her. At the touch of him she pulled herself free as though his fingers had stung her.

'I am sorry,' he said. 'I was truly thinking of your best interests. The inn is well thought of, and Mistress Allen's character is known throughout Ely to be blameless. I beg you, stay and at least drink your wine. See, I'll sit over here, so as not to vex you.'

It seemed rather ridiculous for him to be sitting right beside the door when there was a good fire, so Judith said crossly, 'You may as well come and warm yourself, else I suppose it will be my fault if you catch a chill.'

The Dutchman speedily made himself comfortable by the hearth.

'You haven't said it,' he remarked.

'I haven't said what?'

'Why, the comment I expected to hear—"what on earth are you doing here?"'

'So, what are you doing in Ely?'

'I am here on business.'

'Drainage business?' asked Judith suspiciously.

'What a creature you are for harping upon drainage. It's not a fitting subject for a pretty maid——'

'You promised you would behave,' Judith reminded him.

'So I did. Your pardon. I assure you I am merely here to confer with men of business. Bankers and merchants—and a dull crew they are proving to be... Now it's my turn to ask it. What are you doing here?'

'I am here on business.'

'Ach, I might have expected such a reply. You didn't travel from your home alone, I trust?'

'Of course not.' Judith chose her words with care. It would not do to reveal too much of the purpose of this trip to the Dutchman, but her reply sounded suspiciously curt to her own ears, so she added, 'I am here with Aunt Ketty. We have business with a lawyer.'

'Not a lawsuit, I hope.'

'No, nothing like that. My aunt is getting on in years and wishes to adopt me legally so that my future is secure.'

'Isn't Mistress Kettering your next of kin, then?'

'No, she isn't even a blood relation, which is why she has consulted a lawyer.'

That was no more than the truth, and he seemed satisfied with her answer, for he replied, 'Oh, I hadn't realised your circumstances. How strange we should both be in Ely at the same time.'

'Yes, strange indeed.'

Judith was beginning to wonder if it was not too much of a coincidence. What if the Dutchman had been following them? He might be trying to discover what they were up to. She was thankful that she had not mentioned Adam. At all costs she must not reveal that he was here in Ely buying arms.

'You have been here long?' she asked.

'Some six or seven days, though it seems longer.'

She was relieved to hear it. That meant he could not possibly have been following her—if he were speaking the truth. She was suddenly nervous lest he should begin interrogating her, asking more questions about her visit. Also, there was one more thing that troubled her.

'I still find it incredible that you should have come down that alley just when you did, and just when I needed help,' she said.

'Ah, perhaps that was not quite such a coincidence. I chanced to be walking along the road when I saw a maid of great beauty turning the corner into an alley. I thought that such a paragon of delight dwelt only in Sedgewick. I couldn't believe there could be another of such loveliness, of such lightness of step, such litheness of body, but if there were, then I was determined to make her acquaintance. I hurried into the alley too, to be confronted not by some counterfeit but, to my joy, by the original herself. And, even more miraculous, I was able to be of some small service.'

He had forgotten his promise not to utter extravagant compliments, but for once Judith did not check him. It seemed less and less likely that he had followed them, and all but the faintest of her doubts were stilled.

'I must go,' she said, draining the horn beaker of the last of its mulled wine. 'I thank you again for your timely assistance, and for your hospitality. I must ask you, though, never to reveal to a living soul that I sat here alone with you.'

'My lips shall not utter one word on the subject, and for evermore I shall cherish the fact that we share a secret.'

'I merely request discretion; there's no need to turn this last hour into a conspiracy,' observed Judith.

'Then I shall cherish every minute of this hour all the more because you have scarcely scolded me once.'

There was no putting down this man. 'That's because I was so glad to see you in Ely,' said Judith sweetly.

'Oh?'

'Aye. If you are here you can't be on Hanser Fen starting the draining! Now, if you please, if there is a back door I will leave that way.'

'Surely you aren't afraid of encountering your neighbours from Sedgewick, are you?'

'I encountered you,' Judith pointed out.

There was a back way out of the inn—through the garden and into a lane at the rear. As Judith left by it she met Mistress Allen busy feeding her ducks. She nearly passed by with just a greeting, but then she stopped. This was too good an opportunity to miss.

'It is a very good inn that you run, mistress,' she said. 'Master van de Scheldt was telling me how comfortable he is.'

'Such an easy gentleman to cater for. He's not a spot of bother.' Mistress Allen smiled fondly. 'Every time he comes here to stay I say to him, "If everyone who lodges here was like you, master, my job would be an easy one."'

'So he stays with you often?'

'Whenever he has business in Ely. This must be about his fourth visit. Sometimes it's only for a day or two, but this time he's lain here a full week.'

Judith's last little doubt vanished. She was grateful to the loquacious landlady for offering so much information freely. She had been chary of asking too many questions for fear of raising suspicion.

'They say a good ale needs no bush,' she said with a smile. 'Clearly a good inn needs only satisfied guests to spread its fame. Now, can I beg a favour, mistress? I am a stranger to Ely—if you could tell me where the best spices are to be bought...'

As Judith walked along the lane she wondered if she should tell Aunt Ketty about her meeting with the Dutchman. After a struggle with her conscience, for she never found it easy to withhold things from her aunt, she decided against it. There was no need, was there? It had all been very proper. In fact, the Dutchman had behaved much better than she had expected—though, upon consideration, she never knew quite what to expect from him. She did not even think of telling Adam of how she had spent the last hour—that would have been foolishness bordering upon lunacy. It was as the Dutchman had said: they shared a secret. Judith could not imagine a more bizarre situation in which to find herself. And it was only later that she remembered she had spoken his full name, when she had sworn not to. Moreover, it had tripped off her tongue with great ease, for all its foreignness. If she had had less to divert her she might have found the fact disturbing.

She finished her marketing, then made for the White Hart, where she found Aunt Ketty dozing contentedly by the fire. Of Adam there was no sign. It was nearly an hour before he burst into the room set aside for them, full of apologies and complaints.

'Cursed lawyers!' he exclaimed. 'I've been closeted with them all morning. Their talk has made my head reel! It's been naught but consulting this book here and looking into that stupid book there for hours, and we're still no further forward!'

Judith wished that his greeting could have been less forceful. She would have preferred a loving word or a tender look. But she realised that having been cooped up all morning must have been agony for him. The company of lawyers Adam had been consulting was far more illustrious than Master Nichols, of course, but from Adam's description they did not sound any more efficient.

'But will they take our case?' she asked. 'Do they think we have any hope?'

'They'll take our case, right enough, and our money!' Adam flung himself disconsolately on to a stool by the fire.

'But what did they say? Have we any redress in law?' Judith persisted.

'As to that, they've to look in more books and waste more time before they can give me even the start of an answer. I've to go again tomorrow!'

To Judith the prospect sounded hopeful, and she heaved a sigh of relief. It was typical of Adam to want things settled immediately, when clearly they were going to take time.

Aunt Ketty, who had woken when Adam entered, observed, 'You couldn't expect more. At least they're taking pains. Matters dealt with in a rush are seldom finished satisfactorily.'

Adam's response was to kick irritably at the burning logs and shout for the landlord to bring food.

'And have you no wish to hear how we fared this morning?' asked Judith at last, unable to keep a note of reproof out of her voice.

'How you fared? Oh, aye, you were to see one of these lawyer fellows, too, were you not? The place seems to be crawling with them. I wonder they can all make a living, never mind an honest one. Very well, what did the rogue say?'

'I could have looked for a greater interest in a matter that concerns our future so closely,' she said sharply.

'Aye, you are right!' He took her hand in both of his and pressed it against his cheek. 'I'm sorry, my love. I am interested, of course I am. Forgive me for being such a surly brute. I've a deal to do on this visit and much on my mind, so it angered me that these legal buffoons took a whole morning to say what anyone else could utter in half an hour. I hope your time was spent more profitably so that our wedding draws nearer.'

'Not exactly,' Judith had to admit, mollified by his sudden gentleness. 'He, too, must make enquiries and investigations, but that was no more than we expected. He must seek out my kinsfolk first, but he hopes to have the matter settled by late summer.'

'Well, he's more encouraging than the scoundrels I had to deal with.' Adam's hold on her hand tightened. 'Late summer, eh? So we could be wed at Michaelmas! What better time, with the harvest done and the winter ploughing not begun? We'd have a little time to ourselves to start our wedded life.'

Michaelmas! For Judith the setting of a date made all her dreams much closer to reality.

'Is it possible?' she asked her aunt. 'Could we be married in October?'

'If Master Nichols can conclude matters satisfactorily by that time,' Aunt Ketty replied. 'But best not build your hopes up too much until we see how far he gets.'

It was there again, the slight hesitancy in her tone. Judith knew that her aunt would never go back on her given word that she and Adam could wed, but she wished fervently that Aunt Ketty was more pleased at the idea.

'Oh, of all the fools! I knew I'd forget something!' Adam suddenly released Judith's hand and clenched his fists in a gesture of annoyance.

'Something important?' asked Judith.

'Aye, your betrothal ring! You did say we could be betrothed at once, did you not, Mistress Kettering?'

'I did.'

'I meant to bring the ring for one of the city goldsmiths to make it smaller, but with so much to do I forgot it!'

'My ring? This is the first I've heard of any ring,' said Judith, a delighted smile lighting her face.

'It was meant to be a surprise.' Adam looked a little abashed. 'Still, you'd have had to come with me to get the size right, wouldn't you? It was one of my mother's. Marjorie picked it out for me. It is rubies set in gold.'

'Marjorie picked it out, you say?' Judith felt her pleasure ebbing.

'Aye, and a good thing she did. Not knowing about such gewgaws, I'd have chosen a little band of pearls that belonged to my grandmother, only my sister said it was a tawdry trifle by comparison, not fit to grace the hand of a future Mistress Digby.'

Judith's first reaction was to exclaim that she did not want Marjorie to choose her betrothal ring for her, that she would have preferred Adam's choice, whether it be the band of pearls, a plain keepsake, or even a cheap fairing. But she controlled her tongue with an effort.

Instead she said, 'It was kind of your sister to go to such pains on my behalf.'

She did not dare to catch Aunt Ketty's eye, for she knew all too well what the old lady was thinking.

They stayed at Ely for three days more, but in that time Judith saw even less of Adam than she would have done at home, his time was so taken up with meetings and the buying of arms. The lack of his company apart, she found to her surprise that she enjoyed city life. There was always plenty of interest and incident. Above all, there was news of the rift between the King and Parliament. Each traveller who arrived seemed to bring yet more rumours of quarrels and skirmishes.

One other shadow clouded her visit to Ely: the prospect that she might meet the Dutchman again. Every time she walked out with Aunt Ketty, or Adam, her heart was in her mouth lest she should see him on the street. It only took a tall figure clad in black, or a steeple hat to be visible above the crowd, for her pulse to start racing. She dared not think what might happen if she ever encountered him again in the presence of the others. It was quite a relief when their visit to Ely came to an end without her catching another glimpse of the man who infuriated her so much.

The boat that carried Judith, Adam and Aunt Ketty back to Sedgewick St Peter made slow progress against the receding winter floods. It was heavily laden with powder, shot, and other weapons that Adam had managed to procure. Judith, her legs jammed uncomfortably against a keg of powder, was so cramped by the end of the long journey that she could hardly stand. Adam took this as an opportunity to put his arms about her to help her along the path.

'You go ahead, Mistress Kettering,' he said. 'My men will bring your things, and I will bring Judith.'

'See you do, then!' replied Aunt Ketty, her eyes twinkling. 'But don't think I can't recognise a good excuse when I hear one!'

'It seems as if we've been away for an age,' said Judith, in no hurry to get home now that she was in Adam's arms.

'Aye, we've seen and done so much, yet I doubt things have changed at all. At least, I hope they haven't. It would be just like a thing for the drainers to have come and——'

'We have but five minutes alone!' Judith silenced him with a restraining hand to his lips. 'Let's forget about the drainers, Hanser Fen, King Charles...everything except us.'

'You're right. Why should we waste time on them, when we are so much more important?' Adam edged aside the hood of her cape and traced the line of her throat with hot, eager kisses.

'And interesting, too,' said Judith unsteadily, for his caresses were sending thrills of sharp excitement through her despite her tiredness.

'Aye, interesting...' His hands were beneath her cape now, lingering sensuously over each curve of her body until they came to rest cupped about her breasts. 'Oh, I was a fool to forget that ring!'

'It doesn't matter. It isn't necessary.'

'But it is!' insisted Adam. 'I would have all men know that you are mine!'

'Ah, so you are merely marking your property, eh?' teased Judith. 'The same way you'd clip a cow's ear, or brand a horse's flank.'

'I have better things to do with your flank than put a brand on it...' Adam's fondling began to get more intimate and insistent, but Judith firmly pushed away his hands.

'What right have you to take such liberties?' she asked.

'Why, the right as your future husband, of course.'

'My future husband? Who says so?'

'I say so—and you do, too. Come, don't play the prude with me.' Adam tried to resume his exploration, but Judith laughingly struggled free.

'I never said I'd be your wife,' she said.

'What teasing is this now? Of course you did.'

'Of course I didn't. For you never asked me!'

'What need have we for such foolery? We've always known we'd wed. We've just assumed——'

'*You've* just assumed,' Judith interrupted, 'but a maid needs things to be a bit more definite than that.'

'I'm sure I've asked you to marry me.'

'Oh, yes, when we were children playing at keeping house in a corner of the barn. But when did you ever propose to me since you've been a man?'

'I must have done—I'm certain I did...' Adam floundered, his memory failing him. Then he gave a chuckle.

'Very well, just to keep you happy, I'll ask you now. Judith, will you marry me?'

'That's a very sorry effort. I'll say no if you can't do better than that.'

'What do you want? Have me write a poem to your left ear, or serenade you beneath your window?' demanded Adam in exasperation.

'I'd not put you to such trouble. All I want is a proper, seemly proposal of marriage.'

'Very well, let me see what I can do. Ah, yes...Judith, you're the only woman I've ever wanted, ever loved. I beg you to make me the happiest man in the kingdom—nay, in the whole world, by saying that you love me in return, and that you will be my wife.'

Gently Judith reached out and took his face in her hands. 'I accept your proposal,' she said. 'For you have been my love, my life, my whole world ever since I can remember.'

Suddenly the teasing and the laughter between them ceased, as the importance of the moment overwhelmed them. Enfolded in each other's arms, they stood there in the darkness, not speaking, for no more words were necessary. Only when approaching footsteps heralded the arrival of the menservants did they exchange one long kiss, and part.

CHAPTER FIVE

ADAM was right, nothing much had changed in Sedgewick while they had been away. Lee, the sexton, had oiled the lock of the church tower door, and a few industrious enthusiasts sported baskets of stones and other missiles beside their gates, ready for action, but apart from that the village remained the same. Judith picked up the threads of her everyday life with a new joy now that she and Adam were properly betrothed. Adam, however, was restless.

'There's no sign of them!' he protested. 'Not a hint of a drainer anywhere. Even your Dutchman hasn't been seen in ages.'

His words struck a blow to Judith's conscience. Now that she was safely home again, the memory of her interlude with the Dutchman at Ely filled her with self-reproach. What could she have been thinking of, to have actually sat drinking wine with him? It was no use telling herself that she was bound to be civil to him because he had rendered her a service. Viewed at a distance, her encounter with the two drunkards hardly seemed reason to treat him with anything other than chilly politeness.

'He's not my Dutchman,' she replied, with unnecessary sharpness. 'And, besides, I'd have thought his absence would be considered a good thing.'

'No, while he's here we can keep an eye on him.' Adam lowered his voice conspiratorially. 'It's my belief he's gone to consort with the Devil.'

'Surely not!' Judith was in a quandary. She dared not say that she knew for certain the man was just in Ely. 'I—I heard he was seen heading towards London,' she said.

'London! The Devil! It's all the same!' Adam had only contempt for anywhere beyond the boundaries of the Fens. 'I confess this waiting for action is trying me sorely. Why doesn't something happen?'

For herself, Judith was quite content for things to carry on as they were. She did not know whom she wished to see the least, the Dutchman or the drainers, but so long as they were both absent from Hanser Fen, she was happy. Most of the men from the village shared Adam's impatience for action; however, as day followed day without anything happening the urgency went out of the matter. Some folk even began to think the whole thing had been a false alarm. Then, one day, quite unexpectedly, Judith met the Dutchman again, as she was poling her boat along the river. He was coming in the opposite direction, but there was no chance of avoiding him for the channel was too narrow.

'Mistress Pentelow! This is my lucky day indeed!' he greeted her. 'You aren't in search of a stray cow again, I trust?'

Judith tried to ignore him, in spite of the fact that their boats were forced to pass within inches of one another.

'What, won't you speak to an old friend?' he asked, pausing to lean on his boating-pole, bringing his craft to a halt. Then, when Judith still did not reply, but attempted to continue on her way, he stretched out a long arm and took hold of her craft. Standing in the stern, Judith found herself facing him.

'That's better.' His cool green eyes looked over her assessingly, then registered appreciation. He went on, 'Do you know, you are even prettier than I remembered? So often the mind exaggerates charms, doesn't it? Particularly after an absence. But I am happy to find that my mind and my brain have lagged behind the truth.'

'Am I supposed to feel flattered?' retorted Judith, unable to maintain her silence any longer.

'No, but at least you're speaking to me now. That must give me hope.'

'Aye, hope of a crack on the shins if you don't let go of my boat!'

The Dutchman laughed. 'I forgot how you dealt with that other poor fellow who held your boat. I fancy he still bears the mark of your foot. Those two drunkards at Ely should be grateful to me for arriving when I did. I saved them from a terrible beating.'

'I suppose you're going to throw that incident in my face for evermore,' snapped Judith.

'For evermore? Does that mean we will be meeting frequently in the future?'

'It does not, but it seems I can't go anywhere without stumbling over you. Why must you plague me so?'

'Oh, you're scolding me again—yet at Ely you were perfectly civil—well, almost. That was why I considered we were old friends, drinking companions even——'

'I've no wish to speak of that time at Ely!' Judith retorted. 'I regret it. I wish I'd never seen you that day. In fact, I wish I'd never seen you at all. And if you dare mention our sitting together in the inn I'll—I'll come and box your ears. I don't care if you are two yards high!'

'To have my ears boxed by you, Mistress Pentelow, would be a very pleasurable experience,' he grinned. 'I would have to lift you up so that you could reach, and to have my hands round that tiny waist of yours is one of the greatest joys I can imagine.'

'Oh, you——' Judith ground her teeth in fury. 'Get out of my way, sir, so that I can leave. Why must you block my path so? If it's not your horse then it's your boat! You are infuriating!'

'But if I didn't block your way you would go straight past me,' the Dutchman pointed out. 'Then I would have no chance to talk with you, or to feast upon you with my eyes.'

'Why won't you understand that I want nothing at all to do with you? I have no wish to see you. I have no wish to talk to you. Do I make myself clear?'

'Does that mean that you aren't going to box my ears after all? I don't know how I shall bear the disappointment.'

He looked so crestfallen that if she had not been so indignant Judith might have found the sight funny. Then she realised he had made her angry again.

'There, sir, you have had your sport,' she said, forcing herself to be calm. 'You have vexed me, which was your intention all along, was it not? And having provided you with such amusement I think I've earned the right to go on my way once more.'

'So you shall, Mistress Pentelow, and I must confess were it not for you I'd find your Fens a very dull place indeed. There, see, your boat goes free.'

As he let go and straightened up he seemed to tower above her, so that she was suddenly aware of his physical strength; the powerful muscles beneath the sombre broadcloth; the long sinews of his legs as he maintained his balance in that small craft. He was a man of massive presence, dominating the narrow channel, and everything about him. In that isolated spot, far from human habitation, shrouded by last year's reeds, Judith should have felt afraid—but she did not. It was his laugh which had driven away any apprehension—it held such warmth. He sounded like a man who laughed a lot—when given the chance. Conscious that, against her better judgement, she had spared the Dutchman one sympathetic thought, Judith angrily tried to propel her boat away. But he was too quick for her. He manoeuvred his craft across her bows, forcing her into the reed-bed.

'Well, you can handle a boat, I'll say that for you,' she said, keeping her temper with difficulty. 'Now, if you'd kindly stop playing schoolboy pranks perhaps I could go on my way.'

'A compliment! You have paid me the first compliment! Now, perhaps, I can really hope for an improvement in our friendship.'

His face resumed its customary impassive look, but there was a sharp glint of mischief in his eyes that he could not control.

'Our friendship cannot improve, since it never existed. And I can promise you a soaking if you don't get out of my way,' she snapped.

But still he did not move.

'Will you move?' Driven by exasperation Judith raised her boating-pole and waved it threateningly.

The Dutchman ducked. For such a big man he was very agile.

'You are even prettier when you're angry,' he said gravely.

'Really, sir! This is beyond everything! Keep your compliments for others. I've no need of them, being properly betrothed.'

'Properly betrothed, eh? Yet you bear no ring or keepsake that I can see, to ward off other men. Your foxy-haired lover is a careless fellow, allowing you to run free with nothing to mark you as his.'

'You speak as though I were one of his cattle, and I'll have you know I'm no such thing...' Judith's retort faded.

Not one muscle of the Dutchman's face had altered, there was not a hint of humour in his expression, yet she knew that he was teasing her again. For a fleeting moment she wondered what sort of man he really was. The outrageous manner, the ridiculous compliments, were no more than a mask, and she was suddenly intrigued by the hidden character that must lie beneath the foolery. Then she was appalled. What was she about? She had no business to be intrigued by him!

Angry with herself, she pushed at his boat with her pole so forcefully that he was obliged to sit down hurriedly to prevent it capsizing. By the time he had recovered Judith had made her escape. She was out of sight among the reeds when she heard him call, 'Farewell, Mistress Pentelow, until we meet again.'

'That will be never, if I have aught to say in the matter!' she yelled back.

All she heard in reply was his laughter on the wind.

Adam greeted her news of the encounter with excitement.

'So, he's back!' he exclaimed. 'We'd best look to ourselves now, even earlier than we feared. Who'd have thought that the seasons would have favoured the drainers? That's Devil's work, if ever there was!'

He looked out over a Hanser Fen that had dried out uncommonly early. The spring rainfall had been meagre, and a steady wind had meant that large tracts of the Summer Grounds were free from water, and already sprouting new green growth weeks earlier than usual. In any other year the commoners would have greeted such an occurrence with delight, but fenland that was ready for grazing cows was also fit for the drainer's spade.

Adam set off about the village urging people to be on their guard once again. His warning was timely, for the very next morning Judith was interrupted in her tasks by the frantic jangling of the church bell.

'Surely the drainers haven't come at last?' cried Judith. She and Aunt Ketty stared at each other, then with one accord they seized their cloaks and hurried to the village.

On the green, the first person they saw was Adam.

'To arms, friends,' he was calling. 'Rally at West Gate! See the red flag! That's the way the villains are coming!'

Like sheep driven before a dog, the crowd swerved westward to halt at the West Gate, which was a bridge over the Abbot's Lode, an ancient ditch dug centuries ago to save the village from flooding. Now it proved an excellent focal point between Sedgewick and Hanser Fen.

Judith had long since left Aunt Ketty behind in her eagerness to reach Adam. She barely had time to whisper, 'Take care, my love,' to him in passing before he was hustled to the front of the army of villagers. They looked a ramshackle band, but Judith knew that every man there could give a good account of himself. Adam had now taken charge, issuing his orders with crisp authority.

'Don't forget, save powder and shot until we absolutely need it. If we can drive them off with cudgels and staves we will,' he instructed.

'Where are they? I can't see them!' Thomas the blacksmith was looking out over the fen, his eyes shaded by his hand. 'Ah, now I have 'em. They're on Sedge Bank ... Oh, is that all! There's naught but a handful of 'em.' He sounded disappointed.

Sure enough, out on the fen half a dozen men could be seen, headed by the unmistakable figure of the Dutchman. They appeared to be measuring, sticking poles into the soft earth at intervals.

'The poor souls are sorely outnumbered. Will no one go out and parley with them? Give them some warning...' But this plea from Peter Renshaw was drowned in a scornful outcry.

'Less noise!' hissed Adam. 'We don't want them to take fright and run, do we? Let's go now, lads!'

Making use of his knowledge of the firm ground and old paths, he led his men forward so that they were quite a way into the fen before they were spotted. The drainers had been strung out over several hundred yards until they saw the advancing villagers, then they began to move towards their boat. There was no chance that they could escape, hampered as they were by areas that were still marshy. Adam gave the order, 'Fire!' and a hail of stones fell upon the luckless drainers. More than one was hit and fell as the village men leapt upon them.

With the other women Judith had followed the menfolk on to the fen to get a better view of the skirmish. She saw one of the drainers go to the aid of an injured companion, but as he was struggling to get him to his feet Adam and a group of villagers reached them, cudgels raised. The Dutchman had been fending off a couple of men armed with quarterstaves, but when he saw his men sink beneath a hail of blows he thrust his own adversaries aside with such force that they went sprawling in the mud. Seizing one of their dropped weapons, he dashed into the heart of the fray. He stood no chance, of course. He was too heavily outnumbered. Even so, Judith saw several fenlanders fall beneath his flailing staff before he in turn was felled. Her heart was in her mouth in case Adam was one of the fallen, but to her relief she saw him. He wasn't fighting now, but arguing with Peter Renshaw. It wasn't hard to guess the cause of the argument. Knowing the shoemaker, she was certain that he had intervened to save the Dutchman and his men further punishment. True enough, the villagers began to return, still arguing.

'Scarce worth the bother, that wasn't,' grumbled Thomas. 'We could've got rid of 'em once and for all!'

'Aye, and got hanged for it,' protested Peter. 'They were beaten and outnumbered. There was no cause to kill the poor souls too.'

'Peter's right,' agreed Adam reluctantly. 'It would have been a hanging matter, and no drainer's worth that. It's a shame it's over, even though it wasn't much of a fight.'

'You've a few scars to show for it, all the same,' Judith pointed out, for not one of them had escaped unscathed.

Adam gingerly touched an eye that was rapidly turning black and blue.

'Cursed Dutchman!' he exclaimed.

'He gave a good account of himself, I'll say that,' said Toby, who sported a spectacular bruise on his cheek.

'You don't think he fought unaided, do you?' snapped Adam. 'He had unseen forces helping him. It stands to reason his master, the Devil, came to his aid, else how did he stand so long against eight of us?'

A sigh of apprehension ran through all who were in earshot, but Judith still found it hard to believe that the Dutchman had had supernatural help.

'I thought Sir Walter was his master, not the Devil,' she observed.

'Comes to the same thing!' someone remarked, and everybody laughed.

Immediately the mood of the crowd changed, their fear and disappointment forgotten.

'Well, it wasn't much of a fight, but it'll do for a start!' declared Adam.

'Aye, for a start,' replied a dozen voices as people began to walk back through West Gate to the village.

Judith took one last look out on to the fen and saw the muddied, battered drainers making for their boat. They were moving slowly and painfully, with one man having to be helped along by his friends. As for the Dutchman, he led the way, the unconscious form of one of his workmen slung across his shoulders. She hardly

liked to admit it, even to herself, but she had felt sorry
for those drainers out on the fen. They had been so un-
prepared and outnumbered. She had been glad when
Peter had intervened.

Glad because the drainers had been saved punishment? What was she thinking of? All that concerned
her now was that Adam was unharmed, save for a
splendid black eye. She ran to him, and slid her arm
through his, listening as he and the other men described
over and over again the blows they had dealt and the
injuries they had avoided. She was proud of him, too
proud to point out that a fight which had lasted less
than ten minutes was taking a good hour in the telling.

'Do you think they will return?' she asked.

'Certain to! And we'll be even better prepared for them
next time.'

'You're looking forward to it,' she said accusingly.

'Of course I am! Today was nothing. Next time we'll
show them that we're in earnest.'

By the excited buzz of conversation all about them
she knew that the other men were thinking the same.

'Just so long as you don't get hurt,' she whispered.

'I won't, I promise!'

Adam sealed his promise with a kiss.

The fight with the drainers occupied every conversation for a day or two, then gradually other topics intruded and life returned to normal.

One thing was beginning to niggle at Judith, a job
undone.

'There's naught for it, I must return that tulip,' she
declared to Aunt Ketty one morning. 'Spring's coming
on apace, the road is clear, and if I leave it much longer
I'll be too occupied to go wandering about the countryside. That Dutchman should never have left it!'

'Maybe not, my lamb, but it was a pretty thing while
it lasted. We've had the best of it now, I fear.' Aunt
Ketty gazed at the rapidly shrivelling leaves that were all
that remained of the plant.

'Then what better time to give it back?' declared
Judith. 'I'd best go now, if you can spare me, else it'll

go out of my mind again. You are sure that the Dutchman is at the old Fen Reeve's house?'

'Quite certain. Several folk have seen him there.'

'I'm surprised he dare live so far out, especially after the beating he was given the other day.'

'Ah, there are those who say the place is guarded by an evil demon.'

'Do you believe it?' Judith looked at her aunt in surprise.

'It was Mistress Osborne who told me, and she was certain it was a demon.' Aunt Ketty's eyes twinkled. 'To me, though, it sounded very much like a dog.'

'So I must make up my mind whether I would be bewitched or bitten, eh? I don't much fancy either, so I'll leave the tulip by the gate.'

'Very wise,' chuckled Aunt Ketty. 'Now get you gone, for you've quite a walk.'

The Fen Reeve's house was in an isolated spot, a good way from the village. The road was still muddy in places, but passable, and Judith enjoyed the walk in the mild spring air. She had decided to leave the tulip at the gate long before hearing of Mistress Osborne's warning. Judith was not sure that she believed in demons, and she had not yet met a dog that could frighten her—it was the Dutchman she did not want to encounter. Not that she feared him, either, but deep inside she still felt uncomfortable about the ferocity and one-sidedness of the fight on Hanser Fen—no amount of telling herself that all drainers were her enemies could drive it away.

She meant to walk boldly up to the Dutchman's gate and leave the Delft pot there, but somehow her approach had an air of furtiveness about it. It took surprising control not to drop the pot and then run. She put the tulip by the gatepost, and had started to return home, congratulating herself that she was undetected, when an all too familiar voice called, 'Perhaps you'd care to come in, Mistress Pentelow?'

Judith swung round to see the Dutchman leaning over the gate. She gave a snort of fury at having been found out, well aware that he must have been watching her for some time. But the sharp comment that hovered on her lips gave way to a gasp of concern. One side of the Dutchman's face was livid with bruises, and a half-healed cut ran across his forehead. When he moved it was with stiffness, and the hands that rested on the top rail of the gate were swollen and discoloured.

Poor soul, how can he work with such injured hands? was Judith's first thought. Then she remembered that his livelihood meant ruin and starvation to the Fenlanders, and her brief spasm of sympathy died.

'I came to return the tulip,' she said bluntly.

'So I see.'

'I cannot—will not—accept any gift from you.'

'Oh.' His response was brief, and there was a grimness about him she had not seen before. Even so, he repeated his invitation. 'Won't you come in and take some wine? You've had a long walk.'

'No, thank you. I've come to return this, nothing more.'

Judith picked up the Delft pot and handed it to him, but he did not take it. All he did was to stand there looking at her.

'I—I fear it is dead,' she said uncertainly. 'It will grow again next year?'

He did not even glance at the withered plant.

'Will you take it or no?' demanded Judith suddenly exasperated.

He held out his battered hands, but as he was about to take the pot he vehemently demanded, 'Why? For pity's sake, tell me why?'

'Why what?'

'You need to ask? This!' He held out his misshapen fist. 'Doubtless you saw. A rabble falling upon a few defenceless men, who were only trying to earn a living. All of my men were injured, two of them sorely. And for what purpose? What sort of savages have I fallen among!'

'Savages?' cried Judith incensed. 'We're trying to keep what is ours. If it means bludgeoning a few drainers, then so be it!'

'So you count yourself among their number?'

'Of course I do! They are my people. I am a Fenlander, born and bred, and proud so to be! Did I not warn you to have a care?'

'But why do you oppose drainage? People in Holland cry out to have the marshes drained so they can grow good crops.'

'Then you should have stayed in your own country where your worth would be valued. You're not wanted here!'

'Don't you want the fens improved?'

'We don't want the fens altered at all!'

'But why not? It's beyond my comprehension! You prefer to have poor pasture for half a year, rather than good land which grows grain?'

'I'll tell you why. Because neither the land nor the grain would be ours. Now, although we have pasture only during the summer, it gives grazing to all us commoners. The fish and fowl are there for anyone's taking, along with the peat for our fires, osiers for our baskets, and reeds for our thatch. Once you've done your work, who will it belong to? Your master, Sir Walter, and his rich friends.'

'Can what you say be true...?' The Dutchman stared at her.

'If you doubt me, ask in any part of the fens where the drainers have been. The rich adventurer takes the poor men's ground, and the true owners are left with nothing but starvation.'

The Dutchman seemed taken aback by her words and the vehemence in her voice. 'I hadn't understood this. In my country the land we reclaim comes from the sea or the marshes. No one owns such places, so we're giving the land to the people, not taking it away... I did not understand.' The bitter edge had gone from his voice, and he sounded thoughtful.

'Either we drive you away, or we starve. We have no alternative.'

'So I see. Though that it is little consolation to my men who were hurt. One was without his wits for two whole days.'

'How is he now?' Judith could not hold back her concern.

'Mending slowly, though it was a close-run thing...' The Dutchman continued, talking almost to himself, 'Yet it is unjust to take away people's rights. I'm not happy to be part of it, though I'm not sure what I can do. I am a hired man as much as any of my workers, and must needs earn my bread the same as they. There's no chance of persuading Sir Walter and his friends to abandon their scheme now, but not all of the adventurers are as grasping as he. Some are kindly enough, Master Culpepper for one. You met him on the fen that first day, the old gentleman. He is somewhat over-anxious but he has a kind heart, he would not let people starve. Perhaps I could talk to him privately when next we meet, to see what can be done.'

'You would do that?' asked Judith in astonishment. This Dutchman was being reasonable! Enemies were to be hated, and she did not know how to cope with one who was being sympathetic. In a sudden rush of awkwardness she exclaimed, 'We have a greater reason for opposing you.' Then regretted the words the moment they left her lips.

'Oh, what is that?'

'Some—some oppose you because they say that you must be in league with the Devil.'

'What?'

'I think you heard me clearly enough, sir.' Judith spoke sharply, angry with herself for having started on this tack.

The Dutchman stared at her in silence.

She wondered if, for once, she had punctured that imperturbable demeanour of his. So she had, but not in a way she would have wished, for suddenly he let out a great yell of laughter. Immediately he winced—his lip was still cut from the skirmish—but even the pain could not prevent him from being convulsed with amusement.

His hilarity caused Judith even greater annoyance. 'Well, they do!' she snapped crossly.

The Dutchman tried to speak, only to be overcome by fresh gales of laughter. Judith started to walk away, but he reached across the gate and caught hold of her hand. She had no wish to be touched by him and tried to shake herself free, but he did not release her.

'Pray stay,' he begged mopping his tears with a spotless handkerchief. 'I must hear more. I confess that indeed—indeed I am called Nikolas, Maarten Nikolas van de Scheldt. My mother said it was after my grandfather, but now I begin to wonder.' A fresh wave of hilarity threatened to engulf him. Then, unexpectedly, he raised her hand and placed it on his thick thatch of flaxen hair. 'There, Judith Pentelow! No horns! I'm Dutch Nick, not Old Nick!' His own joke proved too much for him and sent him back into fits of laughter.

'Dutch fool, more like!' Judith snatched her hand away. 'I can't stay here listening to your nonsense.'

'It's your nonsense, not mine. You can't go without telling me more. What else is said about me? Come now, having begun you must finish your tale.'

'Only that your house is guarded by a demon,' Judith said reluctantly.

This information again prevented the Dutchman from speaking.

'Beware, Mistress Pentelow, I fear the demon comes now,' he said, when he had recovered his breath.

From round the corner of the house came an animal, a tiny silken-haired dog, with a red bow adorning its topknot. It was the most un-satanic creature Judith had ever seen.

'Is it yours?' she asked incredulously.

'Heaven forbid! I bought it in Ely for my house-keeper, to keep her company.'

'It could scarce be called a guard dog,' Judith observed, as the tiny animal approached and yapped ineffectually at the Dutchman's boots.

'I agree. I offered to buy her something more fierce but she would have none of it. It was love at first sight, and who am I to reproach her for that?'

'How so?'

'My housekeeper fell in love with that ridiculous dog as immediately as I fell in love with Mistress Pentelow.'

'Oh!' Judith was furious with herself for having fallen into his trap. 'I don't believe a word of it! You say such things only to aggravate me. That dog may be small but it is a good judge of character!'

The little dog was now worrying the Dutchman's ankle with tiny ferocious teeth. Its victim was obviously used to such treatment, for he merely gazed down at his attacker and shook it off. He did so gently, but the dog ran back to the house yelping.

'If ever we're attacked I fear I'll be the first person to be bitten by that animal,' he observed calmly.

'It serves you right for buying a good Fenland dog,' Judith retorted.

'Ah, but I like it for its spirit. The creature is small but it fights back, just like you, Mistress Pentelow. That's why I admire you so much, even though you say I am in league with the Devil.'

'I never said that *I* believe it. It's what I've heard other people say...Oh, I wish I'd never mentioned such nonsense!'

'So, you do not think I am a friend of Satan, Mistress Judith Pentelow?'

'No, I do not, Master Maarten Nikolas van de Scheldt!' She addressed him in similar vein. 'I am convinced that you are a mortal man—rude, saucy, annoying, conniving, treacherous, aggravating, opinionated, stubborn, villainous—but mortal!' finished Judith, regretting that she had run out of invective.

The Dutchman regarded her calmly.

'That is good, I am satisfied,' he said.

'Satisfied?' exclaimed Judith.

'You have called me by my name. I said that you would, don't you remember? And it wasn't difficult, was it?'

'Oh!' For once she could think of nothing to say. She stalked away, the Dutchman's laughter echoing after her.

She was not happy about the encounter. She did not feel that she had come out of it entirely triumphant. Somehow the Dutchman had seemed to manipulate the conversation the way he wanted it, so that even her accusation of diabolical intervention had not had the effect she wished for. Most of all, she was bothered by the amount of time she had spent talking to the man. She could have walked away from him at any time—even when he held her hand she could have pulled away—yet she had not. She had preferred to stand and talk to him. True, she had thrown as many insults at him as she could, but he had not taken them seriously. He had somehow turned the whole conversation into a teasing game... No, not the whole of it. He had seemed serious enough about the drainage of the fens and the trouble it was causing. His offer of help had been unexpected. Her common sense told her that they might be thankful for his assistance some day, but something inside her did not want to be grateful to him, just as she wished she could not still feel the warm pressure of his fingers on hers, or hear his laughter ringing in her ears.

Suddenly she picked up her skirts and began to run, eager to put as much distance between herself and the Fen Reeve's house as possible. With every step she cursed all Dutchmen in general and the one who had come to cause mischief on Hanser Fen in particular.

Once back home it was a relief to confide in Aunt Ketty.

'What is wrong with me?' she demanded of her aunt. 'He is our enemy, yet I can't dislike him entirely.'

'It's not to be wondered at,' Aunt Ketty replied, 'for he's not all bad. Few people are, when you come to look at it. He has an odd manner, true, but taken on his own, doubtless he's a good man. From what you say, the task of draining is a very different matter in his country from what it is here, and I pity him for not being warned of the hornets' nest he was coming to on Hanser Fen. His position can't be an easy one for a man of his conscience. It was kind of him to offer to speak up for us with his masters.'

'Yes, wasn't it?' Judith gave a smile. 'Thank you, dear Aunt. You always make me feel more comfortable. I was feeling quite a traitor to my own people because I couldn't see the Dutchman as all bad.'

'That's the sorrow of it, my lamb. If conflict could be clearly divided between two sides things would not be so bad. It's the poor folk caught in the middle who often suffer the greatest heartache.'

Judith looked sharply at her aunt, sensing that she was not talking of the battle with the drainers alone. Aunt Ketty had never again mentioned her awful premonition of sorrow throughout the land, but Judith knew that she brooded on it.

She took the old lady's hand and held it against her cheek. 'There is no heartache for us, though, nor will there be,' she said. 'We'll defeat the drainers, I'm confident of it. And if the trouble between King and Parliament grows any worse, well, it's scarce likely to trouble us here in the wilds of the Fens, is it?'

'Truly spoken, my love!' Aunt Ketty smiled cheerfully now. 'And if I am a comfort to you, then you are twice as much a comfort to me.'

'Do you think I should tell Adam of the Dutchman's offer to speak for us?'

'Of his offer, aye, but you'd be wise not to repeat any of his nonsense.' Aunt Ketty's eyes twinkled. 'It would be better if your Adam didn't consider the Dutchman to be a serious rival.'

'As if he were any such thing!' protested Judith. Then she laughed, too. 'I understand what you mean, though. And I'll make no mention of demons or witchcraft.'

'Better not. Adam suspects the presence of Dark Forces enough as it is.' Aunt Ketty gave a little sigh.

Not for the first time, Judith wondered if Aunt Ketty's inexplicable reluctance to her marriage with Adam might not have something to do with her own unwanted gift of second sight. There was no denying that Adam was very superstitious and saw the workings of evil in anything he could not understand.

'I will tell Adam about the Dutchman today,' she said. 'But I'll only tell what I think he ought to know, eh?'

'That would seem to be the most prudent action,' Aunt Ketty agreed, and she began to smile again.

As soon as she had finished her tasks Judith went over to Old Place in search of Adam, only to be told that he was down at the church.

'Today? What can he be doing there?' she asked.

'He is looking at the damage,' Marjorie informed her.

'Damage?'

'You mean you haven't heard? Some Dissenters came through here today, the mindless wretches that they are, and desecrated the church! There is no other word for the harm they have done. And in the Lord's name, too, the blasphemers!'

'I've heard naught of this, but then, we've seen no one all day.'

'Well, if you would talk with my brother you must seek him there.' Marjorie brought the conversation to an end with her customary abruptness.

Judith hurried down to the village and, true enough, Adam was in the nave of the church, gazing about him with angry disbelief.

'Can you believe that so-called Christians could do this?' he demanded, when he saw her. 'Goodness knows I've no stomach for Popery, but to see idolatry in every bit of ornament our ancestors left behind is more than I can understand!'

Judith gazed about her in horror. The Dissenters had obliterated the old wall paintings with whitewash, and broken every old statue that they could reach.

'But how could they do it? Did no one protest?'

'I hear they locked the Curate in his vestry, and poor old Lee has a cracked skull for trying to stop them. But there was no one else. They couldn't have chosen a worse time, for most of us men were down on the Abbot's Lode, repairing the stretch that fell with the winter floods. By the time someone fetched Thomas from his forge they'd finished their handiwork and were riding away.'

'Doesn't the place look cold without the colours.' Judith stared at the patchy walls. She knew she would miss the paintings the most, with their flat medieval faces and flowing robes. They had given her pleasure during many a long sermon.

Adam was angry for another reason.

'The fools couldn't even tell the difference between a saint and a soldier,' he protested furiously. He pointed to the tombs of past Digbys around the church. One in particular, of a crusader, hands folded in prayer, crossed feet resting on a dog, had had the face obliterated by many heavy blows.

'The senseless destruction!' Adam was still very angry. 'It would have been better if they'd daubed him with whitewash. At least, we could have washed it off. I daren't think what Marjorie will say. It's not two years since she had a man come all the way from Cambridge to re-do the painting.' Almost tenderly he began dusting bits of stone and grit from the shattered effigy. 'He was an Adam, too, this fellow lying here. We have his sword at home, a huge thing that I can scarce lift, never mind fight with, yet he used it in battles against the Saracens. They say he always fought at the King's right hand. Of course, that was Richard the Lionheart then. What a brave sight Sir Adam must have been wielding his sword, his gilded armour shining and a scarlet plume fluttering in his helmet—he always wore a scarlet plume, you know, and his banner bore the device of a hunting dog worked in silk on a scarlet ground.'

'You speak as though you've met the man,' said Judith in amazement. 'I know he's one of your ancestors, but how can you know so much about a man who's been dead for centuries?'

'Oh, from family stories. Marjorie knows them all, and she used to tell them to me when I was a boy. You should have heard her, you could imagine that you were right there in the Holy Land, in the thick of the battle.'

Judith had never thought of Marjorie as a talented story-teller, yet there was no doubt that the magic she had woven still lingered with Adam.

'So many of the Digbys have been brave knights.' Adam swung his arm in an arc encompassing his ancestors' tombs and memorials. 'Sir John, here, fought so bravely at Agincourt that the King gave him spurs of gold. And here is another Sir Adam, son of the other. Only his heart lies here; his body is buried somewhere on the road to Jerusalem...Oh, how I wish I'd been alive then!'

The longing in his voice made Judith's heart lurch; he had never spoken of her with such passion and emotion.

'In all that heat and dirt?' she asked, determined to point out the blacker side. 'I've heard stories about such places. They say there's no water to be had, it's just a dry, sandy wilderness. Besides, don't you think you're going to get excitement enough with the fighting close at hand?'

'What, against the drainers?' Adam was scornful. 'We'll be lucky to get anything worth calling a fight against them. A few pitiful skirmishes is the most we can hope for.'

'I've something to tell you on that score.' Judith persisted in her efforts to get his mind away from the glories of battle. 'I met the Dutchman——'

'What, is that scurvy dog still around? I thought we'd settled him good and proper the other day.'

'He certainly showed he'd been in a fight. I've seldom seen a man more bruised. He says two of his men were sorely wounded, and one didn't regain consciousness for two days.'

'The pity is he regained consciousness at all!'

'Don't be so hard. It's a good thing the fellow didn't die, else there would have been a rare old bother. But that isn't what I wished to talk about. Seemingly the Dutchman didn't understand the situation here; he didn't know that the land he's been told to drain is common land. When I explained things to him, how we would lose our livelihoods, and probably starve, he was most moved. He said that some of the adventurers who are his masters are kindly enough men who perhaps don't realise the hardship they are causing. He says he'll put the matter to them when next they meet.'

'A drainer offering help to us? And you believed him?' cried Adam witheringly.

'He meant it, I am sure of it.'

'My dear girl, do you honestly think we can trust a drainer, and a Dutchman at that? Can't you see it's just one of his diabolical ploys. Mark my word, he intends to trick us—or worse. He's trying to bemuse us, the better to use his black arts on us. I'm surprised you were so easily taken in.'

'Adam, I'm sure you're wrong——' Judith began, but Adam broke in.

'And even if he is not in league with the Devil we still shouldn't have anything to do with him. We'll have no consorting with Dutchmen or drainers, do you hear?'

'You don't think it might be a good thing to have a voice in the enemy's camp?'

'Not when that voice speaks with a Dutch accent. I wish I'd given the villain an even sounder thrashing. That would have stopped his trickery.'

Judith forbore to mention that he had needed half a dozen men to help him thrash the Dutchman the first time. Instead, she said, 'You'll have excitement in plenty soon enough, never fear.'

'What, here, up to my hocks in fen mud? There'll be precious little glory here.'

His sudden air of despondency alarmed Judith. She had never heard him speak disparagingly about the Fens before. Usually he loudly defended Fenland life.

'We're not so far from the action, particularly if the King and Parliament can't make their peace. I hoped that we were, but the Dissenters found us easily enough, didn't they?'

'They probably came upon us by accident.' He still sounded depressed.

'Adam' she whispered fearfully. 'If things get worse...if matters between the King and Parliament turn to even more bitter bloodshed...you wouldn't think of leaving here, would you?'

'You mean, to go seeking glory? Why, yes, I'd ride off on my white charger, and you'd be my lady, sending me off to battle with your favour waving bravely from my lance and——' He stopped as he caught sight of her face. 'Don't be so glum, sweetest Judith. It's but an idle dream. You don't think I'd be parted from you if I could help it? No, my darling love, we'll be married come Michaelmas, if your lawyer knows his craft. Then, God willing, we'll live here in contentment, raising plump cattle and even plumper babes. Would that please you?'

She only half believed him, and she felt a rising panic. For a moment she pressed her face against his shoulder, letting her fear of losing him drift away. When she raised her head it was to find his mouth seeking hungrily for hers. Knowing that their happiness was balanced on so fragile an edge gave potency to her desperate longing for him, and she pressed against him, hoping that the sensation of her body so close to his would demonstrate her love and reveal her passion. If she could just prove to him how eager she was to be his, then surely he would never leave her?

Gradually her ardour had its effect, so that she could feel his desire for her growing as their bodies pressed closer. The pounding of his heart throbbed with the beat of her own, and his caressing fingers became more urgent.

Suddenly a sound shattered the silence. Someone was blowing, none too expertly, on a hunting horn.

'I must go!' exclaimed Adam.

'Go...why?'

Adam hesitated for the merest second.

'This is a holy place,' he said harshly. 'We should not behave so in a church.'

Judith knew that this was not the true reason.

'Then can't we go elsewhere?' she suggested breathlessly.

The hunting horn sounded again.

'I must go,' Adam repeated almost apologetically. 'We're having a practice with quarterstaves and I'm late already.'

'Fighting! You would leave me for *that*!' she exclaimed, her disappointment too bitter to bear.

'The men are waiting for me.' Adam had already begun to walk away from her.

'Fighting and glory! They're more important to you than I am, are they?' she cried at his retreating back. She waited for an answer, but Adam simply left the church, closing the door firmly behind him.

CHAPTER SIX

THE next day being Sunday, the old church was packed to capacity long before the service was due to begin. It was not eagerness to hear the Curate speak on the matter of their immortal souls that had brought the villagers so early, it was their desire to inspect the damage done by the Dissenters.

'My, doesn't the place seem bare?' commented Aunt Ketty as she got her first sight of the whitewashed walls.

'Yes, it's just like a barn now,' replied Judith. 'I shall miss the pictures sorely. I've always enjoyed looking at them, ever since I was a child.'

'I must take care not to get the wretched stuff all over my best gown.' Aunt Ketty perched herself gingerly on the edge of one of the stools that were set around the church for the elderly and infirm. 'That's it, Judith, my lamb, you stand there by me.'

Judith scarcely heard her, for her attention was directed to watching out for Adam. The memory of his behaviour the day before rankled. She had shown him so blatantly her need for him, and her love, but he had rejected her, preferring instead to go to some paltry arms practice. She did not take such hurt and humiliation lightly. She was determined that Adam would pay for rejecting her.

When, at last, he did arrive, accompanied by Marjorie and a retinue of servants, he smiled and waved a hand in her direction. Judith's response was to toss her head haughtily. The smile faded from Adam's face, to be replaced by a sheepish expression. He knew well enough how he had displeased her. He began to move in her direction. Judith had a string of icy rebuffs ready for him, cool reproaches that had been fostered during a sleepless night, but she got no chance to utter them.

Adam had not taken but two paces towards her before his attention was claimed by Thomas. By the time he was free the service was about to begin.

Afterwards, as the villagers streamed away from the church across the green, Judith found Adam walking alongside her. His fingers entangled with hers before she could pull away.

'I'm sorry about yesterday,' he whispered as they walked step for step. 'You must have thought me the most heartless dolt.'

'I considered you something of the sort,' retorted Judith.

'It's not surprising. Yet didn't you realise that I wanted you? The temptation to have you, to make love to you, to know that you were mine totally and absolutely, was more than I could bear.'

'Yet you managed to resist it!'

'And thankful I am that I did, for your sake. It was your reputation I was considering. Not for the world would I cause you any hurt, surely you know that?'

'Aye, I do.' Judith felt her indignation begin to melt before the warmth of his tone.

'You didn't think that I preferred playing at soldiers to loving you, did you?'

'No, of course not,' Judith replied after a moment's hesitation. She was trying not to remember the enthusiastic look that had appeared in Adam's eye at the first notes of the hunting horn.

'So I am forgiven?'

'What is there to forgive? Only my foolishness.'

'Never call your love for me foolishness, do you hear?' Adam was smiling at her now with such tenderness that all of Judith's niggling doubts vanished.

'I promise I never will,' she replied softly. 'Oh, are you leaving me?' For as they reached the crossroads Adam had paused.

'I must, I fear. Thomas wants a word with me about storing our powder—— Don't look at me so, love. It's very important, else I'd never part from you. He fears

that the place where we've hidden it might be too damp
and——'

'Spare me your explanations,' said Judith shortly. 'You
are so much in demand as a military expert that I must
take second place, I see that!'

'Oh, Judith, that's not the way of it!' cried Adam.
But already she was hurrying after Aunt Ketty, who had
set off at a brisk pace ahead of them.

'Why aren't you walking with Adam this morning?'
asked Aunt Ketty in surprise.

'He has better things to do,' replied Judith so abruptly
that the old lady glanced at her curiously, but wisely said
nothing.

They had almost reached home when swift footsteps
behind them made them turn. It was Marjorie.

'I tried to speak with you after church, but I was delayed.' She tried to disguise the fact that she was
breathless from hurrying, and Judith wondered what was
so important that it needed such haste.

'There now, if we'd known we'd have tarried for you,'
said Aunt Ketty. 'It's too warm to be rushing so, for all
it's still early in the year. Come you in and take wine
with us, while you get your breath back.'

Marjorie seemed thankful to sit down in the cool of
the parlour and sip the elderberry wine set before her.
It was not long before her sharp, restless eyes were
probing every corner of the small room. They rested on
a pot of wild campions that Judith had gathered earlier
in the week. A few of the pink petals were scattered over
the fresh white cloth that Aunt Ketty had laid on the
table in honour of the Sabbath.

'Those flowers are making a mess.' Marjorie scooped
up the petals with her wide capable hands and threw
them into the hearth. 'What do you use them for?'

'We don't use them for anything,' replied Judith.
'They are there because they look pretty. They make a
brave splash of colour.'

Marjorie looked puzzled. She could not understand
anything that had no practical purpose in life. That was
why Old Place was spotlessly clean, yet so cold and drab.

Her eyes continued to travel over the room, taking in the big cracked jug of ferns beside the hearth, and the old bottle that Judith had placed on the windowsill so that it would throw translucent green patterns when the sun shone. To Marjorie they were an incomprehensible waste of time.

Aunt Ketty guessed her thoughts.

'Judith has such a way with things, and I like to see it,' she said. 'The lass is a great one for making the place bright and cheerful, and why not? Our eyes deserve a treat now and then.'

Marjorie looked far from convinced. 'You humour the girl too much, Mistress Kettering, encouraging her to waste her time so. But that is not my concern. I came to speak on another matter.'

Both Aunt Ketty and Judith looked at her expectantly.

'Adam is nearly three-and-twenty, it's high time he was wed. Why cannot Judith and he be married at once?'

The silence that fell on the cottage was total. Neither Judith nor Aunt Ketty had expected such a direct demand.

'So soon upon their betrothal? That would scarcely be seemly, surely?' said Aunt Ketty.

'You are being too particular, Mistress Kettering. If folk want to count the months between their wedding and their firstborn then let them!'

'Already we hope to be wed at Michaelmas,' put in Judith.

'Aye, but as I understand it, matters depend upon some legal nicety. Adoption, is it not? Why you should want to go to law now, when you've had the girl under your roof a good sixteen years or more, is beyond me. What happens if your half-witted lawyer doesn't manage to complete the papers in time?'

'Then we'll wait until he does,' Aunt Ketty replied unruffled. 'I've every confidence in Master Nichols. I'm sure he's a very worthy man.'

'I don't share your faith in him. He can keep us waiting at his pleasure; the longer the time, the longer his bill.

Why the wait? That's what I want to know. Why the wait?'

'Because I would prefer to have things done neatly and legally,' said Aunt Ketty.

'You would prefer——' cried Marjorie. 'Come, mistress, you needs must do better than that!'

'Your pardon, Marjorie Digby, but I needs must do no such thing,' answered Aunt Ketty quietly. 'Though Judith is no blood kin to me, she is all the child I've ever had and her welfare is still my charge, so I will do what I think is right for her.'

The old lady's tone was so gentle but reproving that Marjorie realised she had blundered.

'Your pardon, I did not mean to be so blunt,' she said. 'In truth, I'm very concerned. All this talk of trouble and fighting, both in the village and further afield—it has unsettled Adam. This latest business with the Dissenters has only made him worse. He's so restless these days, it's like living with a caged bear. With a wife and family to care for, with extra responsibilities, I'm sure he would calm down. I know that his choice is Judith, it always has been. I approve of the match, and I'm anxious to see the matter settled, for both their sakes.'

'Nothing would please me more than to see my Judith nicely settled, and *mistress* of her own home,' said Aunt Ketty.

Judith noticed her emphasis on the word mistress, and had to bite back a smile.

Her aunt went on, 'But, as you rightly say, Mistress Digby, we're living in troubled times, and I'd not like to see her hastened into anything because of fears for the future. Let's give Master Nichols a fair chance. If we've heard no tidings from him by harvest time, then I might need to reconsider matters. Until then, however, I see no reason to alter things.'

'But Michaelmas is a long time off,' protested Marjorie.

'And we've a deal of preparations to make if this is to be a wedding worthy of your brother and my Judith, I fancy we'll need every minute from now until October!'

'And that is your last word?'

'It is.'

'You're an obstinate woman, Jane Kettering!' snapped Marjorie.

'Now, there, I think we're two of a kind, Mistress Digby,' smiled Aunt Ketty.

But already Marjorie had stalked out.

'Well, fancy that!' said the old lady, after she had gone. 'Who'd have thought Marjorie Digby would be so eager for this marriage? You'd think she was the bride instead of you.'

'Oh, I'm eager enough, don't be mistaken about that,' smiled Judith.

'Yet you seem content to have a Michaelmas wedding.'

'Yes, but only because I was afeared you'd make me wait until I was of age.'

'Oh, I'm such a heartless old harridan!'

'You know you're not!' Judith flung her arms about her aunt and planted a hearty kiss on her cheek. 'You only say such things so that I will assure you how kind and wonderful you are. All the same,' she went on seriously, her arms still about Aunt Ketty's neck, 'I wish I knew why Marjorie is in such haste.'

'So do I, my lamb,' said Aunt Ketty gravely. 'But you can be certain that whatever it is, it will benefit the Digbys sooner than anyone else.'

That evening when Adam came to call, as usual, his talk was of his own activities. Clearly, he knew nothing of his sister's visit.

'I've finished it at last,' he said.

'Finished what?' said Judith.

'Why, writing out the petition against the drainers that the lawyers are to present for us. And a hard job it's been, too! I can't tell you how many spoilt pens there have been, nor spilt ink. But it's done now and even Marjorie considers it worthy.'

'What happens next?'

'Folk must sign it. I've asked Hal Osborne for the use of his porch next Sunday. Of course, once it's done I'll be off to Ely again. In truth, I'll know the way blindfold soon.' Adam did not look as though he relished the prospect. 'But, at least, there's one more errand I can see to while I'm there.'

'Oh, and what is that?'

'Why, your ring, of course. Had you forgotten?'

Judith had not forgotten. She was eager to see her betrothal ring, even if it had been chosen to some extent by Marjorie, but so far Adam had not shown it to her. Now, she thought she'd waited long enough.

'Am I never to see this ring?' she asked. 'I hear much about it but I'm beginning to wonder if it exists.'

'It's real enough,' laughed Adam. 'I did want to keep it a surprise, but I'll give in to your curiosity.'

From his pocket he took a small leather box and opened it. The ruby ring glowed in the evening sun. The stones were large and opulent. There was no denying that this was a costly piece of jewellery, but the setting was heavy and clumsy. With the best will in the world Judith could only find it ugly.

'It's truly splendid,' she said at last, putting as much enthusiasm into her voice as she could. 'It must be worth a great deal.'

'Marjorie knew you'd be pleased with it,' declared Adam. 'I was all for keeping it a surprise, as I said. I intended to wait until I'd had it altered to fit, but Marjorie said "No, show it to the lass now. It will do no harm for her to see the sort of advantages that will be hers when she becomes Mistress Digby." There, doesn't this make you even more eager to become my wife?'

Judith had to struggle to hold back her anger. The nerve of Marjorie Digby, thinking that she could be bribed into marriage with jewels and trinkets! Swallowing her indignation she said, 'Not even a hundred ruby rings could make me any the more eager to marry you than I am already.'

'The perfect answer!' Adam leaned down and kissed her, his lips hot and urgent. 'Oh, my darling Judith, I haven't got a hundred ruby rings to give you, but I promise that no one on the Fens will have finer jewels or richer gowns than you before I'm finished.'

'I've told you, jewels and riches aren't important, not if I have you.'

'I know you speak truly, and I love you all the more for it, but it would give me such pleasure to be able to deck you out in finery and to adorn you with gold and precious stones. No one, not even the finest London ladies, would hold a candle to you. But such grandeur is in the future. Let's see how this will look on you.' He slipped the heavy band of rubies on to her finger. 'As I feared, it's much too large. What can I use to show the goldsmith in Ely what must be done to make it fit?'

'Take this.' Judith slipped off the little silver ring she wore only on the Sabbath and holidays. 'Guard it with your life, mind, for I treasure it. Do you remember when you bought it for me?'

'Indeed I do,' Adam chuckled. 'One Midsummer Fair, the first time Marjorie ever trusted me to take the cattle to market on my own. I felt a true man of the world, haggling over prices in the market place, then going off to buy a fairing for my sweetheart.'

'And I was so proud and pleased when you brought the ring to me the next day.'

Judith wished with all her heart that she could find the same pleasure in the costly band of rubies. She knew her increasing dislike of the ruby ring had little to do with its ugliness. That would not have mattered if it had been Adam's choice—but it had not. His sister had chosen it. Marjorie clearly saw it as a symbol of the wealth and importance of the Digbys, while Judith wanted her betrothal ring to be a symbol of love.

She watched as Adam put both rings into the leather box.

'They'll be safe there until I go to Ely,' he said. 'And when I see that ruby ring on your finger I'll feel that we're truly betrothed.'

'I hope you feel truly betrothed now!' protested Judith teasingly. 'You're not to go making sheep's eyes at Susan Osborne and the other wenches, simply because I've no ring on my finger.'

'What a woman you are for spoiling my pleasures!' Adam gave a mock groan. 'I can see I'll lead a dog's life once we're wed.'

'Indeed you will! You needn't think you'll rule the roost then.' Judith broke off abruptly, realising that it would not be Adam she'd need to battle with for her share of the hearth.

'What is it? Is something wrong?' asked Adam when he saw the smile fade from her lips.

'I was only thinking that Michaelmas is a long time in coming,' she said.

'Aye, it is that. But it will come eventually!'

Judith wondered if she should ask Adam why Marjorie was in such desperate haste to have them married, but she decided against it. Whatever the reasons, she would doubtless find out soon enough.

In the days that followed she had little time to think about the strange maggots that worried Marjorie Digby's brain. When she could, she helped Adam collect signatures for the petition, going out to the far-flung settlements to catch those who did not come into the village on Sundays. The everyday tasks she did for her aunt were increasing, also, as the fine weather progressed. Seeing to the fowls and the curly-coated pig were perennial chores, but the cows were out on the Summer Grounds now, and Judith had to set out across the fen with yoke and pails to milk them. It was a laborious occupation, needing several journeys by boat and on foot, but she did not mind, for their livelihood depended upon the rich cream and butter that had its source in the sweet Fenland grasses. The more trips she had to make, the more money there was in the family purse.

One fine clear morning Judith set off after the cows as usual. She had grown to know their favourite haunts, and had tracked down all but two animals. By the time she had found them she was far into the fen, in an area that had been inaccessible since the previous autumn.

It was as she straightened her back to lift the brimming pails that something in the far distance caught her eye. It looked like a faint smudge of peat smoke. Knowing that there should be nothing out here but miles of desolate fen, she screwed up her eyes and took a long hard look. The longer she looked, the more certain she was that she could see smoke. If she had not known better, she might also have convinced herself that she could see roofs and dwellings of some sort. That was nonsense, of course, a trick of the light, nothing more; but the smoke did concern her.

Strangely enough for an area so frequently inundated, fire on the Fens could become a tremendous hazard. Once it got down into the layers of peat it could smoulder away for weeks, months, even years, proving impossible to quench. The source of this smoke was a good distance from any habitation, but it was an unusually dry year, and there was no knowing what might happen if a strong wind blew up.

'Smoke? On the fen?' said Aunt Ketty when Judith returned with the milk. 'Best tell Adam, and he can take some men out and see if aught needs doing.'

'But what if I was mistaken?' said Judith. 'I'd look such a fool if they found nothing. No, I think I'll go and have a closer look for myself first.'

'Do you think you should? It might be dangerous.' Aunt Ketty felt anxious.

'I promise I won't do anything foolish. I'll be able to tell whether there's a fire or no long before I get too close. Should it prove a false alarm I'll gather some herbs, then I won't have wasted my time entirely. You were saying only yesterday how the winter had depleted your store of remedies.'

'I can see that you've made up your mind, so there'll be no stopping you,' said Aunt Ketty. 'Only, watch out what you're about. I've no fear of you getting into any danger from fire; it's the ruffians that are abroad these days I warn you against.'

'I'll take care and be vigilant, never fear.' Picking up a basket and slipping some bread and cheese into her pocket, Judith set off.

She enjoyed the walk, unfettered by yokes and pails of milk. The larks overhead were almost deafening in the cloudless, blue sky, while beneath her feet the tortuous path took her round pools bedecked with waterlilies, and by sluggish streams edged with great curds of creamy meadowsweet. Before long the hem of her gown was yellow with pollen as she walked through the flowering grasses. Her basket was soon filled with selfheal and elder flower, horehound and peppermint, and many other herbs, which promised a busy evening for Aunt Ketty and herself.

Sedgewick and the more familiar landmarks were far behind her now. Sure enough, as she looked ahead she could definitely see smoke. More curiously, with every step she was growing convinced that she could see roofs in the distance, thatched with reed that merged into the surrounding fen, but rooftops just the same.

Judith was beginning to grow uneasy. Why should there be buildings out here miles from anywhere? The wildfowlers often built themselves rough cabins in the more remote areas, but they would have no need for the cluster of buildings that was becoming more distinct among the clumps of willow and birch.

Caution made her move warily, and she was grateful for the tall bank of sedge which shielded her. At last, she reached a wide thicket of alder close to the mysterious constructions. Crouching down to make herself even less conspicuous, she peered through the tangled branches. What she saw made her gasp.

A complete settlement had sprung up in the heart of Hanser Fen. 'Cottages' was too grand a word for the rough structures. They were little better than fowlers' shelters, yet they were clearly intended as homes, for she could see men, women and children moving about. Where had these people come from? And why? What sort of men would bring their families to live in such squalor? A squalor which would surely grow worse—

Judith could tell by the feel of the ground beneath her feet that one good shower of rain would turn the place into a sea of mud.

From her hiding place she watched these strangers for quite a time, noting how thin and ill-clad they seemed. Even in the warmth of such a fine day they had a dispirited air about them. She was struck, too, by their numbers—there must have been forty or fifty of them. She began to count them, trying to note the number of men, women, and children. It was not easy, for they were moving about, doing their daily tasks.

Judith was concentrating hard on counting, but not so hard that she did not hear the cracking of twigs behind her. She felt a spasm of fear in the pit of her stomach as, too late, Aunt Ketty's warning about ruffians flashed through her mind. Her fingers groped for a stout stick to use as a weapon, but found only pliant alder roots and osier stems.

Just as she was about to turn and face her unknown assailant a heavy body fell on her, and a hand covered her mouth, cutting off the scream that rose in her throat.

'Good day to you, Mistress Pentelow,' whispered a voice in a familiar clipped accent. 'Don't make a noise, I beg of you!'

Pinioned and deprived of speech, Judith felt panic welling up inside herself. With the weight of the Dutchman's powerful body crushing her to the earth she had never felt so helpless. For the first time she felt afraid of him. As he removed his hand from her mouth, sheer terror made her take a deep breath, preparatory to letting out a scream. Immediately the hand returned.

'For pity's sake keep quiet!' The Dutchman hissed in her ear. 'If they find you I doubt if even I could save you.'

The urgency of his words cut through her fear and she became aware of voices coming closer. Half a dozen men were walking along the rough track. By their rods and nets they had obviously been fishing; by their dispirited demeanour they had been unsuccessful—or was this the habitual bearing of the inhabitants of this

strange new settlement? They passed within a couple of
feet of the place where Judith and the Dutchman lay
hidden, talking to each other in strident accents that
Judith found almost incomprehensible. It seemed an age
before they were out of earshot and the Dutchman took
his hand away from her mouth. Still neither of them
moved.

'Who are they?' she asked at last. 'And what are they
doing here?'

'They are my labourers.'

'*Your* labourers?'

'Aye. Do you wonder that I have to hide them here?'

'You could bring people to live in such conditions?'

'I have to have workers. I could hire no local labour.
I had to bring men from elsewhere. Naturally, their families wanted to come too.'

'But to bring them here. Surely you must know that
after the first rain they'll be ankle-deep in mud?'

'Where do you suggest I lodge them? Do you think
they would be welcome in your village?'

Judith recognised the truth of his words. These folk
would never be allowed within miles of the village. The
only place for them was out on the fen.

'I suppose not,' she admitted. 'But where do they come
from? They talk so strangely.'

'From the poorer parts of London, mostly. And, bad
as the conditions are here, I fear the unfortunate wretches
are used to far worse.'

'Even so, you should be ashamed of yourself for
bringing them here. The poor souls are just heading for
trouble. The minute they start digging we'll attack.'

'So I begin to understand. Unfortunately, so do they,
which is why I feared you were in danger. Feelings still
run high against the people from your village after that
last encounter. I'm sorry if I frightened you, but I could
think of no other way of silencing you.'

'I wasn't afraid of you!' retorted Judith haughtily.

'Then why were you about to cry out?' The Dutchman
asked innocently.

'You startled me a little, that's all!' Then, because she still felt at a disadvantage, she snapped, 'Really, I shall soon begin to believe that you *are* in league with the Devil. You seem to crop up every time I set foot on the fen.'

'How strange you should say that, for I was just beginning to harbour serious suspicions about you! Surely there is more than a hint of the supernatural in the way that every time I come upon the fen, about my lawful business—my lawful business,' repeated the Dutchman, ignoring Judith's snort of derision, 'I seem to come upon you. Why, I can't even look over my own garden gate but there you are! Now, if I were Satan I could think of no better way of ensnaring an honest Dutch lad who is lonely and far from home than with the shape of a comely wench.'

'Such foolish nonsense!' snapped Judith.

'Is it? Then, can you explain to me why you have this basket of leaves and flowers here?'

'Surely that's obvious. For my aunt and me to make our household remedies.'

'Mm, you are knowledgeable about herbs and simples, are you?' The Dutchman shook his head gravely. 'It would not surprise me to learn that you both could ride on broomsticks and see into the future.'

'How dare you accuse us so?' she cried angrily. 'You do nothing but cause mischief with that tongue of yours——'

'Hush! Do you want to draw attention to us?' he whispered urgently. 'I'm sorry. I said those things only in jest.'

'Women have been burnt at the stake through jests like that,' said Judith more calmly. Then she retaliated with, 'I wonder that you aren't afraid to be found here with me, a villager *and* one you suspect of witchcraft, at that. What would your men do if they stumbled upon us?'

'On finding me in such a position, in such a secluded spot, with such a pretty girl...I hope they would have the decency to look away,' he replied impishly.

His words reminded Judith that they were still lying together, in a situation that could only be called compromising. She flushed scarlet at its implications.

'Let me up, if you please,' she demanded.

He did not move. 'In due time,' he said calmly. 'I find this far too pleasant to wish to cease now.'

'I assure you that your pleasure is a solitary one. I don't share it. In fact, I have seldom been in more unpleasant circumstances in my life. Let me go!'

'Do you know you are blushing?' he observed. 'It is quite enchanting to see. The soft flush begins here at your throat and spreads to join the roses in your cheeks.'

With one finger, he began gently to trace the course of her rising colour, until Judith pushed his hand away.

'Stop that!' she exclaimed. 'You are taking liberties.'

'Yes, I am,' he agreed.

'And you are taking a most unfair advantage of me,' she protested.

'Naturally, what else would you expect?'

'From a Dutchman, certainly no better behaviour.'

'Then that's all right. You're not disappointed.'

He smiled down at her, the sunlight glinting on his thick thatch of hair, making it gleam like ripe corn. 'You know how much I have admired you from afar. Now I am at close quarters! I never dared to hope that one day I would be alone with my lovely Mistress Pentelow, in such a place, sheltered from the eyes of the world. I would be a shabby fellow to let this opportunity slip by.'

'And you are not a shabby fellow,' retorted Judith. 'You are a great oaf! Now will you move?'

He received the insult with a grin but made no attempt to free her.

'Oh, your blush is fading,' he said. 'I am sorry to see it go. It told me so much.'

'It tells only that I consider you to be insufferable and impertinent!'

'No, you only pretend that. Your blush doesn't lie. It says you are aware that we are man and maid together, alone, and that my arms are about you and that truly, in your heart, you don't find the situation too distasteful.'

'Yes, I do!'

'Ach, your response was swift. I like that—you protest too much to be entirely convincing. Perhaps you protest to convince yourself?'

'I've never heard such nonsense. Nor have I ever been treated so shamefully.' Judith pounded her fists against his chest. 'Let me go, or I will call for help!' she declared angrily.

'And who will hear? Only my workers, who have little cause to love you.'

'I would prefer to take my chance with them sooner than have to put up with your unwelcome attentions.'

'Would you really? Then shout away.'

Judith glared at him. 'Let me up, then I'll have no need.'

'I don't want to let you up. I am enjoying myself enormously.'

'Oh, so this is another way you get your enjoyment, ravishing defenceless maids, as well as provoking them beyond all endurance.'

The Dutchman managed to smother a shout of laughter.

'I am sorry to disappoint you, but I am not ravishing you. Nor is that my intention. I am just happy for the opportunity to spend time with you in this most amicable way.'

'Well, I refuse to contribute to your happiness. I suppose the more I struggle and protest the more it will amuse you. I simply refuse to co-operate.'

To give emphasis to her words Judith closed her eyes abruptly and lay still. She heard him chuckle softly, then she was aware that his lips were almost brushing her ear.

'Mistress Pentelow, can you hear me?' he whispered.

Judith did not move.

'You can't remain immobile for long, of that I'm certain.'

His face was so close to her now, she could feel the warmth of his cheek against hers, but she did not flinch.

'It's no sport if you don't reply,' he said.

Judith continued to lie still. She felt him back away a little, and something—a blade of grass, she suspected—tickled her chin.

'I had a dog once who could play dead like that. He was more convincing than you, though not so pretty,' he said conversationally.

Judith refused to be cajoled into laughter. She did not move a muscle.

'Or perhaps you aren't playing dead,' he went on. 'It could be that this is how you look when you're sleeping. You have no idea how delightful you appear. It makes me sorry I haven't had the opportunity to regard such a pretty sight before. I should have crept into your bed-chamber long ere this.'

She nearly reproved him for being saucy, but stopped herself in time. She would not respond to his provoking. She would not give him the satisfaction.

There was a pause, then the Dutchman heaved a mock sigh. 'If you're going to spoil the fun in this manner, then I suppose there is nothing for it, I'll have to let you go. First, though, since I've saved you from danger yet again, I think I should claim a reward.'

'A reward?' Judith's eyes flew open in alarm.

Her uneasiness returned. As he had stressed, they were in an isolated spot, away from the gaze of passers-by. Even if she had cried out, as she had threatened, she doubted if the people in the settlement would have taken notice. They would most likely have thought it was only the screech of a marsh bird. She recollected nervously that she really knew nothing of this man who was looking at her now, his face bright with mischief.

'Yes, reward,' he said. 'What should it be, I wonder? Last time I came to your aid you agreed to drink wine with me——'

'Only because I was cold and shaken!' protested Judith.

But the Dutchman ignored her interruption, '...which was very pleasant,' he continued. 'But I feel that we know each other so much better now than we did then. We've

become so close that I think I can ask—nay, expect—
something more...'

'You can expect——' cried Judith, then stopped. She
had been about to say, a box on the ears, but she remembered in time the last occasion when she had
threatened such a thing. The result had been the reverse
of what she had intended.

'I know what you were going to say,' he cried with
delight. 'You were going to say I can expect a kiss!'

'A kiss? You're mad even to think it!' she said bluntly.

'So I am, the anticipation has quite turned my brain.
The thought of your lips on mine. It's a wonder I don't
swoon.'

'No more of your nonsense,' Judith began briskly. 'If
you think that I——'

She got no further, for the Dutchman's lips prevented
her.

She was surprised into stillness. Used as she was to
Adam's energetic demands, the Dutchman's gentle,
almost leisurely kiss was like nothing she had ever experienced before. There was no rough, hasty bruising of
her mouth, no swift snatching of satisfaction; yet he was
far from inexpert, she realised that. He took more than
the single kiss he claimed as a reward, his mouth returning again and again to caress her, and she found she
had no will to refuse him. It was his unexpected tenderness that made her catch her breath, a sweet sen-
suousness in his gentle touch that somehow gave pleasure
as well as took it. Gradually a languorous warmth began
to steal through her, causing her to melt towards him as
if drawn by an invisible force. Of their own volition her
fingers crept up to smooth his face, to entwine about his
neck, and she found her mouth seeking to return his
kisses.

Then some latent instinct flashed a warning. This man
could destroy her peace of mind if she did not take care!

Abruptly she pushed him away.

'That was not a proper thing to do!' she cried. To her
horror she felt her eyes begin to fill with tears.

'One advantage of being a rascally drainer is that I don't need to be proper,' grinned the Dutchman. Then he saw her brimming eyes and immediately his expression changed. 'Oh, I have distressed you. And that is the last thing I intended. It was just my nonsense, nothing more. Surely you know, my sweet Judith, that there is no way I would ever give you pain?'

The sudden tenderness of his voice and his use of her Christian name did nothing to improve matters. She sat up.

'I wish to go home!' she said, in a voice that trembled in spite of all her efforts.

'Aye, it should be safe enough now, but all the same, I'll see you part of the way——'

'No!' she protested vehemently. 'No, I've had more than enough of your company for one day. I'll go alone.'

'As you will.' The Dutchman stood up and helped her to her feet.

He began to raise her hands to his lips, but Judith pulled away. Snatching up her basket, she ran. She was a good way across the fen before she recalled that this was the second time she had fled from the Dutchman in disarray.

Judith told Aunt Ketty about the settlement on the fen, but somehow could not bring herself to mention her most recent encounter with the Dutchman. If Aunt Ketty wondered how Judith knew so much about the colony of newcomers, or why her face bore the unmistakable trace of tears, she said nothing.

'Well, there's a thing!' Aunt Ketty remarked. 'All those poor folk living out there! Whatever next?'

'I suppose I must tell Adam,' said Judith without enthusiasm.

'I suppose you must, my lamb, it being so important.'

Judith gave a sigh. She was not looking forward to passing on this latest piece of news. The fate of those miserable wretches out on the fen bothered her, but the chief cause of her concern lay within herself. She knew that she had not fooled Aunt Ketty with her account of the afternoon's adventures. Adam was far more likely to question her closely, and if he did, how could she reply? With her feelings still in a turmoil, she knew she could not make some casual remark about coming across the Dutchman yet again. She sighed once more.

'You're weary, you've had a hard day,' said Aunt Ketty deliberately misinterpreting. 'Leave it till the morrow.'

Judith was only too pleased to take her advice, but for once her aunt's ability to foretell the future had forsaken her. When the girl went to Old Place next morning it was to find Adam strapping on a sword, while a servant frantically saddled his horse.

'I can't stay, sweetheart,' he replied to her greeting. 'The drainers are on the fen, a huge force of them. I must rally the village!'

'But there was no warning bell?' she cried, bemused. 'I didn't hear the church bell!'

Adam was already in the saddle, urging his mount away. Over his shoulder he called, 'Someone's cut the bell-rope, that's why!'

Judith hitched up her skirts and began running in his wake. Other villagers were also hastening towards the West Gate, urged on by the sexton, who was waving a red flag and yelling from the top of the church tower. As she joined the throng Judith cursed the Dutchman with every step for having made a fool of her. How could she have been so stupid! Letting him take her in with his silly games. Yet again, she had forgotten that he was her enemy, intent only upon draining the fen. Would she never learn!

'There you are, my lamb!' Aunt Ketty came bustling up, her plump face puckered with anxiety. 'No sooner had you left than Toby here came by with the news.'

'Who gave the alarm?'

'Young Charlie Woodley, out on Hanser, cutting a bit of peat,' supplied Toby. 'Came dashing back saying there were hundreds of drainers out there. Mind you, young Charlie's not so good at figuring; once past his fingers' worth, he's flummoxed.'

'We'll soon find out how flummoxed,' puffed Aunt Ketty. 'We're almost at West Gate.'

Considering their scant warning, the villagers had turned out in force. There was confidence and determination on their faces as they greeted Adam, who arrived with a few stragglers.

'Well, Charlie was a bit out in his counting!' he declared, surveying the fen. 'All the same, there's enough of them out there to make it more of a fight.'

Judith regarded the forty or so labourers working steadily on Hanser Fen. Remembering the pallid, weakly-looking men she had seen at the settlement, she felt a spasm of pity for the poor souls. The Sedgewick men could win against twice as many.

'They're not going to make it a proper fight, not them piddling few!' protested Thomas disconsolately.

'There's no pleasing some folks, is there?' declared Adam. 'What do you suggest we do? Ask them to find a few more recruits before we wade into them?' When the laughter died down he called, 'Now, a bit better order today, lads. Last time scarcely counted, but some things did go awry. There's no need for us to injure each other just because we lack enough of the enemy.'

'No parleying this time, Adam!' asserted Thomas.

'Definitely no parleying!' agreed Adam.

Dismounting from his horse, he began to lead the village men on to Hanser Fen, with Judith and the other womenfolk following on behind. They had gone quite a way before the ragged band of labourers caught sight of them. One by one they stopped work to gaze in the direction of the villagers, yet they made no attempt to flee.

'They're going to stand and make a good do of it,' cried Thomas, whirling his great cudgel in the air like a banner.

A cheer went up from the people of Sedgewick, for hadn't they already trounced these newcomers? What they had done once they could do again.

Only Judith watched with silent unease. There was something here she did not understand. Surely those undernourished wretches from the settlement weren't really going to stand and fight? They must know they didn't have a chance. She could easily make out the tall figure of the Dutchman, and the way he stood calmly watching the advance of Adam and his men only served to increase her anxiety. Her dislike of him had returned with a vengeance, but she was certain he'd never risk his men unnecessarily.

The villagers moved forward, getting quicker and quicker as they grew more eager for a taste of action. At a shout from Adam, the boys sent flying a hail of stones, causing the drainers to duck and dodge. But still they did not move.

'There's something wrong!' Judith muttered urgently to Aunt Ketty. 'Can't we call them back? I fear there's some sort of trick.'

'We could call until we were blue in the face, there's no fetching them back now,' said Aunt Ketty.

Fifty yards separated the two bands of men...forty...thirty!

'Oh, Adam, bring them back!' whispered Judith. 'At least stop and take stock of the situation.'

But she knew her prayers could never reach him. Caution was never Adam's way.

The advancing villagers were no more than twenty-five yards from the labourers when their war cries suddenly turned into startled yells, for a host of men seemed to have sprung from the ground at their very feet. One glance was enough to tell that these were no half-starved dregs of humanity from the settlement—they were well-trained fighting men. Each was armed with a vicious pike, and knew how to use it. How long they had been hiding in the crumbling half-forgotten dyke there was no knowing; their emergence was sudden and well-timed. Taken off guard, the Sedgewick men did their best, but they were no match for the small army that had sprung from the ground like young corn.

Judith tried to keep track of Adam in the confusion, but got no more than a glimpse or two of his beloved russet head. In an agony of fear for him she would have run forward to join the fray, as several other women were doing, if Aunt Ketty had not held her back.

'There's no point,' she cried. 'Our lads are routed. Look!'

Sure enough, some of the villagers were fleeing from the battle. Adam must have seen them, too, for suddenly there he was, waving his sword in the air and crying, 'Rally to me, lads! Rally! Rally!'

It was then that a pikeman struck him on the head. Even at that distance Judith winced at the severity of the blow. Horrified, she saw Adam's knees buckle, then he was swallowed up in the mass of struggling bodies.

This time, not even Aunt Ketty could hold her back. She raced out across the fen, her feet hardly touching the rough tussocks of grass, in her desperation to reach Adam.

'Get you home, mawther!' Toby paused in his flight to try to persuade her to return.

But Judith cried, 'Adam? Where is he?'

'Thomas has got him, never fear. Now come you away!'

Just then, Judith caught sight of the bulky figure of the blacksmith lumbering along, a senseless Adam slung over his shoulder. She pulled away from Toby's grasp and ran towards him.

'Is he all right? Does he live?' she demanded fearfully.

But Thomas, his face a sweaty puce from his exertions, had no breath left to reply. She was forced to run by his side, making ineffectual attempts to support Adam's lolling head as she did so.

They were almost at West Gate before their pursuers halted, and even so, no one slackened his pace until they were well over Abbot's Lode. Only then did the men collapse into exhausted heaps on the ground. They were a sorry sight; there was not a man who wasn't bruised or bleeding. Some, like Adam, had had to be carried back by their comrades.

As gently as any woman, Thomas laid Adam down on the grass.

'He got a fair crack on the head, but I think he's just stunned,' he said.

'You think so?' Then Judith noticed that the black-smith's face was grim with pain. 'But you're hurt your-self——'

'A few ribs gone, nothing more. My lass'll strap me up fine, so if I can leave Adam with you, I'll get along to her.'

'Oh, do go! I can manage here. And, Thomas...' What *could* she say to this man who had saved her Adam?

The blacksmith gave a grin that was almost a wince, and waved away her attempts to thank him.

A groan brought her attention back to Adam, and she saw that his eyelids were fluttering. Swiftly she undid the collar of his jerkin and, tearing off strips from her linen undershift, she made a pad to stanch his bleeding wound.

'Oh, my head ... it feels as if it's broke in two!' Adam tried to open his eyes, but the effort proved too much. 'What a sorry mess,' he whispered. 'I should have guessed Sir Walter would take some measure... It was all my fault...'

'It was not!' protested Judith hotly. 'You were a true leader and fought bravely——'

She got no further. She was thrust aside abruptly by a distraught Marjorie.

'I heard that you were hurt!' she cried. 'But never fear, your Marjorie's here to care for you. I've a litter to take you home. I'll tend you. You'll mend, and your poor head will soon be as good as new.'

It was as though she were talking to a small boy, not a grown man.

'I've stanched the blood a little,' said Judith.

But Marjorie did not hear her. She was not even aware of Judith's presence. Her attention was all for her brother. At her command a hurdle was brought, and Adam carried back to Old Place. Marjorie stepped over the other wounded as though they did not exist. Indeed, for Marjorie, nothing existed at that moment except Adam.

Judith watched them go, longing to follow to help nurse him, at the same time fuming with impotence because she knew that Marjorie would never permit it. The thought that this might be the shape of things to come, when she entered Old Place as a bride, caused a cold chill to settle on her heart. At that moment, as she turned to help with some of the other wounded, she was not sure whom she would most like to throttle—Marjorie, or the Dutchman who had caused so much trouble.

CHAPTER SEVEN

ALL night long, Judith fretted about Adam's injuries. She tossed and turned, wondering how he was, fearing lest he was in pain or that his hurts were grievous. The feeling of frustration, knowing that she could do nothing to help him or bring him ease, finally drove her to get up long before time, with the result that her chores were finished unusually early.

'My, you must have been astir afore the lark this morning,' remarked Aunt Ketty, as Judith returned home with brimming pails, the milking finished. Then she noticed the girl's anxious face. 'Ah, you'll be eager to see how young Adam fares, is that it? Off you go then, my lamb. I'll see to the churning today. But don't be surprised if Marjorie won't let you see him. You know how she dotes on him. Talk about a hen with one chick!'

'At least I'll be able to hear how he is, and that's the most important thing.'

Judith deposited the milk pails in the tiny dairy and, kicking off her muddy pattens, hastened to tidy herself.

When she reached Old Place, however, it was to be told by a disapproving Marjorie that Adam had gone into the village. Surprised, she followed after him, and found that, by some unspoken consent, all those villagers whose injuries would let them were congregated on the green. She saw Adam immediately through the subdued throng. He was seated on a bench outside the Lamb, leaning his bandaged head back against the wall in an attitude of exhaustion. Susan Osborne was fussing round him, simpering and clucking with sympathy, but Judith was barely conscious of her. She saw only Adam's deathly-white face and half-closed eyes.

'Should you be here?' she demanded, concern making her voice sharper than she intended.

'Where else?' He opened his eyes and managed a ghost of his normal grin. 'Marjorie was all for me staying in bed, but I'd have none of it. Folks die in bed.'

She knew it would be useless to argue, so she sat on the grass at his feet and took his hand, a gesture that sent Susan Osborne stamping back into the inn. For a while they sat in silence, Adam through weakness, and Judith through relief that he was no worse. Around them the conversation ebbed and flowed. There was only one topic, of course; the previous day's disastrous skirmish.

Old Lee, the sexton, was in his element, declaring loudly that only the Devil could have got into the church tower and cut the bell-rope after he himself had locked up so securely. A few gullible souls moaned and shivered at the thought, until Peter Renshaw pointed out that everyone knew the great key was always left hanging on a nail by the tower door, and the path to it was hidden by a thick yew hedge. Anyone could have got in and out unseen quite easily.

'Those armed men, where did they come from?' asked Judith.

'Seemingly, like many other gentlemen, Sir Walter's been getting together a trainband of his own should matters between the King and Parliament grow worse. Dewdrop Chester spotted them a couple of days ago, but didn't think to tell anyone, the fool! It never occurred to him that Sir Walter might find another use for them.' Adam spoke vehemently, then winced with the pain in his head. 'Though it was my fault too. I should have guessed that our beloved lord and master would try something of the sort.'

'Don't blame yourself, you can't be expected to think of everything,' Judith consoled him, anxious for him not to get agitated. 'After all, you aren't the only person in the village with a head on his shoulders. What's wrong with some of the others taking the responsibility for once?'

'Do you suggest we have Dewdrop at our head?' Adam managed a bitter chuckle. 'A long way we'd get with him as our general. No, the responsibility is mine, and mine alone. They made me their leader and I've failed them. Just look! There's not a man in sight without broken bones or cuts and bruises. Those at home are even worse. Why didn't I stop to think that Sir Walter would bring men in from elsewhere? Though where he keeps them is a mystery.'

'As for his pikemen, I don't know,' said Judith, eager to take his mind off his self-recrimination. 'Probably up at the Hall somewhere. I do know where the labourers live, though. They've built themselves houses right out in the fen, where the Summer Grounds meet Outer Fen.'

'What, all of them? There must have been thirty or forty of them yesterday!' replied Adam.

'There are even more, for they have their families with them.'

'No, surely not! It's beyond belief. Who told you such a tale?'

'No one. I saw them for myself the day before yesterday when I was out milking. I went back afterwards just to make sure. There's a settlement out there, right enough. That's what I was coming to tell you, just as you were riding out.'

'Well, if that doesn't beat everything! If anyone but you had told me this I'd have said they'd been seeing things. A settlement you say... It puzzles me who they are, and where they've come from.'

'They're poor homeless wretches brought from London and such places,' Judith said without thinking.

Adam's eyebrows lifted questioningly. 'How do you know this?' he asked.

'They must be,' said Judith swiftly. 'Have you ever seen such puny bags of bones? And it stands to reason they'd not stay out there on the fens if they had anywhere better to go.'

'Aye, true. A man would have to be pretty desperate to set up home there.' He accepted her explanation without question, and Judith was thankful that there was no need to mention the Dutchman.

Adam continued, 'The dregs of the gutters and poor-houses needn't trouble us too much at the moment. It's those pikemen we've got to get rid of. Oh, I wish this cracked pate would let me think!' He raised a hand to his painful head.

'Haven't you done enough for today?' suggested Judith. 'Go home and rest.'

'Not until we've worked out some strategy. Supposing those fellows come back to finish what they started? They'd find us quite defenceless.'

'I don't think that's likely. Sir Walter gave us a sharp lesson yesterday, and I fancy he'll be content with that.'

'True enough. We're no match for such trained men, though I hate to say it.' Adam was sounding despondent again. 'I don't know what we're going to do, and that's the truth of it!'

During her sleepless night Judith had been doing some serious thinking on that very subject, when she could spare a minute from her anxiety for Adam. This seemed an excellent time to put forward her ideas.

'We aren't likely to beat them in fighting hand to hand,' she said. 'But we don't *have* to play them at their own game, do we?'

'What do you mean?'

'What if we were to turn into bats and owls for a spell? We'd let the drainers dig all they pleased during the day, then fill in their work by night. There'd be other things we could do to them, too—steal tools, let loose their horses, things of that sort.'

'Now there's an idea!' Adam's face brightened. 'Small bands of men going out at night could achieve much like that, taking it turn and turn about. Aye, a splendid idea! That's given me much to consider—— But hold! You said "We".'

'Indeed I did, for this is something where the women could join in.

'Oh no! Far too risky! This is men's work.'

'Stuff and nonsense!' retorted Judith briskly. 'The women of this village know the Fens as well as any men. Better, since we tramp across it more frequently with milk pails and such. Most of us can handle a spade competently, and creep a deal more quietly should the need arise. This is our fight just as much as yours, you know. And don't you think you're going to need every pair of hands you can get before we're done?'

'You've got a point there,' admitted Adam. 'But I still don't like the idea. What if you were hurt?'

'We'd know what risks we'd take. They'd be no greater than the men's. Oh, Adam, if you knew how awful it was just to watch that fight and not be able to do anything to help. I wasn't alone in feeling that way. Lots of the women were very distressed. You couldn't be so cruel as to prevent us!'

'What can I say? I'd be a man of stone to go against you when you look at me with such great eyes.'

'Then it's agreed. The women take their part.' Judith was thankful he'd given in. She wanted to play a part in the fight against the drainers—she wished desperately to be there at Adam's side, no matter what the struggle.

Adam let his hand caress her hair as she sat there at his feet, but their moment of quiet intimacy was short-lived. Thomas and some of the other village men hobbled towards them, still favouring their hurts.

'What's to be done now then, Adam?' the blacksmith asked gloomily. 'We're in a rare pickle, and no mistake. The thought of those cursed drainers getting the upper hand makes every drop of my blood boil with rage. And yet another set-to like the one we had yesterday'd be the finish of us.'

'Never fear, the drainers won't win,' Adam reassured them. 'We're going to change our tactics. It'll mean losing the odd night's sleep, but with luck there'll be fewer broken bones at the end of it.'

At Adam's words, more villagers came crowding over, filled with curiosity.

'The plan is this—we'll give the drainers free rein on the fens during the day, then we'll wreck their work at night. Simple, isn't it?'

'But that's a grand idea!' A smile broke out on Thomas's broad face, as an approving murmur ran through the crowd. 'Trust you to come up with a proper scheme, Adam.'

Only Dewdrop Chester was not keen.

'We won't be able to manage much, not in the dark, we won't,' he wavered nervously.

'Surely a man who can take Sir Walter's game by night can fill in his ditches just as easily?'

Adam's words were greeted with a roar of laughter, for Dewdrop was a notorious poacher. The tension and uncertainty was banished now, as the villagers pressed forward, eager to make plans and talk about the new tactics.

Unheeded, Judith sat quietly beside Adam listening to all that was said. She was so pleased to see the light of enthusiasm back in his eyes, and a touch of colour return to his face, that she was not irritated by the fact that he was passing her ideas off as his own. Even when she heard him comment, 'But why shouldn't the women lend a hand, Thomas? They're eager enough, and capable enough. And, by Harry, we're going to need them before we're through!' she did no more than smile fondly to herself. The villagers still wanted Adam as their leader and were behind him all the way, that was the only important thing.

In the days that followed, the drainers worked steadily on the fen. The Dutchman was always with them, unmistakable, even at a distance, by his size. Judith saw him as she tended the cattle and, though she was careful never to go too close, she had an uncomfortable feeling that those clear green eyes of his were following her. The temptation to shout insults at him, or shake her fists, was strong, but she resisted. Knowing his perversity, he might just take such gestures to be encouragement, and start courting her again. It was safer to ignore him.

Judith waited patiently for Adam to plan a night raid on the drainers' work, a raid which would include her. But he made no mention of one, however, and she presumed he was waiting for his wounds to heal first. She was proven wrong.

'Mercy, here's Adam!' remarked Aunt Ketty one afternoon. 'What can he be wanting so early?'

'The pleasure of my company?' Judith grinned. 'You carry on in the dairy. I'll go and let him in.'

At first sight of him, her heart contracted with concern. 'Are you ill?' she asked anxiously. 'You look so white and drawn. Is your head hurting again? I thought it was mending well.'

But Adam answered her with a cheery enough countenance. 'My head's fine, I thank you. It scarce troubles me at all now. The reason for my sickly pallor is nothing but tiredness, for I had no sleep last night. We had better things to do.'

'You did? And who is "We"?'

'A few of the fitter lads and myself. Out we went to Hanser Fen as soon as it got dark. You know those ditches the drainers have been sweating over all week? Well, we filled them in! Thomas has devised a most ingenious tool that lets us push the soft earth instead of having to dig. It was so simple——'

But Judith did not want to hear about Thomas's invention.

'You went out last night?' she cried. 'But why didn't you tell me? I thought I was to go with you?'

'So you shall, my sweet Judith, in good time. But last night we men took first turn, to see how things went. I know you and some of the other women are eager to have a go, but, really, I doubt if you'll be needed, not if things always go so well. Imagine it! Destroying six days' work in a single night. That was a good idea of mine to alter our tactics.'

'*Your* idea? I thought it was mine!'

Adam was too full of self-congratulation to be deflated. 'You may have put forth the germ of it,' he said. 'But that's a long way from getting the matter organised and carrying it out. Such work is for men.'

'And what is women's work, pray?' demanded Judith angrily. 'To agree with everything you men say and do, without question?'

'No, to drive us poor men wild, and take our minds off our duties by looking so bonny. Being angry makes you look very pretty, you know.'

'Yes, I do know! snapped Judith. 'That's exactly what——' Just in time she held her tongue. In her irritation she had been about to say, 'That's exactly what the Dutchman said.'

Adam, however, did not seem to notice her slip.

'Not that you don't look pretty when you aren't angry,' he went on. 'There's not a comelier lass in the whole of the Fens, in my opinion.'

'Oh, and you are an expert, I suppose?'

'But of course. I thought you knew. I'm renowned for having a good eye for horseflesh, and it's only a short step from there to being able to note the prettiest wenches.'

'Why you wretch!' exploded Judith.

But a laughing Adam had swept her into his arms and holding her so tightly she could scarcely breathe, began kissing her energetically. Usually his kisses left her limp with need of him—today, however, she felt no emotion, other than a vague impatience for him to finish.

At last she pushed him away. 'Aunt Ketty's just in the dairy!' she protested. 'What would she say if she came in?'

'I should think she's guessed by now that I have a fondness for you,' replied Adam cheekily, releasing her. 'And you'll be sorry you didn't take your fair share of love while you had the chance, for it's going to have to last you for a time.'

'Oh, how so?'

'I'm off to Ely tomorrow with the petition. It's an errand that's been put off long enough, waiting for my head to heal. Then, of course, there's our little business to see to as well.'

'Our little business?'

'Don't say you've forgotten! Your ring! I'm taking it to the goldsmith's to be made smaller.'

'Oh, yes, of course.'

At that moment Aunt Ketty did come in, and Judith was surprised at how relieved she felt at the interruption. She had never before failed to respond to Adam's caresses. Her lack of enthusiasm was disturbing, and she hastily tried to find the cause. I'm still angry with him, that's it, she told herself. Going off on a night raid with never a word to me, and then pretending that it was wholly his idea. Aye, he'll leave us women out completely if he gets a chance, for all the assurance he gave me.

But that was not the true reason for her lack of feeling. She did not want to remember it. She struggled against the truth of it. But at the moment when Adam's lips began to kiss her, she could only recall other lips on hers. Why she should suddenly think of the Dutchman just then, she could not imagine. It made her feel very disloyal.

Stricken with guilt, she bade goodbye to Adam with such intensity that Aunt Ketty clicked a disapproving tongue.

With no Adam to occupy her for the next few days, Judith became restless.

'My, I don't know what worm's got at you, so that you can't sit still for two minutes together,' remarked Aunt Ketty. 'But if you're really determined to be up and doing, there's that liniment I've been promising Granny Burns for I don't know how long, and you may as well take a goodly supply of cough syrup as well, ready for the winter. You know what her chest gets like at the least bit of a cold wind. Oh, and you could drop some eye ointment in to old Joseph Rogers on your way. What a good thing you collected those herbs the other day, else I'd not have remedies enough.'

Judith had no wish to recollect her herb-gathering expedition, but she listened thankfully as Aunt Ketty compiled a formidable list of calls for her. It was exactly what she wanted. So eager was she to be active that she did not notice the dark cloud appearing on the horizon. It was small at first but grew with alarming speed, giving the sky an ominous leaden glower, which darkened with each passing minute.

She had just left Granny Burns' house when she first noticed how sultry the day had become. Even the songbirds were silenced, leaving only metallic-winged dragonflies to hover over the green ponds along the way, and great buzzing clouds of gnats to rise from the brackish water at her approach. As she walked on, she liked the heavy colour of the sky less and less, and she debated whether she should turn tail and seek shelter with Granny Burns before the storm broke. By then, she was some distance from the old woman's cottage, so she decided to press on.

It was not a wise decision. She was out on the open fen when the first growl of thunder rumbled across the heavens. It was followed by another and another, and despite her quickened pace she had hardly gone another quarter of a mile before the entire sky was crackling with great flashes of lightning. Then the rain came, huge fat drops, that fell in such a torrent the reeds and blades of grass were flattened beneath their onslaught.

Judith barely noticed how quickly she became drenched to the skin, she was too overwhelmed with panic. Of all things, she feared lightning more than anything else in the world. The idea that those jagged burning fingers could destroy her so cruelly, made her feel extremely helpless. Out here on the fen her vulnerability only served to increase her panic. There was nowhere to hide, only the stands of reeds and a few meagre clumps of alder and willow. In blind terror she hitched up her skirts and began to run, heedless of the direction, in a desperate attempt to find refuge. Her lungs were burning for want of breath and a stitch in her side was agony, but she did not slacken her pace, not until she saw the blurred outline of a house ahead of her. Half blinded by the stinging rain, she hurried towards it.

Her first instinct was to hammer at the door and throw herself on the mercy of the inhabitants. Then she recognised where she was and checked her pace. Without realising it she had come upon the Fen Reeve's house, and she knew that no amount of desperation would make her beg the Dutchman for help. Instead, she pressed herself into the lee of the garden hedge, her hands over her ears to block out the roar of thunder, her eyes tightly shut to keep out the dazzling flashes of lightning. That was why she did not hear the Dutchman approach.

The first she knew of his presence, was feeling herself being swept off her feet by a pair of strong arms. Her squeal of alarm was drowned by a roll of thunder.

'Why in pity's name didn't you come into the house?' demanded the Dutchman, carrying her towards the front door.

'Put—put me down! I was all right where I was!' Judith's protest was not convincing.

Then earth and sky were lit in a sudden blue glare as lightning flashed from the heavens and danced, fizzing and cracking, along the tops of nearby gorse bushes. Thankful for human contact, and grateful that she was no longer alone in the tumult, Judith gave up all pretence and pressed her face against the Dutchman's shoulder. Only when she heard the heavy slam of the front door and knew she was safely indoors, did she raise her head.

'Tildje!' bellowed the Dutchman.

A neat middle-aged woman, in a spotless cap and apron, that fairly shone with starch, came hurrying up. Beside her, yapping ferociously, followed the little dog, its top-knot tied this time with a blue bow.

The woman silenced it in Dutch, then said in English to no one in particular, 'Dat's a brave boy! Always guards his mama vell.'

For a stupefied moment Judith thought that she was refering to the Dutchman, but when she looked at him he gave a chuckle.

'Not me! The dog,' he said. 'Tildje, some mulled wine for Mistress Pentelow.'

'Der young lady, her leg hurts?' enquired Tildje with concern.

'No, not at all,' replied Judith, then realised to her embarrassment that she was still clasped in the Dutchman's arms. 'Let me go, I beg you!' she hissed, her face scarlet as she struggled to free herself from his grasp.

Without a word the Dutchman deposited her on the well-scrubbed floor of the passage way. Tildje pounced, grabbing a handful of Judith's sodden skirt.

'Dat's vet!' she announced. 'Dat's not goot! You come! Vine you have later.'

Painfully conscious that she was dripping water and mud everywhere, Judith followed her up a narrow flight of stairs into a small bedchamber.

'Take off tings!' ordered Tildje. 'You too vet. I get you dry tings, else you get sick. Not goot!' Her command of English was limited, but brooked no argument. Judith slipped out of her clothes while the housekeeper bustled about finding fresh garments, which were all too short and too wide, but clean and dry.

When Judith was respectable once more Tildje regarded her critically, tweaked a highly starched collar into place and announced, '*Mijnheer* vaits! Come!'

Judith wondered if '*Mijnheer*' referred to the Dutchman, but Tildje was already scampering down the staircase, and she had no option but to follow.

The housekeeper threw open a door and announced, 'Go! I bring vine!' and disappeared.

Still somewhat bemused, Judith hesitated in the doorway until the Dutchman's voice called, 'Come in, if you please.'

The room she entered was small and well-furnished, but of a neatness and cleanliness that put even Marjorie Digby to shame. The Dutchman was standing with his back to the fireplace.

'You are more comfortable?' he asked.

'Yes, thank you,' Judith replied, though, in truth, she was not. She was now dry and decently clad, but inside she felt decidedly agitated. The last person she had wanted to see again was the Dutchman, yet here she was with him in his house. The way in which he had picked her up and held her in his arms had done nothing to restore her composure. Concealing her agitation, she wondered whether she dared leave this place and brave the storm once more. A flash of lightning illuminated the garden outside and made up her mind for her. She would stay!

'You will sit?' The request was more like a command, and Judith automatically perched herself on the edge of

a highly polished chair. Her eyes were still drawn towards
the vivid flashes outside. Noting the direction in which
her attention strayed, the Dutchman strode across the
room and pulled the wooden shutters across the windows.
Judith was thankful for the security of the gloom, but
less pleased at the prospect of being alone in a darkened
room with him.

'You've been alone with me before,' he observed, as
though he had read her mind. 'There is no need to appear
so anxious. You look as though you are about to take
flight.'

Judith felt hot colour flood into her face. She remembered far too clearly for comfort the occasion when they
had lain together in the clump of alders and she hoped
that he would not refer to it.

'I recall the time very well,' she said, 'which is exactly
why I'm on my guard. You behaved badly, I recollect.'

'Not badly. I merely responded to overwhelming
temptation, as any red-blooded man would have done.'
The teasing tone in his voice softened as he went on, 'I
am truly sorry I caused distress on that occasion. The
memory of the hurt on your face smites me even yet.
But, that apart, I have no regrets. I fancy that some of
your pain and anger was caused because you did not
dislike it either.'

'So you think that, do you? Well, you could not be
further from the truth; I warn you not to try anything
of the sort again!'

Judith began to edge away from him.

'I know I should give you my word, to put you at your
ease, but I confess, with you looking so pretty, I fear I
would be hard put to it to keep my promise,' he grinned.
'However, if you feel at all threatened you can call upon
my housekeeper for aid.'

'And I can hope for her to come rushing to my rescue?'
she asked sceptically.

'Perhaps not, but her little dog would. He seeks any
excuse to bite me—— Nay, do not go,' he said, as Judith
made for the door. 'You should know my jesting by now.

I'll do my best to behave properly and honourably. There, will that do? I fear it is the most I can promise.'

'And I fear it's not good enough!'

She stalked out of the room, along the passage and flung open the front door, only to be greeted by a heaven split asunder by great jagged slashes of lightning. With a whimper of terror she backed into the house again.

'See! It would be foolishness to try to leave now,' the Dutchman said gently. 'You know it would... Come...'

Meekly, Judith allowed herself to be led back to the darkened room, for once assured that he was the lesser of two evils.

There was a brief knock at the door, and Tildje entered carrying two steaming beakers of mulled wine.

'Drink,' instructed the Dutchman. 'We seem to make a habit of drinking wine together.'

But Judith had had enough of being ordered about for one day. 'I thank you, but no. I've no wish to trouble you. If I can but shelter until the storm passes then I ask no more,' she said.

'But the wine is here already. Why waste it?' He picked up the beaker and placed it in her hands.

Almost against her will she found her chilled fingers curling comfortingly around the warm beaker. Perhaps it was foolish to decline the drink after Tildje had gone to the trouble of preparing it. Lifting it to her lips, she found her teeth chattered against the rim.

'There, you are more chilled than you realised. The wine is just what you need.' The Dutchman spoke with solicitude.

As the gentle warmth of the spiced liquid spread through her, Judith had to agree with him, but she was determined not to admit it.

'Do people always do as you tell them?' she asked.

'Yes, usually,' was the frank reply.

'And what if they don't?'

'Then I grow angry and shout.'

'And a fearsome sight that must be,' Judith replied sarcastically. 'No doubt it makes your unfortunate labourers quake, but how do you fare with those fighting men?'

'The labourers must do as I say, but the fighting men are naught to do with me.'

'Yet you made good use of them the other day.'

'You think we should stand there and let your villagers attack us as they please?'

'No, I think you should not have been there in the first place. You should go back to your own country instead of trying to earn yourself a piece of ours. That's the usual fee for you engineers, I believe. A portion of the land you drain.'

'It is customary—but I'll be paid in gold.'

'Then why don't you take the gold that's owing to you and go? I warn you, we'll never stop fighting back.'

'It isn't for me to say whether I go or stay.'

'Oh, so even the great Maarten van de Scheldt has a master. Sir Walter, I presume?'

'Only in part. Mainly, I am commanded by my uncle. He came here some years ago and made good plans to drain Hanser Fen. They came to naught then, so this time he has sent me in his stead.'

'Aren't you a mite grown to be still tied to your uncle's coat-tails? Are you afraid to seek employment on your own?' Judith taunted him.

'Not at all. I can earn my own bread easily enough, but I have to ensure that my family eats, too. That's not so easy.'

'Oh...' Judith had never thought of him having a family. 'You have children? You are a widower, perhaps?'

'I've never had time to marry. I've been too busy.'

'You must have been busy indeed, not to have had time to seek a wife for yourself.'

'Oh, there was an occasion when I would have wed, years ago, but cautious fathers don't look favourably on poor young men with dependants as sons-in-law.'

'So, for how many do you earn bread?' Judith was finding it more and more difficult to maintain her belligerence.

'As well as myself, for my mother and three sisters.'

'I wonder they could spare you to come to England.'

'Oh, they were glad enough for me to come here to earn some money. Unlike you, they are only too eager to have good marriage portions, or, at least, two are. One sister married last year, and I was able to give her a good dowry. Now the other two can't wait to be married, also, so you see, they are not at all like you.'

Judith recognised that he was setting traps for her, as usual, and decided to put an immediate end to his game.

'If you mean to start some lengthy discussion about my wedding plans, then I fear you'll be sadly disappointed,' she said. 'They're naught to do with you, so I recommend you restrict your interests to guarding your sisters' affairs.'

'But I do!' replied the Dutchman with feigned innocence. 'My youngest sister, who is only fourteen, is already very eager to wed a soldier, but I told her, "No, you are too young. You must wait."'

'How masterful of you!' Judith's tone of admiration matched his innocent look for sincerity. 'How long have you been directing your sisters' lives with such determination?'

'Nigh on fifteen years.'

'Oh, come, sir. You can't expect me to believe that! You aren't old enough.' Judith was jolted out of her mockery.

'It is true enough. I now grow uncomfortably close to my thirtieth year, and my father died when I was fifteen. My youngest sister was born three months later. There was no one else to care for them all.'

'But surely your uncle...'

'Has children aplenty of his own. He was good enough to see to my education, and take me into his business. I couldn't ask him for more than that.'

Judith fell silent. Much as she disliked the man, she realised that he must have had a hard struggle to make his way in the world. There was a long pause, broken only by the persistent thunder above. She decided it would be safer to change the subject.

'This can't be your first visit to England, you speak our language so well,' she said.

'There, you've said something nice about me at last.' The mischievous spark came back into the Dutchman's eyes, and Judith feared that he would start on his non-sensical tack again. However, he must have noted her discouraging expression and thought better of it, for he continued, 'I've been to England many times. For the last few years I think I've spent as much time in this country as my own. There is much land ripe for recla-mation here. I know you won't believe me, but many people are only too happy to have their barren acres drained.'

'Well, don't count the folk of Hanser Fen among them!'

'If I show you my work, perhaps you'll understand. Come!' The Dutchman rose to his feet.

'Where are we going?'

'Only into the next room. It's where I work.' He smiled ruefully. 'Besides, I feel more at ease there. Tildje won't let me smoke in here.'

'You're truly master in your own house!' mocked Judith.

She looked about her, taking in the details of the room properly for the first time. It really was immaculate. It was arranged with an orderliness and precision that she had never seen equalled, not even at Old Place. The fur-niture gleamed with a sheen which spoke of hours of effort; the pieces of blue and white Delft stood on crisp, spotless linen mats; the steel fire-irons might have been made of silver, they shone so; the hearth had been vig-orously scrubbed and holy-stoned to a bone-like whiteness. It was a sight to behold—but far too perfect for comfort.

'Tildje is a remarkable housekeeper,' said the Dutchman, leading the way across the passage, 'but sometimes she forgets that rooms are to be lived in, not looked at. Now, here is my favourite room. Here I forbid her to tidy too much.'

Judith followed him uncertainly, wondering if she could take her leave and go. She felt she had spent long enough in this house conversing with him, and she wanted to get away. It troubled her that, no matter how resolutely she made up her mind to hate him, she had only to be in his company for a short time before a sneaking regard for him began to creep through her defences. After that terrible battle on Hanser Fen she had been determined that the Dutchman was indeed her worst enemy, yet here she was accepting his hospitality and beginning to harbour genuine admiration for the way he faced up to life. It was all very disturbing, and she felt that once she was out of his presence her peace of mind would return.

'Come!' said the Dutchman again, imperiously. He held the door for her so that she had to duck under his arm to enter.

Judith stepped inside and stood transfixed, every thought of leaving suddenly vanishing from her head. It was an untidy room, contrasting sharply with the one they had just left. Everywhere there were maps, rolls of paper and, above all, books. Books in such number that she gasped. It had never occurred to her that an ordinary man could own so many. She put out her hand to touch their tooled leather spines. From their gilded titles she could see some were in English, but many were in foreign languages.

'You've read all these?' she asked in awe.

'Yes. Do you read?'

'Of course!' she retorted, indignant at his question.

'Then you must borrow what you wish.'

'Could I . . .?' she began in delight, then she remembered that she had no wish to accept favours from this man. She continued primly, 'I thank you, but I get little time for such fripperies.'

The Dutchman took no notice. 'Aye, there are some here that will please you, I know,' he said. 'That shelf holds all the English volumes. The rest are mainly in Latin or Greek, with some in Dutch, French or German.'

'You speak all these tongues? And read them?'

'Why would I spend good money buying books I couldn't read? But leave the bookshelves for a moment. This is what I really want you to see.'

He led her to a table, set beneath the window to catch all the light. On it was pinned a large coloured map, with churches, houses and landmarks drawn in intricate detail. It was a work of beautiful craftsmanship.

'Do you recognise this place?' the Dutchman asked, pointing to a minute skilfully drawn church.

Beside it Judith made out the words 'St Peter's Church'.

'Why, it's Sedgewick!' she cried in delighted surprise. 'Yes, look, there's the green, and there's the Curate's house. Oh, and that must be the lane leading to Thomas's smithy.' Her excitement grew as she recognised landmark after landmark, so that outside the lightning flashed across the sky quite unnoticed.

'And do you see the cottages at the edge of what you call the Summer Grounds?' The Dutchman leaned closer to her as he pointed them out. 'I haven't finished the marking of the names yet, but I shan't leave them out.'

'But they're our cottages! That's where we live, and that's Peter Renshaw's!' Judith was like a child in her pleasure. 'Our cottages to the life, down to the sty for the pig and a small boat at the hythes! But you say you haven't finished them—do you mean you made this map?'

'Of course. Who else?'

'I don't know—I didn't imagine—— Why have you drawn it?'

'To show how I mean to set about draining the fen.'

Immediately she drew away from him as though she had been burnt. She deliberately walked away from him and gazed out of the window on to the storm-beleaguered fen.

'I have no wish to look at it any more,' she said coldly.

'I'm sorry to see you frown so. It's very unbecoming, even for you. I beg you come back so that I can explain my work to you.' His voice was gentle and persuasive as he led her back to the table. Too gentle and per-

suasive. She could not bring herself to pull away from
the soft pressure of his fingers. He began to speak,
tracing with his free hand as he did so.

'See, this blue line is the river, and the heavy black
line is the canal I plan to dig to take away the extra water
from the land—not too close to the river, though, so
that there is still room for the winter floods to spread a
little....'

He went on to talk of side canals and sluice gates, of
estuary silting and mud deposits. He spoke with such
authority and confidence that never for a moment did
Judith doubt that he could achieve his aim. He had the
skill and the knowledge to obliterate Hanser Fen.

As he spoke the touch of his hand was giving her a
sensation that came perilously close to pleasure.

'This is foolishness!' she cried suddenly, pulling away
from him. 'Rashness and folly!'

He looked down at her.

'No, I assure you, all this is possible,' he said, misunderstanding the cause of her outburst. 'I know how
hard it is for your people, and I shall indeed seek greater
justice for the commoners at the next meeting in London.
But I fear you can't hold back progress. The more I think
of it the more certain I am that Hanser Fen will be
drained, if not by me, then by some other fellow. It must
come, the transforming of these fever-ridden marshes
into fertile land.'

A sudden depression swept over Judith, bringing her
near to tears.

'Oh, I've made you unhappy!' The Dutchman
sounded so contrite that Judith dared not look up into
his face.

Using anger as her only defence, she snapped, 'What
do you expect, after you've destroyed our livelihood with
a few paltry lines on that map of yours?'

'But it will be for the greater good in the long run!'

'Aye, but only for those who survive the starvation it
brings in the short run!'

The Dutchman gave a sigh. 'I'd hoped to make you
understand my work. We'll never agree, I can see that.

Best speak of something else, eh? I'll find something that will make you look happy again.' He removed the offending map and pinned a fresh sheet of paper in its stead. 'There, that is for you to use. There are colours ready mixed by your side, and brushes in that jar. I'll sharpen a pen for you, then you can begin.'

'Begin what?' demanded Judith.

'Why, whatever you choose. A tree, a flower, a bird...'

'But I've never done such a thing! I don't know where to begin, or what to do!'

'Well, now is your chance to try, and if you should spoil the paper I will give you more.'

He stood over her, waiting for her to begin, but Judith put her hands behind her back like a mutinous child. The Dutchman dipped one of the brushes into a dish that held red colour and thrust it at her so that she had no option but to take it.

'Here!' he said, his old imperious tone returning.

Tentatively Judith let the brush touch the paper, watching as the bright colour transferred itself from bristle to the white surface. The blob that it made reminded her of a goose's head so she elongated it into a neck, then added the full curve of the body. It began as a simple likeness, but as she gained confidence, and learned the possibilities that such liquid colours offered, the bird began to change into a fantastic magical creature, more exotic even than the peacocks which strutted on the lawns at Massingham Hall.

This new activity absorbed Judith more pleasurably, and more fully, than anything she had experienced in a long time. The Dutchman settled himself at his desk close by to get on with his own work, and in some strange way his presence became part of the magic of the afternoon. The scratching of his pen and the fragrance of tobacco smoke as he lit his pipe wove themselves into her feeling of contentment. A hunger within herself, an emptiness she barely knew existed, was satisfied as she painted. Entranced, she tried the red, the blue, the yellow—merging them, mixing them in a way that was a constant delight.

Only when there was no more room on the paper for any more shapes, forms, or colours did she stop to look up. The Dutchman was sitting in her immediate line of vision, and she let her eyes rest on him, wanting to share her feeling of happy contentment with him, yet reluctant to interrupt him. As she watched him she was conscious of his hands as they made the pen move in neat precise characters across the page. They were long hands, well-shaped and capable, with a cleanliness about them that spoke of a fastidiousness that seemed typical of him. He always brought with him the clean scent of good soap and fresh linen, mingled with the aroma of fine tobacco. She had never realised a man could smell so pleasing. Adam usually had a whiff of the stables about him, and she had never seen him when his nails were not broken and blackened. Of course, Adam would see a fondness for soap as being effeminate, but there was nothing effeminate about the Dutchman. He had taken off his coat while he worked, and she could see the powerful swell of his muscles beneath the white linen of his shirt. Yet for all his formidable strength, his face, as he bent over his letter, betrayed a man of much gentleness and feeling. Judith's mind was still concerned with shapes and outlines, and she had to admit that the Dutchman's form was pleasing.

Almost unconsciously she began translating the long lines of his body into a picture, his massive shoulders bowed as he wrote, his muscular body, normally so straight, twisted a little because he sat askew. It was evident that his limbs were as powerful and as sturdy as young trees, despite the fact they were shrouded in broadcloth and worsted.

She had never scrutinised a man so completely before. She was engrossed in tracing the planes of his face and the fan of thick, fair lashes against his cheek, when he looked up and smiled. She should have been embarrassed at being caught staring at him, but curiously she was not.

'You have finished your painting?' he asked.

'Yes, there is no more room on the paper.'

'You enjoyed doing that,' he stated. There was no doubt in his voice, he knew it to be so.

'Yes,' she replied. She did not need to say anything more. He knew how she felt, understood the completeness that had swept over her. It was an extraordinary sensation. She had never before been so totally in accord with any human being, and for a moment words deserted her.

She rose to her feet. 'What a pity that only the rich can enjoy the pleasure of having pictures,' she murmured, looking down at the mass of vivid colour.

'You know I'm not a rich man, yet I own a picture.' The Dutchman got up from his desk. 'It's behind you. Look!'

As though they were children playing a game he put his hands on her arms and swung her round.

'There,' he said. 'Do you like it?'

On the wall hung a picture in an ornate gold frame. It was a street scene, with narrow, unfamiliar-looking houses of red brick, and a canal lined with trees. Judith stared in astonishment, staggered by the skill of the artist who could put such life and vitality into the painted figures that she half expected them to move and speak. The foreignness of the scene intrigued her, too. She had no experience of anywhere beyond the Fens, did not know how other places looked, how their inhabitants dressed, with the exception of the Dutchman himself, of course.

'Is that where you live?' she asked in awe.

'I live in a house very like that one, but in a different part of Amsterdam.'

'Is it as high? And does the roof have such curved shapes at the end?'

'Yes, indeed.'

'Oh.' Once again words failed her. The beauty and artistry of the picture astounded her. She had never expected to see its like but, more than that, it had cast a new light on the Dutchman. For the first time she could imagine him in his own country. In fact, he would have fitted very well into the scene before her, striding along that cobbled street on his long legs.

'You bought this?' she asked, still unable to believe that she knew someone who owned such a marvel.

'No, it was given to me as payment of a bad debt. I drew up some plans for a man who found he couldn't pay. He offered the picture instead, and I was glad to accept.'

'And there are many painters of pictures like this in Amsterdam?'

'Quite a few, and many better. For all I'm very fond of it, and would have to be hard pressed before I would sell it, I know it's not of the highest quality. There are artists in Amsterdam now whose greatness will live on for centuries.'

He began to speak of renowned painters, men with outlandish Dutch names, such as Rembrandt, van de Cappelle, Ter Borch. He was knowledgeable about them and their work, but what astonished her even more was that he actually knew one or two of them by sight. She wondered what sort of place this city of Amsterdam must be, where you could pass such men in the street.

Maarten van de Scheldt guessed her astonishment and chuckled.

'Such things don't happen on the Fens, eh? But this isn't the whole world, you know.'

Judith did not reply. She was just beginning to appreciate how much world there was beyond the flat, watery rim of her own horizon, so many lands, so many wonders just waiting to be explored. In some strange way she felt as though a great window had been opened for her, showing her an existence where books were commonplace, where to create things of beauty was not considered a waste of time. Above all, an existence where life was not bound by mud, cows, and the level of flood-water.

Reminded of the storm, she realised that the thunder and lightning had ceased, and that the sun was shining. She realised something else, too. As they had been looking at the painting the Dutchman's hands had slid along her arms and round her waist, so that she was leaning against the expanse of his chest in what could only be called an embrace. Even as the vulnerability of her situation occurred to her, she felt the soft warmth of his lips begin to trace the contours of her neck. There was no haste, no roughness in his caresses, just a gentleness that sent a melting warmth flooding through her. She did not resist as he deliberately turned her to face him. Nor did she protest as his lips softly covered hers. A vague notion that she should break free stirred in her, but faded into oblivion. She did not want to be free of him—that was the truth of it! In the comforting circle of his arms she had an odd sense of being in her rightful place. It felt natural to lift her face to respond to the sweet sensation of his lips. As if she was in a trance, all outside existence faded for her. She was conscious only of Maarten and of the absurd happiness that had suddenly engulfed her...

Judith returned to sanity with a jolt.

Stunned and breathless, she became aware that these were the Dutchman's arms about her, the Dutchman's lips that were sending thrills of pleasure through her. Shaken, she freed herself from his embrace.

'Enough, sir!' she said, her voice harsh and unsteady. 'That's reward enough for a few hours' shelter from the storm.'

The words were born of her sense of shock. Her compliance had disturbed her to her very heart. But the moment she had said the words she wished them unspoken.

The Dutchman's arms fell to his sides and he stepped away from her.

'Your pardon,' he said immediately. And she saw hurt in his eyes, despite his efforts to appear impassive.

'No, it is I who should beg *your* pardon,' said Judith contritely. 'I had no reason to speak so, and I am sorry. My harsh words—they were really aimed at myself, not you—I shouldn't have allowed...I don't know how I came to act so...Maarten, I am betrothed to Adam!' she finished desperately.

In her distress she did not notice that for the first time she had addressed him by his Christian name.

But he did. His expression softened, and colour came back to his face as he said, 'I can't let you take the blame. The fault was mine, and I know not how to apologise.'

'We mustn't fall out over who should take the blame,' Judith almost managed a smile. 'Perhaps we'd best share the responsibility. It would be better if we put this whole matter from our minds and pretend it never happened.'

'We can try, though, for my part, I fear I can make no promises.' He was looking at her with an expression in his green eyes that she did not want to see. It disrupted her thoughts and put her in a turmoil.

In desperation she made an attempt at her old scornful attitude.

'Oh—oh, you and your nonsense!' she cried. But she didn't sound convincing, even to herself.

'Yes, me and my nonsense,' repeated the Dutchman. He was not convincing, either.

And even the long walk home across the fen was not distance enough for Judith to recover her composure.

CHAPTER EIGHT

THE further away Judith got from the Dutchman's house, the more troubled her conscience became. How could she have behaved in such a way, and with him, of all people? It was as if some madness had overtaken her, subjugating her will. She could have half believed he had indeed used magic against her, if only a persistent inner voice had not kept on affirming that his attraction stemmed from the man himself, and not from any devilish intervention.

In the days that followed she made a deliberate effort to forget the Dutchman, but he had a disturbing tendency to creep back into her thoughts at the slightest provocation. She knew that every moment she allowed herself to dwell on Maarten van de Scheldt was a disloyalty to Adam, and the knowledge made her irritable and out of sorts.

'Are you ailing, my lamb?' Aunt Ketty asked. 'You scarce touch your food these days, and you look as pale as a bowl of milk.'

'It's the weather; you know how storms upset me.' Judith answered hurriedly.

The old lady looked questioningly at the blue sky. It was a perfect summer's day, and Judith realised the stupidity of her reply.

'I'll feel better when Adam's home from Ely,' she amended.

Aunt Ketty seemed more satisfied with this explanation.

'So that's what is fretting you,' she said. 'Well, it's a mercy he's due home soon, so your misery will be short-lived.'

Judith's response had not been completely untrue. She was longing for Adam's return, convinced that his familiar presence would drive away all uncomfortable

174

thoughts of the Dutchman. Once he was back there would be no room in her mind for anyone but him.

The dew was still thick on the grass next morning when Toby came along their path, his ancient dog, as ever, at his heels.

'My, it's turned a spell warm,' he greeted them, fanning himself with his hat. 'Would you have a use for some eels, I wonder?'

He handed a brimming pail to Aunt Ketty.

'Indeed we would!' she cried. 'Mercy, there's enough here for a pie and a good pan of broth besides! Would you have use for a mug of ale in exchange?'

'Those are the prettiest words I've heard this day! But why you bother to ask beats me. Have you ever known me refuse good ale?' Toby settled himself on the wall by the dairy.

'Not that I can recall,' answered Aunt Ketty as she went to fetch the jug.

'I'm surprised to see you still here, mawther,' Toby remarked to Judith. 'I'd have thought you'd be at Old Place hanging round Adam's neck by now.'

'Is he home?' demanded Judith, pausing from her work.

'Aye, he came back last night.'

'Why did no one tell me! Your pardon, Toby, but by your leave——'

'Go, lass, go! Never let it be said I stood in the way of true love.'

Judith fled to wash her face and hands and make her tangled curls into some sort of order. As she did so she looked at herself in the small piece of polished metal, which served as a mirror. Aunt Ketty was right, she did look pale and there were shadows under her eyes.

Not for much longer, she told herself. Not now that Adam was home.

She half expected to meet Adam coming towards her, as eager for her company as she was for his, but she reached the house without catching a glimpse of him. When she entered the courtyard she found out why. Several of the village men, headed by Thomas, were standing there with Adam, talking.

'Judith—well met, my love.' Adam greeted her with the briefest of smiles and an absent-minded kiss on the cheek. Then he turned and continued talking to his companions.

'If you ask me, entering Parliament was the most stupid thing King Charles could have done. Did he think that Master Pym and the rest would stay to be captured, like baited pigeons?'

'What has happened?' asked Judith. 'What have you heard at Ely?'

'Just that our beloved monarch has been a bigger fool than usual.' Adam made no effort to explain, but went on addressing the men. 'Stalked into the House of Commons, did Charles Stuart, bold as you please, and demanded the five members, accusing them of high treason.'

'Which five members?' Judith wanted to know.

But Adam did not hear her. 'Did you ever hear such a trumped up charge? It's Charles Stuart himself who's the traitor, against the good folk of England!'

'Were they taken?' asked Thomas, as Judith opened her mouth to repeat her question.

'Not they! They'd flown in good time, leaving Charles in a rare temper.'

'But which five members?' persisted Judith.

'Do you think there'll be strife?' asked Thomas at the same moment.

'There's sure to be!' Adam chose to answer the blacksmith. 'The King must be the only one in the land who thinks otherwise, else he'd persuade his friend, Sir Walter, to stop trying to drain Hanser Fen...'

The talk turned to more local matters, and a disconsolate Judith gave up all attempts to join in.

This was not how she had envisaged her reunion with Adam. This was not how she needed it to be. She was desperate for him to put his arms around her and talk of his undying love. Only that would drive away the mischievous thoughts that kept creeping unbidden into her mind. Instead, she had to stand by and wait, while Adam related to the others all the rumours he had heard in Ely.

Eventually the men went about their business and she was left alone with him.

He glanced up at the sun and said, 'The morning's slipping by at a rare pace. There's much to do waiting at the farm. These cursed journeys to Ely take time I can't spare!'

'Then you must learn to delegate some of your duties if your hours are so overstretched,' declared Judith.

'You sound angry. What has upset you?' asked Adam in surprise.

'Do you wonder that I'm angry? I've been parted from you for days; I appear to be the last to hear that you've come home; then when I do come to you what happens? I have to wait while you finish talking to the men. Wait and wait and wait while you talk and talk and talk!'

'You don't think that the latest news is worth discussing?'

'Indeed I do! I'd have joined in given half a chance, but you weren't interested in hearing my viewpoint. You preferred to regard the King's squabble with Parliament as men's business.'

'Squabble? Is that how you think of our cause? Have you no interest in opposing a King who leans so heavily towards the Pope, a King with no interest in ruling with Parliament? Don't you consider that our lawful rights, and our true religion, are worth fighting for?'

'Oh, Adam!' Judith felt the tears well up in her eyes. 'You're right, of course! I'm being unreasonable. But I've missed you so sorely, longed for you to be home so very much——'

'And all I did was to give you half my attention and the merest peck on the cheek. I'm a churlish lover, that I am. Come here so I might put matters right.'

All at once she was in his arms, her cheek pressed hard against the familiar roughness of his old leather jacket. Things will go right now, she told herself as she turned her face for kisses. I'll make sure they do now that Adam is back with me.

Her desperation gave an added ardour to her response, so that at last he held her at arm's length, panting and laughing.

'If that's the welcome I get after being away at Ely, I think I'll go more often.'

'No, don't even mention going away again,' she begged. 'I couldn't bear it.'

'Very well, if it will please you. Tell me, what have you been doing in my absence?'

'That would make a dull tale,' Judith said in haste. 'I'd prefer to hear your adventures.'

'Precious few they proved to be. I took the petition to the lawyer and the ring to the goldsmith. The lawyer said "I thank you, Master Digby" and the goldsmith said "I fear this task will take a time". So you see, I must go back to Ely after all, to get your ring. However, I've a surprise for you that's much closer to home.'

'A surprise?' Judith worked hard at expressing her delight.

'Aye. It's something I had put in hand to be done while I was away. I've had the chief bedchamber, the one that's to be ours, refurbished just for you. It's not been used since my father's time, but 'tis all redone, even to new bedhangings.'

'Oh, how splendid! May I see?'

'I'm not sure that would be proper, us not being wed yet.' Adam pretended to be disapproving, but could not hold the pretence and burst out laughing. 'Let's go now, shall we?'

He led the way into the house, to the bedchamber where Marjorie had shown her the ancient inscription. The inscription remained, but the traces of other colours in the mouldings that had intrigued Judith had been obliterated. Only plain dark oak remained. It was a sombre room, ill-lit for all it was one of the grandest in the house. To her eyes it cried out for rich red hangings on the great carved bed, or maybe a warm amber-yellow to bring cheer to the place. Instead the draperies were of a dull brown.

'Marjorie says they'll wear well and still be service-able when we've grandchildren playing about our feet,' grinned Adam, giving the costly material a twitch.

Of course! She might have known that this was Marjorie's idea.

'It is very grand,' said Judith, trying hard not to think of sleeping for the rest of her life in this gloomy place. 'You've worked very hard, you and Marjorie, and in secret too. You've done well to have it ready so long before Michaelmas.'

'About Michaelmas...' Adam looked a little uncomfortable. 'I took the liberty of calling on that lawyer fellow of yours to ask for news. A hard time I had persuading him that I was a truly interested party, but in the end he agreed to talk to me. I hope you don't mind.'

'Truly, I don't,' replied Judith; but she wondered how Aunt Ketty would react. 'Did he have news?'

'Some. He has traced your kinsfolk. They'd moved to York, and even now he is on his way to speak with them. He'll send word to you directly——'

'So the papers will be settled in good time for an October wedding, just as we planned. This is marvellous news,' cried Judith.

'Well, I thought—and Marjorie is in hearty agreement—that since legal matters are so close to completion, and with the state of the kingdom being what it is—I might be called upon to fight for Parliament at any time—we thought that perhaps we could be wed before October. Next month, maybe. That would be long enough to make wedding meats, wouldn't it?'

Adam's speech owed much to Marjorie, but for once she did not mind. She wanted to be safely married, out of the disturbing reach of the Dutchman.

'I will speak to Aunt Ketty about it as soon as I get home,' she promised.

'I'll tell Marjorie, she'll be pleased.' Adam looked longingly towards the bed, and then at Judith. 'If only...' he whispered, his voice husky.

'If only...' she echoed, trying hard to make her tone match his.

'Oh, Judith, even one month is too long to wait for you!'

Adam lunged forward and seized her so forcefully that Judith staggered backwards. She hit her head on the bedpost, but her gasp of pain was smothered by Adam's mouth coming hard on hers. She felt his teeth rake her lips, and the taste of blood came into her mouth.

'Dear heaven, how I want you!' His voice was rasping, his breathing heavy.

Hot, demanding kisses assailed her throat as she felt him tug urgently at the neck of her gown. Judith tried to respond. This was what she had always wanted, wasn't it? To belong to Adam completely? Why, then, was she conscious only of the bedpost pressing into her back and the painful chafing of his unshaven cheeks against her skin? She should have been uttering words of love and passion, but instead she heard herself exclaim, 'You haven't shaved! You're rubbing my face red raw!'

For a moment Adam paused in his tussle with her obstinate bodice lacings.

'Of course I haven't shaved,' he said in surprise. 'It isn't the Sabbath!'

Then desire overwhelmed him again, and he pushed her down on the bed, collapsing on top of her.

'Not shaved indeed,' he murmured, nuzzling against the softness of her flesh. 'Would you have me one of those pretty fellows decked in curls and ribbons and perfumed fit to choke a polecat? Such a one would be no good to you, my Judith.' His voice sank to a whisper. ''Tis a real man you need—there'd be no harm—we're to wed soon...'

His importunate hands, defeated by her laces, slid down and began to tug at her skirts. He was too engrossed in what he was doing, too absorbed to heed Judith's protest.

'No, Adam! Not now, not here!' she cried repeatedly.

'Where better? Our marriage bed...' His words were coming in gasps.

'No, Adam!'

She tried to struggle but he was too strong for her. This wasn't how she wanted to be taken, in a rough, furtive coupling that was fit only for the beasts of the field. Where was the love and tenderness? Where was any consideration for her needs and desires?

'I hear someone coming,' she cried, then added as a last resort, 'I think it's Marjorie!'

It was the one name that could cut through Adam's passion. He lay still and listened. Laughing voices drifted along the passage, a bucket clattered, a door banged shut.

''Tis but the maids doing the cleaning, they won't come in here,' he said, and would have resumed his fumbling under her petticoats, but she restrained his hand.

'Then depend on it, your sister will be along at any minute to check that the work is being done properly,' she said urgently. 'I'd not like her to catch us like this. Please, Adam...'

For a moment Adam remained still, then he rolled away from her with an exasperated sigh.

'I suppose you're right,' he said sullenly. 'Though it's enough to try the patience of any man with blood in his veins, all this waiting!'

Judith knew that it had been the fear of being discovered by his sister, sooner than her own pleas, that had suddenly quenched his ardour. Though, she thought to herself, considering the strange mood that Marjorie's in at the moment, she'd be more likely to dance a jig than be outraged at finding us rolling about on the bed.

Aloud she said, 'The time will come soon enough. It will be worth the waiting.' But she feared that she was trying to convince herself.

'Aye, you're right.' Adam ran a hand through his hair and gave a sheepish grin. 'Well, if we're not to give this bed a proper testing we'd best go.'

'Just let me make myself decent.' Judith brushed down her petticoats and tidied her tumbled hair, trying to hide how troubled she was. She had wanted Adam, or thought she had. Yet being in this room, lying on the great bed, even Adam's eager desire, had not provoked in her any sense of longing for her October marriage. As she tucked the last stray curl under her linen cap she was disturbed to realise that her overwhelming emotion was one of relief—relief to be leaving that dismal room still a maid.

Out in the sunlight Adam kissed her, a very chaste gesture after his recent passion.

'I may not be able to call on you tonight,' he said. 'I've let the drainers have free rein on the fen for long enough. It's time we taught them another lesson, or two.'

'You would go out tonight? Aren't you weary after your journey from Ely?'

'Not too weary to fill in a few ditches.'

'Then I will be one of the party.'

'Perhaps—I'll think on it.'

'There is no need. I've waited a long time to play my part. If you won't include me I'll go alone!'

'Judith!' protested Adam, then his alarmed face changed to a grin. 'You would, too, wouldn't you? Very well, I agree. I'll let you know what's decided before dusk. Will that satisfy you?'

'Certainly it will! But don't tell too many folk. The fewer who know the better.'

'Have you any more instructions for me?' Adam stood strictly to attention and saluted as he spoke.

'Foolish wretch!' Judith gave him a playful thump, glad that their relationship was getting back to something like its old carefree footing. 'I'll see you tonight.'

'Maybe.'

'No! Definitely!'

'Very well, it seems that you are giving the orders!'

Adam saluted her again, then spoilt his military precision by planting a hearty kiss full on her mouth before he hurried off to work.

'Are you sure you want to go wandering about the fen in the dark?' asked Aunt Ketty when Judith explained what was proposed.

'Of course I do. It was my idea. I see no reason why the men should take all the risks.'

'Your mind's made up, I can see that, and I must confess, if I were twenty years younger I'd be champing at the bit to be alongside you.' Aunt Ketty nodded approvingly. She was less happy, however, when Judith told her of Adam's visit to Master Nichols.

'Now I call that being too forward, indeed I do!' she exclaimed, her forehead wrinkling in annoyance. 'I see Marjorie's hand in this. What's she up to now, I wonder? Still eager to have you and Adam at the altar in great haste?'

'Adam did suggest we be married soon,' admitted Judith. 'Seeing that Master Nichols was hopeful of clearing up the matter of my adoption soon.'

'That's Marjorie again! I thought she'd be on that tack before long, especially now she's had their great bedchamber refurbished.'

'You heard about that?' Judith felt herself colour as she remembered her recent visit to that selfsame room.

'Aye. I was having a word with Sukie, one of the maidservants over at Old Place—she's sorely troubled with chilblains, poor lass. I gave her some ointment. She says the chamber's been richly done, but it's so gloomy it will be like sleeping in a coffin. I don't suppose it would have occurred to Marjorie to consult you on such a matter, would it?' Aunt Ketty's annoyance suddenly evaporated. 'But my being in a huff with Marjorie Digby has nothing to do with the matter really, has it? How soon does Adam suggest we have this wedding?'

'Next month.'

'Next month! My stars! I'll allow he has a point, things in the land getting to a pretty pass the way they are, but another four weeks! No, that's out of the question! We'd not have time to prepare the feast——'

'But Marjorie——'

'Aye, I know what you're going to say; Marjorie Digby would like nothing better than to take over the festivities, and doubtless very grand they'd be. But you're my one ewe lamb and I've long dreamed of seeing to your wedding myself. There are your clothes, too. I thought that the next time the pedlar came through—he's due any day now—we'd get a length of really good kersey to make you a gown. What say you? And maybe if he's got some ribbons and laces we could make a fine show, eh?'

'That would be wonderful.' Judith was delighted. 'But how long would the preparations take—so that I can tell Adam?'

Aunt Ketty pretended to consider, though Judith knew that her mind was made up.

'Not much before Michaelmas,' she said. 'Besides, it would be madness marrying sooner, with the haymaking and the harvest coming up. Another month or two will do no harm. And you'll have time to enjoy your first days as a wife, instead of being harassed to death. Would you be sorely disappointed if we held to our plan for a Michaelmas wedding?'

'No, of course I wouldn't.' Far from being disappointed, Judith found that, yet again, she had to quell an unexpected sensation of relief.

'Then that's all that matters. Marjorie Digby can like it or not, as she pleases! Now, as for the kersey, what colour would you like? A deep blue? Or a saffron would be a pretty, warm hue for the autumn, wouldn't it?'

Plans for the gown occupied the conversation all afternoon, as the pair of them went about their work together. Judith tried not to recognise that much of her pleasure in the subject stemmed from the fact that her wedding was some months away.

They were still talking when Adam arrived.

'What's so important that you didn't hear me knock?' he demanded, after having to wait to be let in.

'Nothing crucial, merely my wedding-dress,' smiled Judith.

'Your aunt has agreed to the wedding?'

'To the wedding, aye, but in October, as was first said,' declared Aunt Ketty, coming into the room.

'Oh, Marjorie will be so disappointed,' said Adam, adding hastily, 'As, indeed, I am. I could well be off fighting for Parliament by then.'

'And you could just as likely still be here!' There was a determined note in Aunt Ketty's voice. 'I'm sorry to be disappointing Marjorie and you, but there it is. We can't be ready earlier, us being two women alone.'

Adam opened his mouth to suggest that his sister would be only too happy to help, but saw the glint in the old lady's eyes, and thought better of it. He knew that there was little love lost between Marjorie and Aunt Ketty. He merely said, 'So be it—but now to more urgent matters. If you're still of a mind to come with us tonight, Judith, I'll fetch you as soon as it's dark.'

'Of course I'm still of a mind to come!' Judith exclaimed.

'We'll be a small party, just the two of us, old Toby, and George Boston and his brother—you know, the couple of wildfowlers who live at the edge of East Fen.'

'We'll be enough to do plenty of damage!' Judith was excited at the prospect. 'I'll be ready for you, never fear.'

Some activity to assist Adam and the other Fenlanders,

that was what she needed! Something to dull the image of the Dutchman that kept forming unbidden in her mind.

She was ready long before time, and, being too restless to settle, walked along the path to meet Adam and the others. The Boston brothers looked askance when they saw her, but Adam remarked, 'Why shouldn't we have women with us? Who knows the Fens better?' Judith was forced to hide a smile.

They went by way of the river, a roundabout route to give them most cover. There was no moon, but the sky had a milky opalescence about it that took away the absolute darkness. The air was heavy with the scent of summer flowers, and as they made their way stealthily to the diggings the crushed grasses beneath their feet smelled so sweet that Judith had a hard task remembering that they were on a difficult, and possibly dangerous, mission.

'Where are we going?' she asked in a whisper.

'We decided on the end of the ditch nearest the river,' Adam whispered back.

'What if Sir Walter's left guards there?'

Adam gave a grunt of irritation at her caution, while Toby smothered a chuckle. The two Bostons, however, answered her questions in a more practical way.

'We'll soon find out,' said George. And he and his brother wriggled off into the darkness as silently and as lithely as a pair of eels. They were back within minutes with the news that they had the fen to themselves.

'We'd best get on, then,' said Adam.

As silently as possible, they began work filling in the ditch. It was no easy task. In the poor light it was a simple matter to miscalculate and overbalance or miss one's footing. Judith revelled in the strenuous activity, working as hard as any of the men. In some way she felt she was paying the Dutchman back for having so disrupted her peace of mind. Taking it in turns to keep watch, they shovelled away through the night, having few spells to stretch aching backs and weary limbs.

At last Toby sniffed the air. 'Dawn's not far off, Adam, lad,' he said. 'Time we were gone.'

By what sixth sense he could tell the approach of day Judith did not know, but no one questioned this instinct of his. Silently spades were cleaned off, and the little group made its circuitous way back home.

'There's no need for you to see me all the way,' whispered Judith as Adam made to accompany her the full length of the path.

'But it's so dark. I don't like the idea of you walking alone.'

'I know the way blindfold, and there's naught here that I fear. Get you home and have some rest. You will get precious little before you have to start the morning's work.'

'Aye, that's true. Well, if you're sure?'

'Absolutely.'

'Goodnight.'

'Goodnight, my sweet love.' Adam kissed her, then kissed her again. 'I'm a fortunate fellow to have you as my betrothed. You've worked so hard this night. Once we're married, the two of us toiling side by side, there'll be nothing we can't accomplish.' For a third time their lips met, then Adam turned away to Old Place.

As Judith walked towards the cottage, she felt she had never been so weary. Every muscle complained and her hands were raw and blistered. Nevertheless, she felt a sense of satisfaction that she had taken part in the raid.

She was following the path along the bend of the river, noting the familiar outline of a small thicket of hawthorn, when suddenly a shadow detached itself from the bushes. Vast and terrifying, it loomed towards her, causing her to yell in fright.

'Hush, would you wake everyone?' whispered a familiar voice . At the sound of it her heart gave a treacherous leap of relief, joy, and panic, intermingled.

'Maarten!' she gasped. 'What nonsensical game is this you're playing?'

'No game, I assure you. I'm merely keeping my promise.'

'Promise?'

'Aye, to lend you one of my books. You forgot to take it the other day.'

'And you've come to deliver it *now*?' She was incredulous.

'When else? The days when I could knock on your front door like a Christian are, I fear, long gone.'

'But in the middle of the night! Such foolishness!' She stopped her tirade. 'Listen... I can hear footsteps. Someone's coming! Hide behind that thicket.'

'And leave you here? Nay——'

'Hide, you fool!' she hissed. 'It's Adam. I recognise his step.'

She pushed the Dutchman into the shadow of the hawthorns. By the time Adam arrived he was out of sight.

'Are you all right?' Adam demanded. 'I heard you cry out.'

'It was nothing. I tripped over a root, that's all.' She was surprised that her voice sounded so calm.

'Did you fall? Are you hurt?'

'No, I just feel rather foolish, yelling so, after my brave words.'

'Come. I'll walk home with you. I'll brook no argument this time.' Adam took her arm. Judith was tempted to pull away, but she thought better of it. Meekly she allowed herself to be escorted to the cottage door, permitted herself to be kissed goodnight again, and, as Adam took his leave, waved to him as he reached the garden gate.

Don't let him wait to see me go indoors, she begged silently.

Her prayers was answered; when the sound of Adam's boots was no longer audible she crept back to the hawthorn thicket. the Dutchman was standing on the path, waiting for her.

'Why did I have to hide?' he asked. 'Were you afraid your sweetheart and I would come to blows? I was in no danger. I'm head and shoulders bigger than your Adam.'

'But he is a fierce fighter, there's none better,' Judith retorted.

'Ah, you were protecting me. That's very gratifying.'

Judith gave a sigh. 'I'm in no mood for your tricks and games,' she said. 'Just stop pestering me and go away.'

'I've no wish to pester you,' said the Dutchman.
'Surely you know that? I simply wanted to bring this
book and leave it on your doorstep. I'd no idea that you
would be abroad at this hour. I won't ask you what you
were doing. Your poor hand tells its own tale.'

In the darkness he had taken hold of her hand.
Abruptly she pulled it away.

'Please,' she begged, 'please go.'

'Not until I've given you the book.'

'I don't want your wretched book!'

'What a pity! In that case, I'll throw it in the river.'

Judith saw his arm swing upwards, the book clasped
in his hand.

'No!' she gasped, appalled at such waste.

'Then you must take it!'

He passed the book to her, and she knew he'd had no
intention of throwing it in the water.

'Now, will you go?' She was terrified in case Adam
or one of the others came back.

'Are you so desperate to be rid of me?' There was a
warm vibrancy in his voice, and she knew that he, too,
was remembering their last meeting.

'Yes!' she said. Then, because she couldn't bear the
harsh dismissal of that one word, she added imploring-
ly, 'Have you any idea what would happen if you
were found here, with me?'

'So, you truly are concerned for me?' His question
held such a note of longing.

'Yes,' she said again, wishing it were a lie.

'It makes me so happy to hear you say that. You can
have no idea how much.' His voice was soft and held in
it a serious note she had never heard before. 'It makes
me hope a little——'

'I don't want to hear your hopes,' she cut in brusquely.

'Not even when they involve you?'

'Especially not when they involve me! Maarten, you
must understand, I am bitterly ashamed of how I behaved when I last saw you. It was wrong. It was unfair
to both you and Adam. If I could go back and undo
my actions then I would. Since that is impossible, I must
seek to pretend they didn't happen. There never was a

storm; I was never at your house; we were never alone together; and I never... I never behaved like a wanton!'

'Nay,' he protested. 'There was never aught of the wanton about you, and I'll not have you disparage yourself so!'

'It does not matter what name I give to my behaviour; the fact remains I should not have acted as I did, and nothing you say will make it otherwise. I beg you to forget all that happened, and in so doing, help me to forget it too.'

'It is asking a great deal, expecting me to eradicate so much from my memory.'

'But try, I beg you, and so must I, else neither of us will ever have an easy conscience again. I am betrothed to Adam! We are to be married at Michaelmas!'

'Now that is something I would be only too happy to forget.'

'Please, Maarten, don't jest. Not now.'

'I wasn't jesting. I was never more serious in my life.'

'Please go.'

'Judith!'

In the darkness she sensed him reaching out to her and she backed away. 'Don't,' she said fervently. 'I've had enough of such madness. I beg you to leave me alone.'

'If that is what you want...'

'It is.'

'And you have nothing more to say to me?'

'Only, thank you for the book.'

Judith clutched the leather-bound volume to her, conscious that Maarten had made no attempt to go. The silence between them hung heavily. She knew he was waiting for her to speak soft words to him, to give him some encouragement. She realised that it would be sheer folly, yet she could not prevent herself from adding gently, 'You must never do such a reckless thing again. Calling on me in the middle of the night! To be so foolhardy. What were you thinking of?'

'I was thinking of you,' said Maarten simply. 'I was only going to leave the book on your threshold. I had no intention of trying to see you; that indeed would have been stupid. Don't you know I would never do anything to put you at risk?'

'But you have put yourself in great danger. There are—there are people abroad on the fens even at this time of night—people who would wish you harm,' Judith said hesitantly.

'I'll not ask who they are, or what their business is. For your sake I won't try to guess.'

'It is better you do not, just as it is better if you never come here again.'

'But when can we meet?'

'Meet? Don't even suggest such a thing! It would be the greatest folly. It's too dangerous, anything could befall you, and not for the world would I have your blood spilled on my account.'

'So you do care?'

His voice was soft and imploring, and even in this lunatic situation his presence was having its magnetic effect on her. In spite of all her resolutions, she knew that if she did not make a superhuman effort she would find herself irresistibly drawn to him.

'Oh, Maarten, I implore you, don't seek to read things into my words. I don't want to be the cause of you getting hurt. I don't want to be the cause of anyone getting hurt. Let that be enough. Go now...'

'Very well, I'm going, but don't set too much store on not seeing me again.'

Before she could prevent him he had seized her hand and pressed it to his lips. Then without another word he disappeared into the darkness. Judith stood transfixed until she heard the quiet splashing of oars and knew that he had really left. Only then did she walk slowly to the cottage door, holding the book tightly against her breast with folded arms.

'You're back safe then, my lamb?' Aunt Ketty greeted her. 'All went well?'

'Aye, all went well,' said Judith wearily.

'There, you sound worn out! Just hold a minute till I light a rushlight or two. I thought it best to keep the place in darkness in case prying eyes marked that we weren't abed. That's better... Why, what are you holding, child?'

In silence Judith laid the book on the table. The well-tooled leather binding and the gilt lettering glowed like jewels in the spluttering flame of the rushlight.

'Where did that come from?' asked Aunt Ketty. 'Surely Adam didn't give you such a thing?'

Judith shook her head. 'No, the Dutchman. I met him not five minutes since, on the path by our hythes.'

'No!' Aunt Ketty's eyes grew large in astonishment. 'Whatever was he about, coming here at this time of night?'

'Bringing the book. When I took shelter in his house, that day of the storm, he promised to loan me one, but I left without taking it.' She had told her aunt only a little of that episode. 'It seems he's a man of his word. He was going to leave it on the doorstep, but I arrived at the vital moment.'

'Mercy on us! Did he know what you'd been up to? Will he say aught to Sir Walter?'

'He'll say naught.' Judith was confident on that score.

'But the risk he ran!'

'Aye, Adam nearly caught him. If he had, then there would have been bellows to mend, sure enough.' Judith sank down, her exhaustion becoming almost unbearable.

Aunt Ketty eyed her with a concern that had little to do with her physical state. 'Get you to bed, my pet. You need sleep now more than anything.'

Judith lifted the book and read the title, *Sir Bevis of Hampton*.

'What's to be done with this?' she asked, almost too fatigued to speak.

'Best keep it out of sight,' advised Aunt Ketty.

With an almost imperceptible nod of consent, Judith took the book and slid it under her pillow. Within minutes she had undressed and was in bed, certain that oblivion would claim her immediately. It was not to be, however. Sleep just would not come. It was not her blistered hands or her aching limbs that kept her awake, so much as a sore heart. Why had she happened upon the Dutchman tonight of all nights? The satisfaction she had gained from her activities had dissipated with the sound of his voice. Silently, in the warmth of the big bed she shared with Aunt Ketty, she condemned herself for not having sent him away with a flea in his ear, for having consented to listen to him. Above all, she cursed herself for having again found pleasure in his company.

'Why, oh, why do you have to plague me so?' she demanded aloud.

'Wassermatter...?' murmured Aunt Ketty, wakened from her slumber.

'Nothing, Aunt dear. A bad dream, nothing more,' Judith soothed her.

Aunt Ketty went back to sleep again almost at once. But it was a long time before Judith closed her eyes.

The weather seemed determined to match her mood; it turned unseasonably cold and wet. Judith finished the milking drenched to the skin, so that Aunt Ketty insisted she sit by the fire and get warm again. Even with dry clothes, and her chilled hands and feet warmed by the glowing peat, Judith's spirits remained depressed.

'This rain doesn't seem to stop,' she protested, pacing up and down the tiny cottage parlour.

'I agree, it's miserable,' said Aunt Ketty. 'What we need is something to cheer us up. A drop of elderberry wine? Some blackcurrant cordial? No? Then, how about if you read a page or two from that book?'

'No!' said Judith vehemently. 'I'm determined not to open it. The nerve of that plaguey Dutchman, to thrust it upon me!'

'I wonder how he knew what a fondness you have for a good tale?' observed the old lady calmly. 'And me, too. There's naught I like better than a story told, or read, beside the fire. I've always regretted I have no skill in reading and the like. The pennies I laid out to have you taught when you were a child were money well spent, I reckon.'

'Oh, very well! I give in!' exclaimed Judith, unable to withstand this gentle onslaught. 'Though, I warn you it will probably be dull and boring.'

'Well, it will do no harm to try it,' said Aunt Ketty, satisfied that she had got her own way. 'After all, it's only loaned, not a gift. You go and get it while I set a couple of stools by the fire. And a beaker of elderberry wine apiece will do us no harm, either.'

Judith was determined to hate the book, for no better reason than it belonged to the man who was causing her so much anguish. The thought that at some time she would have to find a way of returning it, along with the clothes she had borrowed from Tildje, did nothing to improve her belligerent frame of mind.

With her being out of practice, her reading was halting and disjointed at first, and she stumbled over some of the longer words, but as page followed page her fluency increased and with it her interest. The book was a tale of knightly exploits, and soon Judith and Aunt Ketty were totally absorbed in the battles of Sir Bevis against the dragons and giants. Only when the failing light made it difficult to see did Judith close the book with an aggressive snap. Against her will, she had enjoyed it! It seemed typical that something belonging to the Dutchman should give her pleasure, whether she wanted it or not.

'What a wondrous thing!' Aunt Ketty was still enthralled by the recollection of the story. 'The afternoon has gone by in a flash.'

'Which proves what a wondrous waste of time it is,' said Judith. 'I think we've had enough of such things, don't you? That book can stay shut for ever as far as I'm concerned.'

'If you say so, dear.' Aunt Ketty sounded a little disappointed. 'But you must admit, there's no greater cure for the miseries. Takes you right out of yourself, it does, so that you can't dwell on these troubled times we live in.'

If only that were true, thought Judith. As far as I'm concerned that book is trouble in itself—and its owner is a greater problem to me than anything else.

A general air of gloom seemed to settle upon Sedgewick and the surrounding area. The change in the weather had spoilt the hopes for a bumper hay harvest. Because of the rain, the gathering of the last crop on the cutting fen was a hurried, miserable affair, with none of the singing and joking which usually made it such a festive activity. The same thought was in everyone's mind—will our fen be here next year? The wider troubles in the land were worrying, too, but above all, everybody was tired. Parties were going out regularly to destroy the drainers' efforts, but no matter how Adam tried to organise it so that everyone took his part, it was growing increasingly exhausting now that the farm work demanded more attention.

'It's no use, we can't keep this up,' Adam said gloomily to Judith one day. 'Even with you women joining in it's too much. Everyone's worn to the bone now, and come harvest it will get worse. In addition, we've the pikemen to contend with. There's no knowing when they'll suddenly pop up in the middle of the fen.'

'Aye, there seems no rhyme or reason to them,' agreed Judith.

She had now taken part in several more raids, and on at least two occasions had had to take flight across the dark fens because of Sir Walter's men. The pikemen had materialised out of the night too often for coincidence, and there were mutterings of careless talk and gossip reaching the Hall.

She went on, 'I can't argue with you on the other score, either. I confess I feel a hundred years old because of weariness alone, and I know others in the village who are just as fatigued. We've reached our limit, I fear. We must change our tactics yet again, though what to do this time I've no idea.'

'I've had a few notions on what we could do,' said Adam. 'That lawyer of ours at Ely put a thought into my head last time I was there——'

'And you've just thought to mention it?'

'There was no need. We were managing so well with the night raids that I decided to keep this notion in reserve. And a good thing I did, for now we need it. It really is a splendid plan, one of my best!'

Judith tried not to notice the way in which Adam had promptly claimed the idea as his own, when she guessed it had come entirely from the lawyer.

'Well, am I not to hear about it?' she asked.

'Of course you are! I tell you it's masterly. It will sweep the drainers from the fen quicker than anything else we've done, and be safer and less tiring for us, too. All we need to do is turn the tables on them.'

'As simple as that?' Judith's eyes widened in mock astonishment. 'I wonder we didn't try it at first and save ourselves weeks of effort!'

'There is more to it than that. I've no illusions it will be easy—but it will be effective. I'm sure of it.' Adam spoke quickly, an almost over-eager note in his voice.

Judith regarded him quizzically. There was something strange in his manner that she could not fathom.

'Am I never to know the details?' she prompted.

'Indeed you are! We must get out on to the fen ahead of them for a change, setting traps and snares for them before they get there. With the poachers and wildfowlers we've got among our number, we should be able to devise some rare contraptions—they wouldn't take much time or effort to set up. But they would be useless if we don't know where the drainers intend to dig next . . .'

'So you will need to know their plans first. How do you propose to find out about those?' asked Judith.

Adam was silent for a moment, as though he were reluctant to give an answer.

'I was hoping we might rely on you for that,' he said at last.

'How so?'

Adam answered her with a question.

'Does the Dutchman still sniff after you?'

'No man sniffs after me! I'm not a bitch on heat!' retorted Judith.

'Does he still try to woo you? Come a-courting? Sing beneath your window? What does it matter how I put it—is the Dutchman still interested in you?'

'Hadn't you best ask him that?' Judith was suddenly wary.

'There are many questions to which he holds the answers, besides that one.'

'Then why did you ask? What is it that you want of me that you are so reluctant to put into words?'

'I need to get into the Dutchman's house, to search it. He's sure to have papers and such there, giving his plans for the draining of Hanser Fen.'

'And you expect him to stand meekly by and let you?'

'No. Which is where you come in . . .'

'Oh?' Judith's wariness had changed to distinct unease. For a dread second she was afraid that Adam had heard something of her visit to the Dutchman's house. But his next sentence drove all such fears away.

'I want you to lure him from home.'

'What!'

'Don't look so horrified. Hear me out. We're agreed that I must search his house, aren't we? And I can't do that while he is there. There is one person who can persuade him to leave, and that is you.'

'But that's nonsense! He'd never——'

'Come, love, no mock modesty. We both know that he would dandle after you, given half a chance. We'll give him that chance. Surely your nimble brain could think of some reason for meeting him?'

'No, I couldn't!' said Judith, then broke off. She still had Tildje's clothes to return, and that wretched book.

Adam noted her change of expression and didn't believe her.

'Think of it,' he urged. 'I'm sure something will come to you ... And once inside his house you could drop a hint to him that you're longing to go to—to the Midsummer Fair over at Wellham, say. My guess is he'll jump at the chance.'

'Wellham? Why on earth should I want to go there? It's miles away from here.'

'I hear the Fair's a merry enough thing. And as for the distance, the farther the better. It will take you a whole day to get there and back, giving us long enough to search the place and be clear away before your return. Also, you would be unlikely to meet anyone you know so far from home.'

'Adam, I could never do such a thing!'

At first, Judith had not taken him seriously, but now she was beginning to realise that he was in deadly earnest. Hastily she cast around for excuses.

'I can't go gallivanting about the countryside with that man. Surely you must see that? You, who are so convinced that he is in league with the Devil!'

'You should be safe enough if you carry that bit of the Scriptures I wrote out for you. Believe me, I do not like this any more than you do, but the more I think of it the more it seems the best way. By your action you would be saving our efforts, maybe even our lives. Most of all, you would be playing a major part in saving our fen. That's what you've always wanted. At least, that's what you've always *said* you wanted.'

Judith ignored this last barbed statement.

'No, I won't do it!' she said. 'I won't even consider it! It's too deceitful!'

'Deceitful? That's a poor excuse when you might save some poor Sedgewick man from being injured. Besides, when have we had to be so considerate towards one of Sir Walter's toad-eaters?'

'Don't ask it of me, I beg you! I'd play the part badly and spoil everything. And I know Aunt Ketty would disapprove.'

'Do you have to tell her anything about it?' Adam gave a sigh of resignation. 'I thought you wanted to do something for us; you've spoken about it often enough. Yet here is a chance where only you can serve, and you develop a tender conscience. I suppose I could ask Susan Osborne, she'd be willing enough I dare say—but I've little hope of her succeeding. It's you that plaguey Dutchman's sweet on, and has been ever since he set foot here.'

He sat very still, his face turned away from her, reproach in every line of his body. Suddenly he said, 'There's nothing for it, then, is there? I'll ask Susan. Don't blame me if the plan falls apart and some of us end up in Ely jail—or on the gallows. Susan would try her hardest, I know she would—but she isn't you. With you baiting the trap we would be certain of success. We could be in, do our search, and be out again without stirring the dust. But you won't do it, so there's an end to it! Even if—— '

'Very well, I'll do it!' Judith cried in desperation.

Every word he spoke had been a hammer blow to her already sore conscience, and she could not bear it. Here, perhaps, was a chance to make amends. It would certainly serve as a bitter penance.

Adam, however, did not notice her stricken expression as he flung his arms about her and swung her round.

'Sweetest Judith, I knew I wasn't mistaken in you,' he said setting her on her feet again. 'In fact, I'm very glad you proved so reluctant. If you had fallen in with my plan too eagerly I'd have been suspicious that that long black streak of a Dutchman had replaced me in your affections!'

He meant it as a joke, but Judith had to fight not to wince openly.

'He—the Dutchman—has a housekeeper,' she pointed out, eager to turn the conversation to practicalities.

'So I hear... Never fear, we'll deal with her easily——'

'You'll not harm her?'

'Of course not! When have I been an attacker of women? No, we'll find some way of getting her out of the house, too, so that we can have a good look round undisturbed. I promise you, the Dutchman won't know we've been.'

'You speak of "we". You aren't going alone?'

'No, that wouldn't be prudent. I thought I'd take a couple of the lads to stand guard, and maybe a couple more to help search—not many.'

'You will need men who can read, then, so they can recognise what they are looking for.'

'If I can find any in the village.'

'Peter Renshaw has some knowledge of reading.'

'What, that soft...' Adam, seeing the look on her face, decided that he had tried her temper enough for one day. 'Very well, I'll ask Peter Renshaw to be one of the number.'

The idea that gentle, reasonable Peter would be in the party comforted Judith, but only a little. As for her own part in the venture, she was filled with a sick dread every time she thought of it. It threw her into a mood of permanent despondency, that caused Aunt Ketty to glance at her anxiously from time to time. Her aunt never asked the reason and she never confessed. A dozen times a day she wished she had not agreed to take part, but she had given her word to Adam and would abide by it.

The need for her to make a move grew more urgent. Not only was Midsummer Day approaching at an uncomfortable speed, but out on the fen the villagers were proving no match for the drainers, who were gaining ground each day. Already the difference could be marked in the new swiftness of the river currents, and several shallow meres and marshes had dried up completely for the first time anyone could remember, their brackish waters having run off into newly dug ditches.

More than once Judith tried to make the effort, but every time Aunt Ketty saw her putting the book, along with Tildje's clothes, into a basket she would protest, 'Why take it back now, my lamb? We haven't finished it. I declare that if I don't find out soon how Sir Bevis got out of that last sorry pickle, I'll be wondering about it until my dying day. The Dutch lad didn't say he wanted it back urgently, did he?'

Judith had to admit that he had not, noting how, as Aunt Ketty grew more engrossed in the story, her references to Maarten van de Scheldt became more amiable. No longer was he referred to curtly as 'the Dutchman'. He was now 'the Dutch lad' or 'Master van de Whatshisname'.

As she opened the book yet again to read a further episode of the tale, Judith knew that she was only too glad to fall in with her aunt's wishes. The longer she could put off that dreaded visit the better. On the other hand she was reluctant to touch the smooth leather binding or open the pages, for they reminded her too strongly of Maarten himself. The fine quality of the paper held a ghost of his tobacco smoke, and the thought that his hands had touched these same leaves, his eyes had read the same words, aroused in her feelings she fought hard to suppress.

At last, though, the tale was finished, and all of Judith's excuses for further delay disappeared. One June morning she set off towards the old Fen Reeve's house, her basket clasped firmly in her hand. The air was fragrant with the scent of woodbine and dogrose in the thickets, and a lingering freshness still haunted the stubble of the cutting fen. Yet Judith noticed none of it. Her mind could only dwell upon the distasteful business ahead of her.

When she arrived at the house she hesitated. It took all her resolve to knock at the door. Presently she heard

Tildje's felt-shod feet shuffle along the passage. To her mingled relief and trepidation she was shown straight into the room where she had painted the bird. Maarten was there in his shirt-sleeves, busy at his desk.

He looked up, and she wished his face did not show such genuine pleasure at the sight of her.

'So, you have come back again,' he said, rising to his feet.

'Only to return Mistress Tildje's clothes and your book.' Judith answered in what she prayed was something near her normal voice. 'My aunt and I enjoyed the story, and we thank you.'

'Then you shall have another.'

'Thank you, no,' she said abruptly, then added, 'It's a busy time of the year; I've no leisure to read at present.'

He looked at her with a glint of amusement in his green eyes.'

'That's a pity, for I've already picked out a book I'm certain you would enjoy. See, here it is.'

He handed her a copy of *The Shepheardes Calendar*.

Dutifully she turned the pages until her attention caught an illustration. It was beautifully engraved, far more skilfully executed than any of the stiff little woodcuts on the ballad sheets she occasionally bought from the pedlar. Almost hungrily her eyes began to take in the intricate lines.

'I thought that would interest you.' Maarten could not keep the triumph from his voice. 'There are more further on in the book. Let me show you.'

He leaned across, his arm touching her, his fingers closing over hers as he made to turn the pages. In that instant the tricks and the subterfuge that she had been planning for days to bring the talk around to the subject of the Wellham Fair withered away, and she felt herself being drawn towards him. The sensuous, heady attraction she had experienced on her last visit began to overcome her, and it was only with a tremendous effort that she managed to recollect her mission.

Pulling herself away, she went over to the window, putting as much distance as she could between herself and Maarten.

'It is indeed beautiful,' she said, taking care to gaze out at the garden and not at him. 'You are fortunate to own so many fine books. But I must decline the loan of any more.'

'Then, if you won't take a book, let me call for some wine. I can't let you walk all the way back to the village without your taking some refreshment.

Judith's first reaction was to refuse. All she wanted was to complete her assignment and get away as fast as possible. Then she reconsidered. It would be much easier to introduce the subject of the Midsummer Fair into the conversation if she had a glass of wine in her hand.

However, when Tildje entered, carrying a tray, it bore not only wine but an iced cake. The somewhat crumbled pink sugar surface bore strange words picked out in white.

In spite of herself Judith was intrigued.

'I've never seen a cake like that before,' she observed. 'What do the words say?'

'I'm not surprised that you have never seen its like because it is a Dutch cake. My mother sent it, and my sisters too, of course. That's why the message on the top says "Our Dear Maarten".'

'Oh...' She found the homely gift, with its simple message, strangely moving. The purpose of her visit suddenly seemed doubly deceitful.

'Your family must miss you,' she said.

'Of course.' He smiled. 'I know they don't forget me. My two young sisters were devoted enough to make this shirt for me. They are so fond of me they must do a sleeve each. Unfortunately they were not so devoted that they could agree on the measurements. Look.' He stretched out his arms to reveal that one sleeve was a good three inches longer than the other. 'Ach, I've got ink on it already! They will be angry with me if they find out,' he observed.

'I fancy you aren't the dreadful tyrant towards them that you would have me believe,' said Judith, wishing that she had not encountered this intimate domestic aspect of Maarten's life.

'Perhaps not,' he agreed with a grin. 'Let me help you to some cake and wine.'

'But the cake was meant for you.'

'It was meant for me to share,' he insisted, cutting her a piece.

It was delicious cake, rich in eggs and butter. It had taken much loving care to make such a confection, and great pains to have it transported across the German Sea. Judith tried hard not to think of the qualities that had inspired such devotion. If she started to regard Maarten as a caring son and an affectionate brother then she knew her mission was doomed.

She finished the last crumbs of the piece of cake, even though it had lost its savour for her.

'That was excellent,' she said, her voice formally polite. 'Was it made for your birthday?'

'No, for our *kermis*. That's a special celebration rather like your English fairs, but much more exciting.'

Judith almost choked over her wine. Such an opening—such a chance! It was almost too good to be true!

'It sounds an interesting festival,' she said. 'Does every town have one?'

'Aye, and just about every village as well. Large places, such as Amsterdam, have two; everyone enjoys them, rich and poor alike. It's a time for families to get together for a holiday and enjoy themselves. There are entertainments, music and dancing, and feasting too. Oh, how we feast! Herrings, smoked eels, special *kermis* cakes like this one, and many other delicacies you can't get in England. Of all things in Holland, with the exception of my family, I think I miss the *kermis* most.'

Judith looked at his face, alight with the memory of past pleasures. It made her task no easier to discover that he was homesick. But there was no going back for her.

'You Dutch don't have all the good celebrations,' she pretended to protest. 'Our fairs can be good too. The one held on Midsummer Day at Wellham is really famous. It's judged to have the finest music for miles around. There will be singing and dancing in the streets right until dusk. They say that you can hear the music and laughter a full two miles away.'

'You have been to this fair?'

'Alas, no. It's a place I've always longed to visit, but it is some distance from here, and my aunt does not care for the journey.' She put as much yearning in her voice as she dared.

'What of your sweetheart, the foxy-haired Adam? Won't he take you?'

'Adam Digby doesn't care for music or dancing.'

'Digby? His name is Digby? Is that a common name in these parts?'

'No, I don't think so. Why?' Judith was alarmed at this sudden turn in the conversation.

'I just thought that I had come across it somewhere... Perhaps it was in London.' Maarten was silent for a moment then, to Judith's relief, he said, 'And how do you get to the fair at Wellham?'

'By boat would be the simplest way. It's on the river, towards Lynn.'

'And you wish to go?'

'Aye, but it's too far on my own.'

'Suppose someone else took you. Another man. Would your Adam object?'

He was taking the bait. She could hardly believe it.

'I don't care whether he does or not! If he won't take me then he can scarcely complain if I go with someone else, can he?' Somehow she managed get a defiant, aggrieved note into her voice, as though she had fallen out with Adam.

That was obviously the interpretation Maarten put upon her reply, for his eyes glinted with humour. To Judith's regret there was something else in his expression—she feared it was hope.

'I will take you!' He spoke with all his old forthrightness.

She longed to cry, 'Yes!' and get the whole dreadful business over swiftly, but she knew that she had to play her part convincingly.

'Indeed you won't!' she retorted.

'Why not?'

'Because it would not be proper, being alone with you.'

'You are alone with me now. You've been alone with me before——' Maarten stopped abruptly, the colour rising in his face, and Judith knew he was recalling the last occasion when they had been in this very room together.

'Judith,' he said, his voice low and appealing, his arms reaching out to her. 'Judith——'

'No!' She backed away from him. 'No, that is the very reason why I cannot go with you!'

She heard herself speak the words and wondered if she had gone mad. Wasn't it exactly what she wanted? To lure Maarten? To entice him? Oh, why had she agreed to do this awful thing!

'I'm sorry!' Maarten let his arms fall to his sides. 'I promise that won't happen again. Please say you will come with me to the fair. Please!'

She turned her face away from him, not only because she did not want to see the tenderness in his expression, but because she was afraid he would see the deceit in her own.

'It would be foolishness.' She was appalled at the coyness in her tone.

'Then be foolish for once.'

She paused, pretending to consider, when all the time there was only one answer that she could give.

'Very well,' she said at last.

There, it was done! She had set herself upon a path of deceit and intrigue. She should have felt proud and happy to be aiding Adam in the fight to save Hanser Fen, yet as she trudged home once more from the Fen Reeve's old house she knew that she had never felt more wretched in her entire life.

CHAPTER NINE

JUDITH prayed earnestly for something to prevent her from going to the fair at Wellham. Perhaps she would fall sick, the festivities would be cancelled because of the parlous state of the country, or even a great thunderstorm might make travelling impossible. It was to no avail. Midsummer Day dawned fine and warm, and she had never been in better health. No hindrance at all presented itself. She had to go.

Aunt Ketty made no objection to her proposed visit to Wellham. Her only stipulation had been that she should be home before dark. Nevertheless, the old lady knew something was amiss. She was not taken in by Judith's vague reply to her query about who else was going. Seeing the troubled look on her aunt's face, Judith was hard put to it not to blurt out the truth, and she was obliged to hurry from the cottage before she ruined the whole enterprise.

Maarten did not hear her approach, for he lay sprawled nonchalantly in his boat, his hands behind his head, whistling soundlessly. He was dressed in a fine coat of green broadcloth and a very handsome tabby waistcoat with silver buttons. Divested of his usual sombre attire, he looked a different person from the serious Dutchman who controlled the drainers with such authority. The smile with which he greeted her was almost boyish in its delighted anticipation. There was also a ray of deeper happiness there that Judith tried not to see. She hated herself for being its cause and making him so uncomfortably vulnerable.

'You're in good time. Splendid!' he said, leaping to his feet, setting the boat rocking perilously. 'Now we can have a good, long day together.'

To Judith the day already seemed interminable. Aloud she said, 'Yes, it would be a shame to waste time. Here,

take the basket, if you please. I've brought us some food,
and a bottle of my aunt's blackberry wine.'

She meant to step into the boat unassisted, as she was
accustomed to do, but he leapt on to the bank and
handed her in, at once attentive and protective. Judith
was not used to such behaviour—Adam had known her
far too long to play the gallant—and she found herself
pleased by the courtesy. It made her feel like a fine lady
to be so cherished. But then she remembered the implications of being cherished by Maarten, and sat down
heavily.

'To your oars, sir!' she cried with forced gaiety.

Grinning like a schoolboy, Maarten did as he was bid.
He enjoyed rowing, so much was evident from the
expression on his face as he pulled on the oars, and there
was an easy competence about his movements. His coat
was soon discarded and, with the warm breeze ruffling
his thick straw-coloured hair, Judith had to acknowledge
that this carefree, relaxed Maarten was likely to cause
quite a few female heads to turn. She was bound to be
an object of envy to every woman with eyes in her head.

If only they knew, she thought disconsolately.

Judith, too, wanted to appear casual and at ease, but
try as she would she could not manage it. She sat rigid
and upright, her tongue seemingly cloven to the roof of
her mouth, unable to think of anything to say. The silence
between them felt as though it would go on for ever,
until, at last, Maarten shipped his oars.

'You regret that you've come,' he said, as the boat
drifted on the current. 'You would like to go back.'

'Why do you say that?' she demanded.

'Because it's written on your face. It's all right. I understand. You have quarrelled with your sweetheart, and
so, to make him angry you keep company with the worst
person you can think of—the plaguey Dutchman! But
now that your anger has cooled you are having second
thoughts.'

'If that's what you believe, I wonder you brought me,'
Judith protested.

'For a long time I have been envious of that Adam
of yours. I didn't see why he should not be jealous of

me, just once.' He smiled a bleak little smile. 'Never fear, I'll not hold you to your word. We'll go back.'

Dipping one oar in the water, he began to turn the boat.

'No, that's not how it is at all!' cried Judith, and she thought how ironic it was that those would, mostly likely, be the only honest words she would speak all day. 'If you please, I wish to go to Wellham Fair with you,' she said more quietly.

'You are sure?'

'Yes, I am sure.'

'Then so be it.'

Maarten turned the boat once more into the current, but it was some time before the puzzlement left his eyes and his holiday mood returned.

The nearer they got to the little town of Wellham the greater the traffic grew on the river, as other folk beside themselves made their way to the fair by boat. Among such a throng, with so much to notice and comment upon, Judith began to feel her tension lessen. The conversation flowed more easily, so that by the time they had found a place to tie up for the day she was confident that she might make a passably agreeable companion.

Maarten surprised her. She had seldom seen a man set about pleasure with a greater concentration. From the moment his feet touched the riverbank he seemed determined to enjoy himself, no matter what. There was not a side-show they did not visit—from the two-headed sheep to the deadly serpent from Araby—and no delight they did not sample, whether it was sticky twists of barley sugar or gilded gingerbread. Maarten proved to have a very sweet tooth, and they acquired a formidable collection of sweetmeats in their journeying about the booths.

Judith found that such constant variety did help, but time and again her mind was drawn back to why she was at this fair with Maarten. Then misery would settle in the pit of her stomach like a clenched fist.

'This is a good fair,' Maarten remarked suddenly. 'But where is the music you promised me? Come, I wish to dance.'

Judith had shamelessly exaggerated the quality of the music at Wellham. In fact, until that day she had not known if the little market town possessed so much as a lad with a penny whistle. Much to her relief, she thought she heard the beat of a tabor above the cries of the cheapjacks.

'I think it's this way,' she said, pulling a willing Maarten across the town square to a patch of green.

She was in luck. In the shade of a large oak a band of musicians, bravely decked with flowers in their hats and ribbons at their elbows and knees, was just beginning to strike up a tune. On the grass the sets were already made up for the first dance. As she stood watching the people dancing and laughing she could not help thinking that in other circumstances she would have been truly enjoying herself. The music was lively and she dearly loved dancing. She knew that she was looking her best in her Sunday gown of periwinkle blue, and her escort was one of the most well-favoured fellows at the fair. What more could she want? Only that things were different, and that she was not playing this miserable charade!

The music soon came to an end—too soon for a ruddy-faced farmer in the nearest set.

'We'll have that again!' he demanded cheerfully.

'Who says so?' The tabor player wanted to know.

'A jug of ale for you merry lads says so!' The farmer fetched a coin from his breeches pocket and sent a small boy scurrying to the nearest inn. Then, as the musicians began to tune up he called to the onlookers, 'What are you waiting for, all you with two sound legs? There's no fun to be had gawping when you can dance.'

'The fellow's right,' said Maarten. 'I'm eager to see if my Dutch feet can dance to an English tune. Shall we join in?'

He did not wait for Judith's reply, but seizing her hand led her on to the green.

She was not loath to go. Any activity that helped the time to pass was welcome.

Maarten's determination to enjoy himself extended to joining in the sets and the measures of the dancing place. He proved no great dancer, but he was agile and quick to learn, so they got through their paces very creditably. As dance followed dance it was no coincidence that whichever set contained the Dutchman was the one that rang with most laughter when things went wrong. Even when one entire set finished in a dusty and undignified heap on the ground because of one of his mistakes it was all very good-humoured.

Judith was surprised to find her own laughter genuine as she extricated herself from the tangle of limbs and brushed herself down. Half of the day was already gone, and it had passed better than she could have hoped. Perhaps her worries had been for nothing—after all, Adam had promised to be careful in his searching. Maybe Maarten might never suspect that his house had been entered. She began to relax, and even permitted herself to enjoy the dancing.

Her downfall was swift and totally unexpected. She and the Dutchman were at opposite ends of the set, separated temporarily by the measures of the dance. As she waited to be swung down between the twin rows of dancers she happened to glance towards him. Maarten smiled at her. That was all. One single, solitary smile. But it was a smile so charged with emotion that Judith stood rooted to the spot. The unswerving adoration in his expression made her catch her breath. There was no hint of his usual flirtatious nonsense, there was only genuine, unflinching love. No one had ever looked at her in such a way before. Judith was held by his gaze; for her the music of the dance receded, the raucous sounds of the fair ceased to exist. From deep inside her came an instant response, a sensation of complete and utter happiness, that welled up from the depths of her heart. It was as if the most wonderful thing in the world had just happened to her.

An answering smile slowly spread across her face, lighting her features with a glow of absolute joy. It took a moment for the significance of her reaction to register. How could one smile, one look affect her so? There was only one solution. She was in love with Maarten!

How long she had been fighting the fact, she did not know. She could not even tell when the first uncomfortable attraction she had felt for him had toppled over

the brink into full-blown love. All she knew was that
she loved him. It was no use trying to pretend that it
was his foreign ways or worldly manners. It went deeper
than that. It was the man himself she loved. She had
thought she loved Adam—she still did, but it was very
different from the intense emotion she now felt.

As if from a long distance off she heard voices
shouting, and with a jolt she realised that they were
shouting at her. Her new partner in the dance, a gangling
lad with a bad complexion, was frantically trying to
manoeuvre her to their place at the bottom of the set,
while the other dancers noisily attempted to break into
her reverie.

'Never mind, my pretty, young Luke'll get you back
to your sweetheart before some other wench runs off
with him,' called the ruddy-faced farmer. Then he added
wistfully, 'My, but I'd give a year's harvest to have a
pretty lass look at me in such a way again!'

To the accompaniment of laughter a scarlet-faced
Judith scurried down the set with more haste than style.
But Maarten was waiting there for her, his arms open
wide. She went to him, content to be enfolded by him,
to allow him to swing her round in the dance, anything,
so long as she was close to him. And all the time he
gazed down at her, not speaking, but with a face so alight
with love that words were not necessary.

With one accord they left the green at the end of the
dance, and wandered hand in hand along the riverbank.
As the sounds of the fair began to recede Judith knew
that she was suffering from some form of lunacy, but
she was past caring. This was the only day she would
ever spend with Maarten—it was not even that, for it
was long past noon. Half a day's happiness was not much
to ask, surely? With a resolution she never knew she
possessed she shut her mind to Adam, to Sedgewick, to
her normal everyday life. She concentrated only on
Maarten, resting her head against him, and feeling his
arm steal about her waist. They found a quiet spot
shrouded by willows in a forgotten backwater. The only
witnesses were a pair of dabchicks, foraging at the water's
edge, as Maarten laid down his coat upon the grass for
Judith, then flung himself down beside her. Then, and

only then, did he take her in his arms properly and claim her mouth with his.

'This is madness, of course,' he said softly as her fingers traced the line of his chin.

'Undoubtedly,' she answered, and they both laughed because it was so unimportant.

Her hair came unbraided and tumbled down across her shoulders. Maarten twisted a strand about his fingers before gently brushing it back. His lips were soft and insistent on the base of her throat, sending shivers of pleasure along her spine. Slowly his hands moved across her, following the swell of her breasts until he found the laces of her bodice and began to unloose them.

'For a man who has never had time to wed you're very expert,' she teased.

'I never said I had no time for aught else, though,' he pointed out.

She tried to retort, 'Philanderer!' but he had pulled her gown free of her breast and the word was lost in her sharp intake of breath as she felt his touch on her flesh. Her response was immediate and passionate as she clung to him, her body throbbing with emotions too powerful to control.

Her whole world had suddenly become encompassed by Maarten alone, by the weight of his body against hers, by his urgent need of her, but most of all by his love. Her lips savoured the warm, salt taste of him as her mouth explored his neck, his shoulders, his chest. Her senses were aware of the bands of hard sinews beneath his white skin as their bodies craved closer and closer contact, until, at last, they fused together in an explosion of love.

Afterwards, drowsy and overcome by a languorous serenity, Judith felt that she had never experienced such a sense of completeness, of happy fulfillment. She gazed up at the delicate green lace of the willow tree etched against the blue sky, at the elderbush that still bore its creamy clumps of blossom. She imprinted it all on her memory so that she could treasure this one perfect, beautiful moment within herself for ever.

With a contented sigh, Maarten propped himself up on one elbow and, brushing away a stray curl from her cheek, said, 'Judith Pentelow, I love you.'

'So I should hope!' Fondly she pulled his face down so that she could kiss him. 'I'd be most concerned to find that you behaved in such a way with a wench for whom you had only a passing fancy.'

'And what of you?'

'I?' She still held his face between her hands. 'What can I say that would explain how I feel now? That this is the most wonderful part of the most wonderful day of my life is inadequate. I would need new words to describe it, words that no one else has heard or understands, save only you, for I would say them to you alone.'

Maarten leaned down and began covering her eyelids and her cheeks with soft kisses.

'But until we invent these new and wondrous words we must make do with the old ones, I fear,' he whispered.

'There speaks a practical man,' replied Judith, then she amended it with a smile to, '*My* practical man.'

'Aye, ever yours, while I've breath left in my body— and beyond, if God be willing. All I wish to know is, do you love me in return?'

'Yes, oh yes!'

'Then, what need have we for new words? Those say all we need.' Her kisses put an end to his talking for a while, but when he spoke again his tone was serious.

'There are other things we must talk of, though,' he said. 'What of that fellow Ad——'

Judith's hand swiftly touched his lips to silence him.

'No!' she begged. 'Let's not talk of such things now, today. This is our special time, yours and mine. It's perfect. Nothing must spoil it.'

'You're right!' He enfolded her in his arms and drew her close again. 'Such matters can wait for another day. We have enough to occupy us here, with just the two of us.'

'Just the two of us,' echoed Judith. 'The world is naught to us, not today.' And she put her arms about him, clinging tightly to him. Her fragile happiness had teetered precariously on the brink of destruction for a moment, and it took a while for her to push back the difficulties that suddenly loomed about her like fearsome monsters. Gradually, though, the sensuous pleasure of Maarten's closeness and the growing insistence of his caresses once again filled her mind, and to the exclusion of all else she gave herself up to her love of him...

As she lay indolently beneath the willow trees, Judith's thoughts dwelt solely on the gentle, tender man whose arms now held her. She wanted to know about his life in his own country, his family, his friends.

'Who was she?' she asked suddenly.

'Who was whom?' Maarten turned his head and lazily kissed her on the ear.

'The girl you wanted to marry. The one whose father refused to give his consent.'

'You remembered that?'

'I remember everything you've told me about yourself,' Judith replied, realising with a shock that it was true.

'Why do you want to know?'

'Because I'm curious. I want to know everything about you.'

'I thought you had no wish for the world to intrude on us today? Besides, I'm a very boring subject.'

Maarten seemed far more interested in nibbling the lobe of her ear.

'Nothing about you is boring to me,' Judith insisted, punctuating her words with kisses. 'Particularly not your other women.'

'My other women?' Maarten fell back with a laugh. 'You make me sound a real libertine.'

'For all I know, you are!'

Maarten grinned, and his hold tighten round her. 'If that is what you think then I fear you are doomed to disappointment. It is true that in my youth I wished to marry—the daughter of a glove merchant, since it interests you—and I confess I have not lived the life of a monk, but a libertine is an exaggeration.'

'Was she pretty, this glove merchant's daughter?'

'Of course. Would I love a maid who was plain?'

He was teasing, yet Judith was startled by the pang of jealousy that assailed her.

'And—and do you ever see her now?' she asked hesitantly.

'Yes, indeed . . . She and her husband live not far from us. I saw her walking with her children the day before I sailed for England and she looked...' Maarten paused, his eyes bright with mischief.

'Fat and dowdy?' supplied Judith hopefully.

'She looked delightful.' He tried to keep his face serious but failed miserably. Laughing, he showered her face with kisses. 'Oh, Judith, my Judith! You've no notion of how happy I am that I didn't marry the glove merchant's daughter. If I had I could not be lying with you like this, kissing you like this, loving you like this...'

Her momentary disquiet calmed, Judith reached out to him and drew him close, too unaccountably near to tears to speak, or to tell him how much she loved him in return.

For a while they lay silent, enfolded in each other's arms. The sweet scent of the elderflowers and crushed grass hung on the drowsy air, the soft cadence of the bees working the flowery canopy above them providing a constant buzzing chorus. Half-suspended between wakefulness and sleep, Judith knew that nothing in her life would ever surpass this moment for beauty and love and complete happiness. She felt as though she were drowning in sweet contentment, and she was savouring every second.

'What are you thinking of?' Maarten asked softly.

'Of the day when I took shelter in your house. The day of the thunderstorm.'

'What day? What thunderstorm?'

'Surely you remember it?' Judith half sat up and looked down at him in alarm. 'You must!'

'Not I!' Maarten shook his head gravely. 'For, as I recall, you bade me put the whole incident completely from my mind. And I always obey you, else you box my ears,' he finished, his prim expression dissolving into laughter as Judith began to pummel him.

'You wretch!' she cried. 'How I ever came to love you, I'll never know!'

'Nor will I—but I'm eternally grateful that you did.' Suddenly serious, Maarten tightened his hold on her, drawing her down until she was resting on his chest. 'I feared at one time that you would never come to care for me. There were so many obstacles barring the way.'

'Was that why you hounded me so? It seemed as though I couldn't even walk to the fowl yard without encountering you somewhere on the way.'

'Now there you give me credit for greater powers than I possess,' he said fondly. 'I wish I had engineered those meetings, but I confess that they were mere chance. Dame Fortune was smiling on us, I fancy.'

'So she was. Just think, if I hadn't gone on the fens that day, and got caught in the storm when I did—— And don't keep up your pretence that you don't remember! I give you full leave to recall every moment...If I hadn't come to you that day I might never have realised how much I'd begun to love you. For I'm sure that was the day when I first began to feel...when I began to suspect...to know that...I was already...in love with...you...'

Judith's speech had become disjointed as Maarten's fingers caressed her back, gently fondling her spine and exploring the soft expanse of her bare skin in a way that seriously disrupted her thoughts.

'I knew long before then,' Maarten's voice was no more than a whisper.

His body began to cleave to hers, hungry and passionate. Her response was immediate, answering his every move, his every demand, with a desperate intensity that was almost startling. She had never expected to be so pleasured by a man, nor to be overtaken by the urgent need to pleasure him in return. It was as though she was being consumed by some instinct, some ancient knowledge within herself that was desperate for release. When at last desire overwhelmed her, and her need for him reached limits beyond her comprehension, she knew that this was how it should be between a man and a maid—with tenderness, with compassion, but above all with love.

The shadows in their leafy refuge began to lengthen, casting a deep green glow over everything.

'The afternoon is fading,' said Maarten with a sigh.

'It can't fade!' protested Judith. 'Today is too perfect ever to end.'

'I wish it were so.' Maarten planted a kiss on the back of her neck. 'But wishing won't hold back the night; if I'm to get you home before dark we must make a move now.'

'I suppose so.' Judith was still reluctant.

'Our consolation must be that we've a long journey ahead of us.'

But to Judith that journey was still far too short. She managed to hold the world at bay for the first few miles, concentrating on Maarten as he bent over the oars, taking in the beloved lines and angles of his face, as if she were determined to draw his portrait from memory. But the first familiar landmark on their route home shattered the dream-like shell she had woven about herself. From then on reality encroached relentlessly, and she was powerless to withstand it.

'You are silent,' observed Maarten. 'Perhaps you are tired?'

'Aye, that's it.' Judith seized on the excuse.

As they drew closer to the end of their journey the fear of what would be awaiting them loomed large for her, overshadowing everything else. She had to know the outcome of Adam's raid on Maarten's house. Was it possible that it had gone exactly according to plan? That Maarten could return home and be unaware that he had had intruders? The chance was slight, she knew, but, oh, how she longed for it to be so. Then, at least, he would be ignorant of her part in it.

With each tedious mile Judith's anxiety grew along with her misery. When they reached the secluded mooring where they had started from, so many long hours earlier, she stepped ashore knowing that the most sensible thing would be to go straight home, but she was long past doing the sensible thing. She knew she could not rest until she found out exactly what had been going on at Maarten's house.

'This is where we say farewell.' Maarten took her in his arms and held her close. 'For the present——' He got no further, for she silenced him with a kiss.

'No mention of the future,' she begged, scarcely able to contain her tears.

He did not argue, but held her more tightly. It took a time before she could control herself enough to speak again.

'Maarten, can I ask a favour of you?' she whispered.

'Aye, of course, anything that's in my power.'

'It—it is in your power. It is the book you showed me not long since, the one with the pictures. I would like to borrow it after all, if I may?'

'Is that all? Can't you ask for something difficult, like my life's blood, or my right arm, so that I can demonstrate how much I love you? A book is not much of a challenge.'

'But it will do, for it will please me.' How she kept her voice sounding normal she did not know.

'Then the book it shall be. But you must come to the house for it, unless you want me to make another moonlight visit to your home?'

'No, I'll come!' Had she sounded too eager, too unconvincing?

Together they walked the short distance to the old Fen Reeve's house. As they strode along Judith slid her hand into his. The gentle pressure of his fingers told of his pleasure at the gesture.

At first sight the house seemed normal enough in the gathering dusk, there was even a thin curl of smoke rising from the kitchen chimney. Judith was almost allowing herself to hope when she saw that all the windows had been flung open so they swung free in the evening breeze. The front door stood open and a broken Delft pot lay smashed on the path. Maarten paused only to give Judith a questioning look then they both began to run.

Inside they were shocked into immobility.

'I promise you the Dutchman won't know we've been,' Adam had said.

His promise had not been worth a handful of dirt! The neat, well-scrubbed little house had been turned into a scene of utter chaos. Clothes, papers, and broken dishes were strewn everywhere.

Maarten was speechless. With Judith in his wake he strode along the passage and threw open each door.

Every room was in a similar state of turmoil. But his work-room was worst of all. The leather-bound books had been tumbled from their shelves and ripped, his beautiful picture leaned drunkenly against a chair, the canvas slashed to ribbons. Of his meticulously drawn map there was no sign.

He swung round on Judith in horrified bewilderment—but before he could speak a sound came from the room above. It was a thin wail of grief and terror.

'Ach, Tildje!' he exclaimed, and rushed upstairs, kicking aside a broken stool as he went. Judith could do nothing but follow him, feeling sick.

They found a dishevelled Tildje in one of the bedrooms. She did not look up but stayed seated. She was minus her cap and her hair was tumbled in disarray over her shoulders. In her arms she held a bundle wrapped in a shawl, and she talked to it softly in Dutch as she rocked back and forth. Quite unexpectedly she uttered another grief-stricken wail, before going back to murmuring in Dutch.

Stunned, Judith watched as Maarten dropped to his knees beside the housekeeper.

'Tildje,' he said, then when she did not respond he shook her very gently and repeated, 'Tildje!'

At last recognition came back to her shocked blue eyes.

'Mijnheer?' she said hesitantly. 'Mijnheer! Oh, Mijnheer!' Words in Dutch streamed hysterically from her lips, while Maarten listened, his face looking more and more grim.

Stirring at last from her immobility Judith made a move to get a blanket to put around the shaking housekeeper, but Maarten seized her by the wrist and pulled her down beside him so fiercely that she winced.

'Oh, you aren't leaving!' he said through tight lips. 'Say it all in English, Tildje! In English, so that Mistress Pentelow can understand!'

Tildje, however, had gone back to her rocking.

'He tried to save his mama!' She addressed the bundle in her arms. 'He is so little, but he vould not let der vicked men hurt his mama. Dey kicked him, you know!' Her eyes, wide and blank, fixed on Judith. 'But his mama vill make her darling better.'

Judith drew in her breath as Maarten gently reached out and pulled back the shawl. The bundle was too still, too quiet. As she had feared, once free of the wrapping the small silken head lolled distressingly, the neck clearly broken. Without a word Maarten replaced the covering and Tildje continued to rock, relapsing again into Dutch.

Judith still could not think of words to express her feelings. She was only conscious of Maarten's iron grip on her wrist and the blank stare of that poor woman.

Quite unexpectedly Tildje spoke up again.

'Dey come in, *Mijnheer*! Dey come in. I say "No, no," but still dey come. Five, six maybe. Dey trow tings. Dey tear tings. Dey find your money chest, and dey vould have it. I say "No" again. Dey vould have struck me but one man come. He say "No, dat bad ting. Not to touch voman. Not to touch gold".'

'This man who came to help you, what did he look like?' Judith had to know.

'Look like?' For a moment Tildje was surprised out of her grief. 'He not pretty. Very tall, very narrow, very dark hair about de face. He not pretty—but he good man. He put me in here and say "No one hurt you now. I stay by door." He bring *Mijnheer's* gold. Den he find shawl to wrap my poor darling. He good man. Der only one.'

Judith's heart was heavy enough already, but now it sank further. She had hoped it might have been Adam who had helped Tildje, but from the housekeeper's description it was Peter Renshaw. How typical of Peter to speak out against the whole sorry business. He was the only one who had acquitted himself creditably. For the rest—and she included herself—they had precious little to be proud of.

Maarten's fingers released their grip on her wrist, and he stood up. Judith stood up, too, and went to pull a blanket from the bed for Tildje, but with a sharp gesture of his head he indicated that he wanted her to leave the room, and quickly. As she passed through the doorway she saw him put a warm coverlet around the house-keeper and heard him speak reassuringly to her, then he left the room, closing the door behind him.

For a moment they confronted each other in silence. Judith longed to explain, to excuse her part in this sorry affair, but she did not know where to begin. Above all, she wanted to comfort him. She had never seen any man's face so ashen with distress as Maarten's was now. What could she say to ease his anguish? Nothing that he would believe.

It was Maarten who spoke first.

'I must be the biggest fool in Christendom,' he said, 'to have been taken in so. What a gullible, stupid fool!'

He spoke quietly, and that made it worse. Judith could have borne it better if he had shouted and raged.

'No!' she protested. 'That wasn't the way it was!'

'You mean it was not your task to lure me away from home, while your lover ransacked my house and attacked my housekeeper?'

'Yes—no——' She tried to answer but it was so difficult. 'Maarten, hear me out, I beg of you. They shouldn't have done this. But it wasn't all lies, truly it wasn't.'

'You are going to tell me that your talk of love was true? I give you credit for persistence, but surely even you couldn't hope to succeed with the same ploy twice. I believed you once. Aye, once too often. Let that be enough, and leave.'

'Maarten!' She had to find some way to explain, to take that agonised look out of his eyes. But he took her by the shoulders and gently but firmly turned her towards the door.

'Go!' he said. 'For pity's sake go!' He spoke with the voice of a man nearing the end of his tether.

Stifling a sob Judith hurried down the stairs. As she reached the door, however, he called after her.

'You can give Adam Digby a message from me; tell him that in my country we don't send the maids we would wed on such errands as he sent you today. We have jades and trollops who would serve just as well. I would never have used someone I loved so——' At that point his voice cracked under the force of his hurt and humiliation.

Judith could not bear it. She turned and put one foot on the bottom stair.

'Maarten, I love you, truly I do,' she cried.

But Maarten just looked down at her, his eyes a startling green in his pale face.

'Go back to your foxy-haired lover,' he whispered. 'You deserve each other.'

Then he moved out of her sight. She heard a bed-chamber door close and a bolt ram home.

'Maarten!' she cried. 'Maarten, hear me!'

But there was no reply.

She was too unhappy for tears as she made her way back home across the fen. All she could see was Maarten's face, so hurt, so vulnerable; all she could feel was a great, white-hot pain inside herself, a pain she knew matched his. A pain she feared could never be healed.

Aunt Ketty's kindness when she reached home was more than she felt she deserved. The old lady listened in silence as Judith sobbed out her story—or, at least, part of it, for she still felt unable to tell even her aunt of her love for Maarten.

'That young Adam!' Aunt Ketty snorted when she could no longer contain her feelings. 'He'd no right to put you in such a situation. It seems to me that you would not have been right whatever you did. And that young rascal had no business to make you go across your conscience. Forcing you to do such things! For make no mistake about it, that's what he did! I'll have some sharp words to say to Master Digby, that I will!'

Judith wiped her eyes and blew her nose.

'I think I must tackle him, don't you?' she said.

'Well, if you think it right. But use firm words, mind. Don't let him wriggle out of taking the blame.'

'I won't, I promise you!'

'Best see if you can get some rest now.'

Judith was reluctant to go to bed; she felt that she would never be enough at peace ever to sleep again. She steadfastly refused Aunt Ketty's offer of a sleeping-draught, however, with the result that yet again it was dawn before she closed her eyes.

She was knocking at the door of Old Place as soon as it was respectable. Marjorie wanted to turn her away, pretending that Adam was away from home. But Judith would have none of it.

'No, Marjorie!' she said, pushing her way into the cross-passage. 'I can see from your face you know all about yesterday's events. It's no use trying to let him hide behind your petticoats this time. I want to hear from Adam's own lips why he broke his promise to me, and I'll not be put off.'

Marjorie was clearly disconcerted by the firmness of her tone. She hesitated for a second, then reluctantly went to fetch Adam.

'Judith, my love, you're abroad bright and early.'

Adam sounded over-hearty as he came into the room. He strode over to kiss her, but she evaded him.

'You owe me an explanation,' she said.

'An explanation? What about?'

'You know very well!'

'Ah, yesterday's little outing. It went splendidly, thanks to you. You were magnificent! Because of you we now have an exact idea of the Dutchman's plans. It was a great success!'

'It was not! And don't try to fool me with pretty words! You promised me there would be no damage. "The Dutchman won't know we've been." That's what you said, but you didn't keep your word. You wrecked his house, destroying things that had nothing to do with the draining. Worst of all, you attacked his housekeeper.'

'I didn't attack her. It was——'

'I don't care. They were your men and you did nothing to stop them. If Peter had not been with you there's no knowing what might have happened.'

'I should have known! You've been talking to that long streak of nothing, Renshaw!'

'I have not.'

'Then how do you know all this?' Adam was suddenly suspicious.

'Because I went back to the Dutchman's house and saw everything with my own eyes.'

'Oh, so you didn't get enough of him at the fair, you must needs go home with him too. What did you intend? To spend the night in his bed?'

'Don't take that tone with me!' blazed Judith. 'You were at fault, and don't try to avoid it. I blame myself, too, for letting you bully me into falling in with your plans. I should not have been so weak, but goodness knows I'm suffering enough for it now! My conscience has never troubled me more. That poor woman! And her little dog! She really loved it, you know. Did one of your louts have to kill it?'

'It was a dog, that's all.' Adam shrugged. 'I don't see why you should be so bothered about a stupid, pampered lump of meat.'

'I'm not just bothered about the dog. I'm bothered about an innocent woman who was almost frightened out of her wits! I'm bothered that you didn't keep your promise to me! And most of all, I'm bothered because you don't appear to understand why I am upset!'

'No, I don't!' yelled Adam in a fury. 'You women are all alike. Whatever a man does is wrong! If he's strong and determined then he's being cruel. If he gives way then he's weak. You want to get rid of the drainers, don't you? Then don't quibble about my methods. First it was Marjorie whining that I'd get hurt. Now it's you mewling about how wicked and rough I've been. You make me weary, the pair of you!'

Judith stood facing him, tense and angry.

'You still don't understand, do you?' she said.

'I understand that we are quarrelling about a dead dog. Come, sweet Judith, no dog is worth that!' Adam smiled at her persuasively, the sort of smile that once would have won her over completely—but not now.

'We are quarrelling over much more than that,' she said quietly. 'I've never disagreed with you before, Adam, not really, but I do now. What you did was wrong. Frightening innocent women and killing lap-dogs isn't going to drive away the drainers, and you know it. But your broken promise—that is another matter. You knew I'd find your scheme ugly and distasteful, so to persuade me to do what you wished you gave a promise you had not the slightest intention of keeping.'

'How else would I have got you to do it?' Adam stared at her in bewilderment.

Judith gazed back at him, distress and frustration rising within her.

'Then there's nothing to be said!' she cried, and stalked away.

'Not one word or regret or apology!' she exclaimed angrily to Aunt Ketty as she recounted her meeting with Adam. 'He truly could not see why I was angry. The lies I've told—the deceit, and the suffering and humiliation it has caused—and he couldn't even say he was sorry.'

Judith was so beside herself that she was striding about the cottage parlour. She did not say that the suffering and humiliation were Maarten's, and that every hurt he felt she now felt a hundredfold.

'Maybe Adam will come round to it in time,' said Aunt Ketty.

'When? Next week? Next year? Well, I don't want him to! He can go to the Devil for all I care! I never want to see him again!'

Judith stopped pacing, realising what she had said. This was Adam she was talking about, the man she was supposed to be going to marry... marriage to Adam. For most of her life that had been her dream—now she could only think of it with misgivings. It was not just because of Maarten. She loved the Dutchman, but she knew he was lost to her. She had said she would wed Adam and she would keep her promise. In an age when arranged marriages were common she would not be the first maid whose bridegroom was not the man she loved. No, strangely enough, love—or the lack of it—had precious little to do with her trepidation. It had more to do with viewing the world differently and wanting different things.

'Oh, you'll make up your tiff with Adam before long,' said Aunt Ketty comfortably, then she saw the expression on Judith's face. In a more cautious tone she asked, 'Or perhaps this is more than just a lovers' quarrel, eh?'

'I fear so,' admitted Judith.

'Hm!' Aunt Ketty pursed her lips. 'Young Adam's not come out of this business at all well. But that's not why you are fretting yourself to the bone, is it?'

Judith shook her head.

'This Dutch lad,' went on Aunt Ketty, 'am I right in presuming that he didn't behave as he ought, either?'

'No, he didn't!' cried Judith, suddenly unable to hold back. 'But I'm glad! I encouraged him, and don't regret it one bit!'

Aunt Ketty gave a sigh.

'It's as I guessed,' she said. 'I feared that was the way the wind was blowing. Well, here's a pretty bother, and no mistake. You don't think it's because he is different from the common run of lads hereabouts? Novelty can be very appealing... But, no, I can see that's not the way of things. What do you propose to do now?'

'I don't know. I wish I did.' Judith's voice dropped to a whisper. 'One thing is certain, you needn't fear that Maarten will come a-courting. He will never come near me ever again—— Oh, Aunt Ketty, why did I hurt him so terribly, when I love him so much?'

And for the second day running, Judith, who had never readily sought refuge in tears, buried her face in Aunt Ketty's lap and sobbed out her heartbreak, until it seemed she would never stop.

CHAPTER TEN

JUDITH awoke to brilliant sunshine and wondered what o'clock it was. Then she wondered what day it was. It had been just past noon when Aunt Ketty had packed her off to bed, insisting she take a sleeping draught. Now it seemed to be close on noon again, judging by the sun. Surely she had not slept for a whole day? As she slid from the warmth of the bed her mind was still so clogged with sleep that anything seemed possible. Splashing her face with cold water revived her a little, though dressing was a slow, vague business. There was no sign of Aunt Ketty, so she took some bread from the crock and was about to cut herself some when her aunt came hurrying in, a basket on her arm.

'Oh, so you're awake at last!' she exclaimed. 'Do you feel better?'

'I'm not sure. My head seems stuffed with sheep's wool and my limbs refuse to obey me.'

'That will be my sleeping mixture,' chuckled her aunt. 'The effects will soon wear off once you've got some food inside you. Slice a bit of that bread for me while you're about it, my lamb, will you?'

'I hope you're right,' said Judith, trying to focus clearly on the loaf in front of her. 'Just at this minute I don't believe I'll ever think clearly again.'

'I'll admit I gave you a strong dose, but it was what you needed—a good long sleep. You haven't fooled me, you know. You haven't had a decent rest since goodness knows when, and I'd no intention of having you sicken with brain fever.'

Judith wanted to say that it was not her brain that was sick, it was her heart, but she felt too weary.

'Here, let me spread a bit of honey on that for you.' Aunt Ketty took charge of the uneven slice of bread,

cutting it into strips just as she used to do when Judith
was a child. 'There, get that down you. You'll feel better.'

Judith was certain she was too sleepy to eat, but after
the first few mouthfuls she really did begin to revive.
She was surprised at how hungry she felt.

'No wonder! I must have slept the day round,' she
said. 'How have you managed with the milking?'

'A couple of Peter's lasses lent a hand. We managed
well enough.' Aunt Ketty settled herself at the table and
began to eat too.

'Have I missed anything of note by being such a lie-
a-bed?' asked Judith.

'You certainly have! Such excitement! Sir Walter's
soldiers have found the powder and shot that Adam
brought from Ely!'

'Found? You mean, they were searching the village?'
The enormity of the loss penetrated Judith's still foggy
brain.

'No. That's the mystery of it. They marched into the
crypt of the church and put their hands on it straight
away. There's no doubt that someone must have told
them where it was.'

'Surely not! Maybe it was in a noticeable place, easy
to see.'

'It was not. It was in an old tomb; and not one of the
Digbys', either. Adam says he deliberately chose against
one of his family's for fear it would be too obvious. The
whole village is a-hum with it, I can tell you!'

'And no wonder! But who would betray the hiding-
place? There were precious few who knew of it. Even I
only knew it was somewhere in the church.'

'That's what everyone would like to know. It's gone
beyond careless gossip reaching the Hall. This must have
been deliberate. Yon Adam's ranting and raving and
charging about the place like a pig in a fit. I fear you'll
not see much of him today, if that's what you're hoping.'

Judith paused before she replied. She decided that she
did not want to see Adam, not that day nor in the fore-
seeable future, and the knowledge distressed her.

'I think it's best if we don't meet for a spell,' she said.

'I agree.' Aunt Ketty brushed some crumbs off her embroidered apron, and Judith suddenly realised that she was dressed in her Sunday best.

'Who have you been visiting at this time of day?' she asked.

'Oh, I just made a few calls...' Aunt Ketty continued to brush at crumbs that were long gone.

It was so unlike Aunt Ketty to be evasive that Judith stared at her.

'Surely you haven't been meeting a secret lover...' she began, then the smile died from her face as she realised the truth. 'Oh, you didn't go there—— Surely you didn't!'

'I felt I had to.' Aunt Ketty was apologetic. 'I couldn't bear to think of that poor woman alone out there after all she's been through, with only the Dutch lad to look after her. I thought she might be glad of a bit of womanly comfort, her not being among her own folk, poor soul.'

'Oh...' Judith felt ashamed, because she had given no thought to Tildje's subsequent welfare. 'How is she?'

'Much recovered, and busy packing her things. Can't get back to her own country fast enough, and I don't blame her. I'll say this for the Dutch lad, he seems very capable. Cared for her like a son, she said, from what I could understand of her. He's got a maidservant over from the Hall until he can make other arrangements.'

There was one question Judith just had to ask.

'Did you see...' No matter how she tried she could not bring herself to say Maarten's name.

'I did.'

'And how was he? Did he use you kindly?'

'Aye, he was courtesy itself and thanked me for showing consideration to his housekeeper.' She did not add that his courtesy had been chilling enough to have frozen the flames of Hell.

'But—but how was he? Truly now. I must know.'

'Very quiet, and not a drop of colour about him. You're right, lass, he's suffered a hard knock; but then, these quiet, serious men often injure more easily than they'd ever admit.'

'But he's not quiet really, and only serious sometimes. He can be very merry when he chooses, and he has a great love of music, particularly for dancing...' Judith pictured a happy, laughing Maarten at the fair, the enjoyment on his face as he danced, his helpless merriment when he created such chaos among the other dancers. At the thought of him she felt a sharp, cutting pain that could not be eased by all the remedies in her aunt's cupboard.

'Advise me. I don't know what to do,' she said. 'I love Maarten so very much, yet it is Adam I've promised to marry. It's such an awful muddle, and I'm so miserable.'

'So it seems at the moment, no doubt. But it will all work its own way out. One day...' Aunt Ketty seemed about to say something else, then changed her mind. 'The best advice I can give at the moment, my love, is the hardest to follow. Do nothing for a while. Let tempers and passions cool a little, so you can see things more clearly.'

'I suppose you're right. It would be the best course. But you're right, too, when you say it's the hardest way. Any action would be preferable to sitting still!'

'Well, I'm afraid that's exactly what you must do. You're not to lift a finger for the rest of the day. Peter's lasses are coming to help me. All you're to do is sit in the sun.' Aunt Ketty's voice was firm, and Judith knew that there was no point in arguing when she used that tone. Obediently she took a stool outside and, leaning against the cottage wall, drowsed in the warm sunshine.

Aunt Ketty had been right, the rest and sleep did help. She still carried her pain with her, but at least she was no longer weighed down by desperation. Stretching, she rose and went in search of her aunt. She found her busily hoeing between the rows of vegetables.

'I should be doing that,' she said.

'Don't worry, there will be plenty of these plaguey weeds for you to tackle tomorrow. Take advantage of your holiday while you've got it. You're looking a bit better, less like a pale cheese on a dark shelf, but see if you can get a rose or two in your cheeks.'

Judith had to laugh.

'I don't like your description of me much,' she said. 'Have you no prettier words to waste on me?'

'Not I, nor on these dratted weeds, either—— Hello, if I'm not mistaken I hear the girls coming to lend a hand.'

It was not Peter's daughters who came running down the path, however, but a small boy whom Judith recognised as one of Thomas's children.

'Good day to you, Jackie. We don't often have the pleasure of your company,' she greeted him.

'I'm looking for my father. Do you know where he is?' said the boy.

'Thomas? No, I've not seen him these several days. Isn't he at work?'

Jackie shook his head.

'Not today. He's gone after vermin, and Ma says you'd know where he'd be, seeing as you're the one who found 'em.'

'I am? I can't think what you mean. Is he after rats or polecats, or what?'

'Don't know.' The boy shrugged. 'I just know he's gone out on the fen after vermin with Master Digby and some others, and Ma wants him back. There are soldiers in the village and their horses need shoeing. Ma says he can go burning vermin any old time, but the soldiers and their silver won't stay drinking Hal Osborne's ale for ever, so he'd best get back.'

His words echoed his sharp-tongue mother so exactly that Judith grinned.

'I've still no idea what you mean. The only creatures I've had trouble with were the rats that got in among the hens. But that was before Easter, and it certainly wasn't out on the fens.'

'Judith, did the lad say "burning vermin"?' asked Aunt Ketty quietly.

'Aye, you did, didn't you, Jackie? Though what creatures apart from wasps can be cleared by burning I don't know.'

'Two-legged creatures, perhaps,' said Aunt Ketty. 'How many others were there with Master Digby and your father?'

'Nine—ten.' The boy was not sure.

'You don't need ten men to destroy a wasps' nest, nor do you need to march on to the fen to do it.' Aunt Ketty's voice was a mere whisper.

'Surely you can't mean...? Oh, no! They wouldn't do such a thing!' Judith suddenly understood what her aunt was suggesting.

'What else is there out on the fen they would consider worth burning?' asked Aunt Ketty.

'But there are women and children out there, as well as men. Adam wouldn't—— Thomas wouldn't—— They wouldn't try to burn——'

She looked down and saw Jackie listening intently. 'Tell me again! Where have your father and Master Digby gone?' she demanded.

'Out on the fen to burn vermin,' insisted Jackie. 'According to Ma, Father said you were the one to find the nest. A fine big nest,' he amended.

Judith did not want to believe it, but what other solution was there? The only 'nest' she had found out on the fens was the drainers' settlement. And one thing she knew for certain was that the ramshackle huts and the surrounding fenland would burn fiercely at this time of the year.

'Go back to your mother, Jackie,' she instructed. 'Tell her I'll go after your father myself.'

'What do you propose to do?' asked Aunt Ketty when the boy was out of earshot.

'Why, go and argue with Adam. Make him stop, of course.'

'Do you think you'd succeed? He was in a rage this morning after losing the powder and shot. And you know what he's like when he gets in one of his tempers.'

Judith knew, only too well.

'Then I must try to get to the settlement first.'

She made to set off immediately but Aunt Ketty held her back.

'I'm not happy about you doing that,' she said. 'After all they've suffered I fear they'd attack you, or use you harshly, long before you could give any warning.'

'What are we to do then?' cried Judith. 'We can't let those poor souls be burned alive.'

'No. I'll go and fetch Peter. He'll round up Toby and some of the less hot-headed men to go after Adam, to try to talk some sense into him.'

'And what am I to do?'

'There is only one place you can go for help.'

Judith guessed where her aunt meant, and she was horrified.

'No,' she cried. 'Not there. He'd never believe me. Please, don't make me!'

'I'll not make you, love...'

Judith knew that she had no alternative. She had to go to Maarten. How she was going to persuade him that she was telling the truth she did not know—but she had to try. Reluctant as she was, she set off immediately.

Her former lethargy forgotten, Judith ran until her burning lungs slowed her to a halt, then she walked for a way before running once more. Even so, the old Fen Reeve's house seemed a terrible distance away. When she did reach it, hot and weary, she was greeted by a slatternly woman who opened the door. On seeing the grubby apron and the greasy hair poking from beneath an equally grubby cap her first incongruous thought was, Oh, poor Maarten, how he'll hate being tended by such a one. But then the urgency of her mission reasserted itself.

'I must see your master,' she gasped.

'Oh, must you?' The voice and the stare were insolent.

'I've no time for games!' Judith snapped. 'Fetch your master at once!'

'He isn't here,' the woman replied.

'Then where in heaven's name is he?'

'How should I know? I in't his keeper,' retorted the woman. Then seeing the fierce look on Judith's face added, 'He's taking food to his workers on the fen.'

Her ribs were aching and her legs felt like lead, nevertheless, Judith set off in the direction the woman indicated. She decided to break away from the track. If she cut across the fen she would stand a better chance of intercepting Maarten. The trouble was that the route was dotted with shallow pools and marshy stretches. Before she had gone much further she was soaked and filthy with spattered mud, but she could not let that stop her.

When she saw the train of pack-horses ahead of her she nearly wept with relief. As she grew closer she could easily make out Maarten on a tall bay horse, and with him were two other men in charge of the animals.

One of the packmen noticed her first, and directed Maarten's attention towards her. Even at that distance she was sure she saw him stiffen with anger. He continued to ride on, but she hurried to overtake them, confronting them by standing directly in their path.

'You are confident I won't run you down,' Maarten said coldly, signalling for the train of pack-animals to stop.

'Aye...' For a while that was all her tortured lungs would let her utter. Then she managed to gasp, 'You're too much of a man to do that.'

'Too much of a fool!' Marten's face had lost none of its bleak hurt and anger. 'What is it you want?'

'The people at the settlement, they're in danger. Men are going there to set fire to the place!'

'Men from your village, no doubt, headed by your lover, Adam?' The scorn in his voice cut through her like sharpened steel.

'Oh Maarten, please believe me! I've no idea how far ahead they are. They might be there already. Please do something.'

'What mischief are you up to now? It would be better if you came straight out with it, instead of using your usual deceitful methods.'

'I'm not lying! You've got to believe me! Please...' she begged. 'Those poor people——'

'Ah, here come the embellishments to lend credence to your story. It is rather less spectacular than your last attempt to dupe me. But, then, I am a wiser man now.'

'Maarten!' she was almost screaming in her desperation to make him believe her. 'Maarten, think what you like about me. But warn those people!

'And fall into some ingenious trap set by that red-haired scoundrel?' Maarten's eyes burned with contempt. He swung his horse to one side, and would have ridden past her, but the two packmen did not move.

'Master, what if she's telling the truth?' asked the elder of the two. He spoke in the strident accent of the settlement people. 'Look at the state of her! She'd not run herself to such exhaustion for the sake of a lie, surely?'

'You've no idea what these Fenland women will do for the sake of a lie, Joshua!' Judith knew that he was trying to wound her with every word—and he was succeeding. Joshua, however, still held his ground.

'I've got a wife and four little ones at the settlement, master,' he said.

'And I've my mother and sister there,' added the younger packman.

Maarten glared at them, then, unable to withstand their anxiety, growled, 'Very well. Unload the two fastest animals and, Joshua, get you to the settlement and raise the alarm. You, Matthew, must go back to the Hall and rouse the pikemen. But don't blame me if you fall into some deadly snare.'

'We'll take care, master.' Already Joshua was unbuckling the load from a skewbald horse. 'But what of you?'

'I think I'll go across the fen to meet up with these fine upstanding men who fight women and children so valiantly. I've a word or two I want to say to Master Adam Digby, that's long overdue.'

'You mustn't do that! Not alone!' cried Judith in alarm.

'Why not?' Maarten's eyes were as cold as green glass. 'Wasn't that part of the plan, to get me by myself?'

'There is no plan!' Judith insisted. 'Please believe me, I'm not trying to trick you, truly I'm not. But don't go and face Adam and the others on your own. It's too dangerous.'

'Such sudden concern for my welfare! I'm much moved.' Maarten's voice was heavy with sarcasm.

Exhaustion had forced Judith to her knees on the muddy earth. Now she struggled to rise. Only by clutching hold of the nearest animal for support did she manage to regain her feet.

'You don't know the mood Adam is in,' she cried. 'He's so angry at losing the powder and shot. He has a fearsome temper when he's roused. He's capable of anything.'

In an attempt to restrain him she put out a hand to grasp the bridle of Maarten's horse, but he edged his mount away from her.

'I've no doubt you know your sweetheart's temper well enough,' he said icily. 'But you need not fear. I've no intention of meeting him alone. You are coming with me!'

'She's too far spent to walk,' observed Joshua.

'Very well, unload another animal!'

Maarten did not ask her if she could ride, nor did he make any attempt to help her get up on the animal. That was left to Joshua. Only when she was mounted did he rein close to her and say in a voice that was low and heavy with threat, 'I promise you, if this is another of your tricks, I'll hang for the pair of you!'

Judith was too weary to reply. She could only urge her mount forward with her aching, muddied legs, and follow him across the fen.

They had little difficulty in finding Adam and his men in that flat landscape. Adam called a halt when he saw them, making them approach him. His angry eyes raked over the pair of them. But it was to Judith that he spoke.

'What's this?' he demanded. 'Have you brought the Dutchman to help us in our day's sport?'

'This is no laughing matter,' said Judith as she slid stiffly from her mount. 'Adam, you must not do this thing. It's too cruel and barbaric.'

'It is practical,' stated Adam. 'If you wish to rid yourself of rats you destroy their nest, young and all. That's simply what we're going to do to the drainers.'

'But they aren't rats, they are Christian souls. They are people! Adam, you can't do this!' Judith pleaded.

'Can't? And who's to stop me?'

Adam turned his gaze to Maarten, his eyes glittering.

'Aye, I'll do my best to prevent you.' Maarten dismounted.

'You fancy your chances, Dutchman? One against so many?' Adam mocked.

'The odds aren't in my favour, I'll admit. But it's my hope that blows will be unnecessary,' said Maarten. 'Think what you're about, man, attempting to kill the innocent. I do not believe that you or any other Christian man could be so cold-hearted.'

'You don't believe it, eh? Yet Judith persuaded you to come. You have to admit, she has coaxing ways—as you know to your cost!'

Maarten stiffened at Adam's jibe.

'That's a score you and I will settle privately,' he said menacingly. 'But it's a score that will wait. This matter won't!' He looked round at the others in the group and his eye fell on Thomas. 'Have you killed many children?' he demanded. 'Doubtless it pleases you to snuff out their little lives. What do you do? Squeeze the breath out of the babes with one movement of your great hand, as another man might get juice from an orange? Is that how you get your pleasure?'

'It is not!' declared Thomas vehemently. 'I've never hurt a child in my life. I don't even punish my own, fearing to do them harm, me not always knowing my own strength. I leave such things to my wife!'

'Then what makes you think you can destroy women and children today?' asked Maarten quickly. 'Any of you, have you really got the stomach for such a fearful task? Go home, all of you, before there's harm done. The alarm has gone out to Sir Walter's soldiers. Leave before they get here.'

'Aye, and if you hearken to his pretty speeches you'll know what will happen. The fen will be drained and we'll be starving,' cried Adam. 'Don't listen to him. Let's get on with it!'

The men shuffled uncomfortably, gazing at the ground. All except Dewdrop Chester.

'Seems he's right about Sir Walter's soldiers,' he observed. 'Leastways, there's a body of folk coming this way.'

'Are you happy with your meddling?' Adam demanded of Judith. 'I never thought you would turn traitor to your own folk, sending for the soldiers.'

Before Judith could speak Maarten said, 'All Judith wanted to do was to save lives. I was the one who sent for the soldiers. Did you really think that you could kill and burn indiscriminately without someone trying to stop you? If so, you're a fool as well as a blackhearted villain!'

At these words Adam took a step forward, his fists clenched aggressively. It looked as though the battle would start there and then. But Dewdrop suddenly called out, 'No. It's not Sir Walter's men. It can't be, for there are women with them. If I'm not mistaken I can see your sister, Adam.'

'Marjorie?' In his surprise Adam dropped his arms.

A crowd of men and women were hurrying towards them from the village. At its head strode the stiff, upright figure of Marjorie Digby. Judith could pick out others, too. Peter Renshaw, easily recognisable because of his long skinny frame, and the squat outline of old Toby, his dog at his heels as usual. She felt quite giddy with relief. Never once had Maarten flinched, in spite of being outnumbered, but Judith knew all too well what the outcome would have been if the villagers had not arrived so promptly.

She glanced swiftly at Maarten and met his eyes. Hopefully, she managed a half-smile—but it met with no response.

The villagers were upon them now, and Marjorie strode forward until she faced Adam.

'What foolishness are you up to this time?' she demanded. 'Have you no thoughts in that addled pate of yours? Anyone would think I had nothing better to do than trip across the Fens from morn till night preventing you from getting into trouble!'

Judith had heard her use the same scolding tone of voice on Adam a hundred times when he was a small boy, whenever he had torn his clothes or broken something. But he was not a small boy now, and the circumstances were more serious than torn breeches. Adam's face grew more and more mutinous as his sister harangued him in front of his men, but Marjorie did not seem to notice. She went on.

'We've come to a pretty state of things when I've got to thank a Dutchman for saving you from your own folly. Aye, and Judith too, for this day's work would have ended with a hangman's noose as sure as fate. All I can say is the sooner you marry Judith Pentelow the better. You need a wife with some sense, for you've precious little of your own!'

Some of the men sniggered, and that proved too much for Adam.

'Oh, scoff all you like, Marjorie!' he cried, angry at having been made to look foolish. 'When have you ever taken notice of anything I say? Well, you'll have to take notice of me now. The rest of you may be lily-livered, but there's one person man enough to fight for his rights. Me! And I'm going to finish what I set out to do.'

'Don't be such an idiot, Adam lad,' said Thomas. 'No harm's been done. Let's turn round and go home.'

But Adam was now beside himself with fury. 'I wasn't an idiot when I led you against the drainers, or when I went out time and again on night raids! I wasn't an idiot when you all still had backbone enough to fight! If we hadn't been prevented we would have been at the settlement by now, and the deed done. And who prevented us? This plaguey Dutchman! Things have gone wrong from the minute he set foot on the fen. Now he's bewitched Judith so that she goes running to him with every titbit of gossip.'

'That's not so!' protested Judith. 'How can you say such a thing. This is the only time I've ever betrayed your plans. On this occasion my conscience wouldn't let me keep silent.'

'So you say!' sneered Adam. 'But my guess is that he's been getting information from you all this time by witchcraft. How else would Sir Walter's men have known where we were going to strike on our night raids, or where we kept the powder and shot? I've said all along that he's in league with the Devil. Well, if I can do naught else, I can rid the Fens of this Devil's disciple!'

As if in a nightmare, Judith saw him raise his pistol and aim it straight at Maarten. She knew him too well to believe that he was bluffing. He was going to kill Maarten!

'No!' she screamed, hurling herself forward.

She never reached Adam. She was too far away. As she fell to the ground there was an almighty roar that sent the marsh birds wheeling and crying into the sky. Then there was silence.

Winded by her fall Judith looked urgently for Maarten. He was still standing there unharmed.

'Thank God,' breathed Judith. Then she saw that his face bore a horrified expression. Incredibly, he was holding out his arms to catch Marjorie, who clutched a great gaping wound in her chest as she fell.

'Marjorie!' Adam's anguished howl was like the baying of a wounded animal as he rushed forward. He thrust Maarten aside, crying, 'Don't you dare touch her!' Then he cradled his sister in his arms, rocking her and crooning softly in a way that reminded Judith painfully of Tildje.

'Judith! Judith!' Aunt Ketty's voice broke through the nightmarish scene as she came puffing across the fen, far behind everyone else.

It was Maarten who helped Judith to her feet and said quietly, 'She is unharmed, Mistress Kettering.'

His grasp on her arm was reassuring. Judith hated for him to let go, she needed the comfort of his touch. But it was not to be. As Aunt Ketty reached them he released his hold and stood back.

'Oh, heaven preserve us!' Aunt Ketty caught sight of Marjorie's prone form lying in Adam's arms. At once the old lady tore off her apron and tried to use it to stanch the bleeding. But one look at Marjorie's waxen face told its own story.

Marjorie Digby clung on to life. Her lips moved, but it was some moments before any words were discernible.

'Mustn't stop them...the drainers...will make our fortune...' The words were faint and disjointed. 'Not Judith... It was I told Sir Walter... Lose so much if draining is stopped... Digby family never be great...again...' Marjorie loosed her last breath in a sigh.

'She's not dead!' Adam protested. 'She's not! She's not!' Then his anguished tone turned to one of desperate persuasion as he asked, 'She's not, is she?'

In answer Aunt Ketty gently closed the sightless eyes.

Adam bowed his head over his sister, still cradled in his arms, and sobbed, his whole body racked with grief. Again and again he cried, 'Marjorie! Marjorie!'

It was pitiful to watch, and Judith's heart went out to him. It was true, they had had serious differences of late. She scarcely dared to think that it might have been

Maarten lying there lifeless, but her close brush with grief
made her feel Adam's all the more. Both he and Marjorie
had been part of her life ever since she could remember,
and she could not harden her heart to him now. She
moved forward to comfort him. But suddenly his head
went up and his sobbing ceased.

'You killed her, Judith Pentelow!' he screamed. 'It's
your fault she's dead!'

'No!' cried Judith. 'No, that's not true!'

'You killed her! Murder's writ all over your face!'
Adam's voice went on and on, 'Murderer! Murderer!'

His words bore relentlessly into her head. Then, as if
from a long way off, Toby's voice cut across Adam's
hysterical screaming. 'Come, lad, let's get poor Marjorie
home with fitting respect.'

'I didn't kill her,' whispered Judith.

'No, but the poor soul had to blame someone, I
suppose.' That was Aunt Ketty.

Thomas and some of the other men lifted Marjorie's
body and began the slow, sad walk back to Old Place.
As Adam took his place at Marjorie's head he turned
and glared at Judith.

'Murderer!' he cried once more.

Judith flinched and took a step back.

Toby put a consoling hand on her arm. 'Don't take
it to heart, lass. Young Adam was certain to kill someone
before the day was out, the mood he was in.'

'I didn't even touch him. I just screamed,' Judith
insisted.

'Aye, so... And that pistol of his always did pull to
the right.' Toby was determined to comfort her.

But in spite of her protests, Judith knew very well that
it had been her scream that had distracted Adam and
spoiled his aim. She also knew that, at that range, he
could not have failed to hit Maarten if his attention had
not wavered. Perhaps it had been destined that there
would be a death on the fen that day, but the thought
did not lessen her terrible regret at her part in it.

'What was it Marjorie was muttering at the end?
Something about her telling Sir Walter,' muttered Toby.

'The poor woman's mind was wandering,' said Aunt
Ketty.

'Marjorie Digby's mind wandering when she was about to meet her Maker? I think not.' Toby was definite on that score. 'My guess is that she was trying to tell Adam something. It sounded as if she wanted him to encourage the draining of the fen, not stop it. But I don't know how that could be.'

'She had good reason,' said Maarten quietly. He had been standing back, watching but not speaking.

'You know something, Dutchman?' asked Toby.

'Aye. Mistress Digby put a deal of money into the draining. She was one of the adventurers, along with Sir Walter,' Maarten replied.

'Marjorie? Surely not!' protested Judith.

'I assure you it is so, Mistress Pentelow. I can show you the written proof in Sir Walter's papers.'

So, she was Mistress Pentelow to him now, was she? His formality gave one more blow to her battered heart, even though his voice had lost some of its coldness.

'There now! Wouldn't that be just typical of Marjorie? Bent upon restoring the Digby fortunes no matter what the cost?' Toby was in no doubt about Maarten's information. 'And so she was the one who gave the game away about our powder and shot, and all the rest.'

'I have no knowledge of that, but I think it is likely,' said Maarten.

'Aye, more than likely.' Toby nodded his head in agreement. He looked towards the cortège, which was still visible across the fen. 'We've given them a good enough start, I think the rest of us had better be getting home. We don't want to tangle with Sir Walter's pikemen for naught, do we?'

'I think I can see them on the horizon,' said Maarten. 'Perhaps it would be best if I went that way and headed them off.'

'We'd appreciate that, lad. Let's be going.' Toby took Aunt Ketty's arm and they followed the other silent villagers who were making their way home.

Judith made to follow them, but Maarten held out a restraining arm.

'One minute of your time, if you please, Mistress Pentelow,' he said. 'I owe you my thanks. You saved my life.'

Judith tried hard to catch some warmth in his words, some echoes of love, but failed.

'You owe me nothing,' she said.

'Indeed, I do, for as well as my gratitude I must give you my apologies. I doubted your word when you came to raise the alarm. I'm sorry.'

'You had reason enough for your doubts,' said Judith bitterly.

'There was more hurt pride than reason in my reluctance to act.'

For one hopeful moment Judith thought she detected a hint of emotion, but when she looked into his face he was as grave as ever.

'I must bid you farewell, Mistress Pentelow,' he said. 'I remain in your debt.'

He prepared to ride away, and Judith feared that she would never see him again.

'Then pay that debt,' she cried. 'At least call me Judith when you say farewell, not "Mistress Pentelow" as though I were a stranger!'

Maarten was in the saddle now, and he looked down at her for what seemed an eternity.

'Farewell, Judith,' he said softly. And in his voice there was a great sadness.

Judith turned and ran after Aunt Ketty and Toby, for she could not bear to see Maarten ride away from her.

There was a strange, unreal quality about the rest of the day. Neither she nor Aunt Ketty had the heart to do much and, when the animals had been attended to, they sat in the parlour talking.

'At least most of my troubles are at an end,' said Judith bitterly, as they went over the events of the day yet again. 'I've managed things beautifully, haven't I? A week ago my problem was that I had two lovers. Now, neither of them will give me the time of day. I never want to think of love again, it's too painful by half. It's easier by far to live and die a maid.'

She was close to tears and Aunt Ketty took her hand. 'You'll not do that, my lamb,' she assured her. 'You've a fine happy life ahead of you, never fear.'

'You sound very certain.'

'I am. I've known for a long time that Adam wasn't the man for you. That was the main reason I delayed matters as much as I could. Your future never lay at Old Place. In fact, your future lies away from this country altogether.'

'Away from this country?' For a moment Judith's surprise overrode her depression. 'You've seen this? You've had one of your feelings?'

'I have, the same thing, more than once, and so clear and definite ... I never saw the man you will marry, but I know he'll give you the sort of happiness few women are lucky enough to experience. And the house he'll take you to is so fine. Not grand like the Hall, but new-built and——'

'But what of the country?' Judith was not interested in the house; she wanted some hint that her future lay across the German Sea with Maarten.

'That was the strange part of it. It's a new land that I've seen, fine and fertile, but it has been hard-won from the elements. Where it is, I'm not certain, but it may be in one of those new plantations in America.'

'America!' Judith could not contain her disappointment.

'It's a fair way off, I've been told, but your journey will be worthwhile. So don't despair of the future, my love. Times are hard for you just now, but things will right themselves soon.'

'Thank you, Aunt.' Judith tried to sound cheerful. But if her future did not include Maarten she did not see how she could ever be happy again.

The village of Sedgewick St Peter heard the news that the country was now officially embroiled in a civil war with numb acceptance. Everyone was still too stunned by the tragedy of Marjorie's death to respond to the knowledge that King Charles had raised his standard at Nottingham, declaring his intention to fight Parliament. Even though it meant that the draining of Hanser Fen must stop, it made little impact.

After Marjorie's funeral, however, the wider events became too insistent to ignore. On the same day that the labourers were reported to be moving out of the Fenland settlement Sir Walter rode off with his trainband to join the King. Already the young men of Sedgewick were preparing to fight for Parliament.

Judith had seen nothing of Adam, but she had not expected to. She had not even deemed it prudent to go the funeral, for fear of unleashing another outburst. Then one morning there came news that he had gone.

'His bed was empty, his horse taken from the stable,' announced Aunt Ketty. 'Not one word did he say to anyone. No instructions left about the running of Old Place. He's gone off to the war and, seemingly, he's no wish to come back!'

With Adam's departure Judith felt that part of her life had departed too, the happy childhood days when she had followed wherever he had led. She preferred to block her mind to more recent memories of a ruthless, determined Adam—an Adam she could never have loved, unlike the boisterous, carefree companion of her girlhood.

What she wanted most now was news of Maarten, but none came. The digging on the fen had ceased, and she no longer caught casual glimpses of him across the broad levels of the rough grazing land.

Even so, there was not a waking hour of any day when he did not creep into her thoughts. She tried hard to picture him happy—at Wellham Fair, or lying with her under the willows—but often, when her mood was at its blackest, she saw only his face grim with hurt, his eyes filled with anguish.

'If only I could talk to him and explain,' she would cry to Aunt Ketty when this painful image of him haunted her to distraction. 'If only...'

In the end she could stand it no longer.

'I must go and see him,' she told Aunt Ketty. 'I'm sure he wouldn't turn me away without a hearing at least. I don't expect him to love me again, or even feel kindly towards me. I just want to explain.'

'If it would set your mind at rest then that's what you must do,' said Aunt Ketty gently. 'But, my lamb, what if he has gone from here?'

'Then...' Judith shrugged her shoulders, unable to express the hopelessness she would feel if he had departed.

The route to the Fen Reeve's house had become very familiar to her, yet the way now seemed interminable. Hope and fear battled within her at every step—hope that she would see Maarten again, fear that he had gone from her life for ever.

Surely, she reasoned, fate did not allow us to meet and fall in love only to drive us apart?

Strengthened by this thought, hope began to gain the upper hand as she reached the house. Nervous anticipation hastened her footsteps as she reached the gate— the gate from which he had mockingly greeted her on the day she had returned the tulip. She pushed it open, and stood very still, disappointment causing her to keep a tight hold on the gatepost. No smoke rose from the chimney, shutters barred the windows. Already the house had a forsaken air. She walked up the path and hammered at the door. But she knew it was no use. All she could hear was the sound of her own hammering echoing through the empty rooms.

Maarten had gone; she would never see him again.

If the way to the Fen Reeve's house had seemed long, the road back home was even longer, burdened as she was with misery and despair. As she trudged across the wide expanse of the fen the sombre clouds of an approaching rainstorm matched her mood exactly.

A strange boat was moored alongside their hythes as she passed. Curiosity intruded briefly into her unhappiness as she noted the boxes and the bags that were stowed on board; she would have questioned the boatman, but he was sleeping so soundly she had no wish to disturb him. Deciding that it was probably a customer come to order new shoes from Peter Renshaw, she hurried on her way home.

But the visitor was no customer of Peter's.

Aunt Ketty was not alone when Judith entered the parlour.

'Mistress Pentelow. Judith.' Maarten rose to greet her.

'Oh!' Startled, Judith was deprived of speech. 'Oh,' she said again.

'See who is here, my lamb,' Aunt Ketty broke in hurriedly. 'What a good thing you got back again so soon.

I was just telling Master Dutchman here that you had stepped out for a moment and should not be long.'

So Aunt Ketty had not revealed her destination—Judith was not sure whether to be glad or sorry. The first icy chill of shock receded, and she felt hot colour rise to her face.

'Good day to you, Maarten,' she said in a voice that sounded strange and unreal.

They stood facing one another awkwardly, not knowing what to say.

'Sit you down, Master Dutchman—you'll forgive me calling you that, but I still can't manage your name. Yes, sit you down while I get you a bite to eat and some wine.' Aunt Ketty fairly gabbled the words to ease the tension that was in the room.

'I beg you not to trouble,' replied Maarten doing as he was bid. 'I must be on my way soon.'

'On your way?' said Judith faintly.

'Aye, to Lynn. I hope to sail to Holland on the morning tide.'

At his words the hope that was beginning to stir in Judith's breast faded. He was going home... Yet he had come to take his leave. That had to mean something.

'There now, we can't let you go such a distance without nourishment,' declared Aunt Ketty. 'It will not take above a minute to get you something.'

As she bustled out she caught Judith's eye. Now's your chance to speak to him, her expression said, more clearly than any words.

When she left, however, another heavy pause fell upon the room.

Judith longed to look up into Maarten's face, but awkwardness kept her eyes fixed on her hands as they lay in her lap. Eventually, unable to bear the silence any longer she said, 'Maarten, I must speak. About the day we went to Wellham Fair—— '

'Aye, in truth, that was what I came about.' Maarten sounded relieved. 'I could not go away without knowing...without being sure—— After that day—if there should be a child...'

A child! So that was why he'd come. She should have remembered he was a man accustomed to responsibility.

He was not likely to shirk any new obligations, such as a bastard child! She had been foolish to imagine even for one second that he had come because of any feelings for her.

'There is no chance of a babe,' she said curtly.

'Are you sure? You would not let pride...?'

'Pride has naught to do with it. It is a matter of nature.'

'Oh.'

Judith expected him to look relieved, but he did not. Once again there was silence between them. Neither of them looked at the other.

This time Maarten broke the silence. 'I never did approach Master Culpepper and the other adventurers on behalf of the commoners,' he said. 'I got no chance...'

'And now there is no need,' completed Judith.

Silence descended once more.

'You began by mentioning Wellham Fair,' said Maarten suddenly. 'What were you going to say?'

Judith still could not bear to look at him. She had to acknowledge that he no longer cared for her. How could he when she had killed his love so mercilessly? The most she could hope for was his forgiveness.

'I wanted to ask your forgiveness for having behaved so deceitfully towards you,' she began. 'If I explain things, then perhaps you will no longer think badly of me——'

'There is nothing to forgive!' exclaimed Maarten. 'Nor are explanations necessary. I've had much time to think on things lately, and I see how it was for you. You were fighting for your home, your land, for everything you hold dear. Of course you used every weapon against me that you could. Knowing your spirit and your courage, I would expect nothing less of you.'

'But that's not exactly how it was,' protested Judith. 'I took no pleasure in deceiving you.'

'I am sure you did not. Just as I am sure now that you did not condone the attack on poor Tildje, or the wrecking of my house.'

'He promised there would be no damage. He said he only wanted to know your plans.'

'By "he" you mean Adam Digby, of course. Aye, I can imagine how he persuaded you to fall in with his scheme. And you, who care so much for your beloved Fens, did not worry what sacrifices you made. Such selflessness does you credit.'

Judith glanced up at him sharply. There was no hint of sarcasm in his expression, nor was there any warmth.

'You may say that there is nothing to forgive,' she said. 'I must insist otherwise. All I can say in my own defence is that I never wanted to give you pain.'

'You gave me a sorely bruised pride. No man ever died from that,' replied Maarten brusquely. 'Let us not speak of the matter any more, eh? You have your Fens, I am going home, so all is ending well.'

All is ending well! Judith longed to cry out, but I love you—what of that? She did not, of course. There was nothing in Maarten's demeanour to encourage such an outburst. She had destroyed his love for her. The fact that she still loved him must serve as her punishment.

Aunt Ketty came back into the room bearing a jug of wine and a plate of honey cakes. As she set them before Maarten her kindly eyes went from him to Judith. Seeing no kindling of happiness in the girl's face, she gave a sad little sigh.

'Eat heartily of the cakes, Master Dutchman,' she said. 'They were new-baked this morning by Judith. So, what's to become of you? Will you have difficulty in earning your living now that the draining here is abandoned?'

'Indeed, no! My uncle will have employment enough for me. We Dutch are never satisfied with our land, we always want more. There are sufficient areas in need of draining to see me to the end of my days.'

Judith noticed that though he sipped his wine he did not touch the cakes. Remembering with a pang his fondness for sweet things at the fair, she wondered that he should leave them. Was it because she had made them or because he had no appetite? He undoubtedly looked thinner.

'Well, that's a blessing, anyway,' said Aunt Ketty. 'No doubt your family will be glad to have you back. You have a mother living, I think you said?'

'Aye, mistress, and three sisters.' Politely Maarten answered Aunt Ketty's gentle questions.

At last, he drained his cup and rose, seeming to fill the tiny parlour with his presence.

'I must take my leave of you,' he said. 'I thank you for your hospitality, Mistress Kettering, and you, too, Judith.'

Judith longed to say something to detain him—but what words would have such power?

At the door, however, he paused, and putting his hand in his pocket he took out a book.

'I would like you to have this,' he said, and handed it to her.

For a second their fingers almost touched on the leather binding as Judith took it—almost, but not quite. Looking down she saw that it was *The Shepheardes Calendar*. Somehow it had escaped the onslaught of Adam and his men. Surely his wish to give it to her meant that he still had some warm feeling left for her? But it was too late now. The time for hope had gone.

'Thank you——' she began, but an exclamation from her aunt interrupted her.

'My stars! What a fool!' Aunt Ketty clasped her head with her hands, setting her cap askew. 'Master Dutchman, the house where you live with your mother, has it a front door painted a fine green?'

'I beg your pardon, mistress?' A startled Maarten stared at her in bewilderment.

'I know you think I'm ripe for Bedlam, but humour me, I beg of you, sir. The house where your mother is, has it a green door, and a garden before it of coloured stones set in clever patterns?'

'I fear not, Mistress Kettering. We have no garden in the front of our house. It is set direct on the road. And the door, unless it has been repainted, is black.'

'Oh!' Aunt Ketty's face fell. She looked at Judith. 'I had a thought, my lamb...but it came to nothing. Such a pity!'

Once more Maarten took his leave, but once more he paused at the door.

'Mistress Kettering,' he said, 'I've no idea why you are so curious about our front door but, if you are interested, my eldest sister has just such a garden as you describe.'

'And where does she live?' Aunt Ketty's hands were clenched.

'With her husband, of course. They farm land some distance from Amsterdam.'

'And this land, would it have been wrested from marshes or some such?'

'Why, yes!'

'Then your mother is there with her at the moment.' It was not a question but a statement.

'Most likely, for my sister is with child and my mother will be there for the lying-in about now. How did you know?' Maarten's bewilderment was growing, but Aunt Ketty gave no explanation.

Instead, with a triumphant cry, she hurried to the hearth and lifted the stone underneath which she and Judith kept their valuables. She removed a leather bag and thrust it into Judith's hands.

'Your dowry!' she exclaimed. 'And forgive me for being such an ignorant, foolish old woman!'

'What do you mean?' Judith was as puzzled as Maarten now.

'Don't you see? My thoughts were dwelling so much on you going to the Americas I didn't stop to think that there might be new land elsewhere. In Holland, for example! It all fits! The house, everything, though it's not his house but his sister's—not that it matters, for his mother will be there and that's where you must go——'

'Mistress Kettering!' Maarten's voice, at its sternest, suddenly cut through Aunt Ketty's voluble chatter. 'Will you please calm yourself and explain what you are talking about?'

'I mean that you must take Judith with you. There, is that plain enough?'

'Aunt, please don't speak so!' cried Judith in an agony of embarrassment.

'It's—it's impossible!' Maarten too was taken aback.

Aunt Ketty faced him. 'Why is it impossible?'

'You do not know all—— You do not understand——' he protested.

'I know that you two are meant to go through life together. And if you'll do naught about it then I must. Master Dutchman, as you are an honest man, tell me, do you love Judith?'

Judith stood transfixed as, for the first time, she dared to look into Maarten's eyes. He was a long, long time answering.

'As I am an honest man, I must say yes,' he said, his gaze not wavering from Judith's face.

Judith heard his words but did not—could not—let herself believe them.

'Now you, Judith! Tell this great fellow that you love him,' insisted Aunt Ketty. 'Tell him that you were so desperate for the sight of him that you went to his house this very morning, only to miss him on the way. Tell him that you've been pining away like a spent candle for the sake of him——'

'Well?' demanded Maarten, in a near parody of his old blunt manner. 'Well, is it true?'

Judith held out her hands to him, the book and the money-bag falling from her grasp.

'It is true,' she said. 'I love you. I believe I have loved you from the first moment we met.'

'Can it be so?' Maarten seemed unable to comprehend. 'I have said harsh words to you of late, behaved so coldly——'

'No more than I deserved—nothing you could say or do would stop me from loving you.'

'Do you care enough to come with me? To live in a strange land, among people who are not your own?' Maarten had grasped her hands and was pulling her slowly towards him.

'If I am with you then that will be all the happiness I want,' Judith said softly. 'For without you my life would be unbearable.'

'Oh, Judith...' Maarten's voice shook. 'I thought you no longer loved me. Worse still, I feared that you had never loved me. That all those tender moments between us had been a mockery and a sham. That was what tormented me so.'

'I swear to you that every word of love I ever spoke to you was honestly said, and came straight from my heart,' whispered Judith. She was in Maarten's arms now, close to him, as she had feared she would never be again.

'And will you be my wife?'

'If you will have me.'

'If I will have you? Such a question, after I have loved you so ardently for so long.' Maarten's mouth covered hers softly, hesitantly, tenderly, as if neither of them could believe in their present happiness. 'You are sure?' he asked when their lips parted.

'Absolutely sure.' Judith's voice was definite.

'Of course she's sure!' There was no hesitation in Aunt Ketty's voice. 'Doubtless there will be explanations and apologies and forgivings to be got over, but they'll while away the journey to Holland, which I dare say is a tedious one. But if the pair of you intend to sail tomorrow we'd best get Judith's things together, and promptly.'

'But I can't go!' Judith gave a sudden cry of anguish. 'How could I be so thoughtless! I cannot leave you alone, Aunt Ketty, not with the country at war!'

'I won't be alone. I've decided to wed Toby after all; he's asked me often enough. As for the war, I don't suppose it will affect a pair of old uns like us overmuch.'

'But I'll be far away,' protested Judith.

'Not so far as the Americas, though, for I hear they are very distant. I'll miss you, my lamb, of course I will, but if you'd gone to the Americas I'd never have seen you again. Holland is different. It can't be too great a journey, not judging by the way these Dutchmen seem to come and go as they please. You'll be back when the strife is over, bringing me pretty babes to fondle, and my, won't we have a joyous time!'

Aunt Ketty rounded on Maarten and her tone became authoritative. 'You are to take my Judith straight to your mother, mind, at your sister's house! Never bother how I know. I care not what has passed between the pair of you before; things are to be decent and proper this time, and I trust to your mother to see that it's so. I know you big lusty lads. You're so eager to get a wench to bed the church is liable to get missed on the route. To your mother, do you hear?'

'Yes, Mistress Kettering.' For the first time Maarten smiled, a faltering lighting of his features, as though he had got out of the way of doing such things.

Judith watched him, delighting in the laughter that suddenly sparkled in his eyes and the happiness that suffused his whole expression.

'Now let's be starting on your things, Judith.' Aunt Ketty began to bustle about. 'I could have wished we were further on with your new gown, but perhaps Master Dutchman's sisters will be kind enough to help...' She stopped, for she might as well have been talking to thin air.

Maarten and Judith were in each other's arms again, oblivious to the whole world, conscious of their love for one another and of the wonderful future that stretched before them.

With a smile that held more than a hint of tears Aunt Ketty left the room and closed the door on them.

'Never mind, my lambs,' she said softly. 'I can manage the packing by myself.'

THE IDEAL TONIC

Over the past year, we have listened carefully to readers' comments, and so, in August, Mills & Boon are launching a *new look* Doctor-Nurse series – MEDICAL ROMANCES.

There will still be three books every month from a wide selection of your favourite authors. As a special bonus, the three books in August will have a special offer price of **ONLY** 99p each.

So don't miss out on this chance to get a real insight into the fast-moving and varied world of modern medicine, which gives such a unique background to drama, emotions – and romance!

COMING SOON FROM MILLS & BOON!

Your chance to win the fabulous

VAUXHALL ASTRA
MERIT 1.2 5-DOOR

Plus

2000 RUNNER UP PRIZES OF WEEKEND BREAKS & CLASSIC LOVE SONGS ON CASSETTE

SEE
MILLS & BOON BOOKS
THROUGHOUT JULY & AUGUST FOR DETAILS!

Offer available through Boots, Martins, John Menzies, WH Smith, Woolworths and all good paperback stockists in the UK, Eire and Overseas.